LIGHT OF DAY

HT
DAY

ALLISON
VAN DIEPEN

HARPER TEEN
An Imprint of HarperCollinsPublishers

HarperTeen is an imprint of HarperCollins Publishers.

Light of Day
Copyright © 2015 by Allison van Diepen
All rights reserved. Printed in the United States of America.
No part of this book may be used or reproduced in any manner whatsoever without written
permission except in the case of brief quotations embodied in critical articles and reviews.
For information address HarperCollins Children's Books, a division of HarperCollins
Publishers, 195 Broadway, New York, NY 10007.
www.epicreads.com

Library of Congress Cataloging-in-Publication Data
Van Diepen, Allison.
  Light of day / by Allison van Diepen. — First edition.
    pages cm
  Summary: When high school senior Gabby learns that men are drugging girls and
forcing them into prostitution, she fights back using the popular radio show she hosts and
captures the attention of X, a mysterious gang member determined to get pimps off the
streets of Miami, who, in turn, captures her heart.
  ISBN 978-0-06-230348-6
  [1. Prostitution—Fiction. 2. Gangs—Fiction. 3. Radio talk shows—Fiction. 4. Latin
Americans—Fiction. 5. High schools—Fiction. 6. Schools—Fiction. 7. Family life—
Florida—Miami—Fiction. 8. Miami (Fla.)—Fiction.] I. Title.
PZ7.V28526Lig 2015   2014042506
[Fic]—dc23   CIP
                                                                            AC

Typography by Ellice M. Lee
17 18 19 20 21   PC/LSCH   10 9 8 7 6 5 4 3 2 1
❖
First paperback edition, 2017

MYSTERY GUY

HE WAS WATCHING ME FROM across the club. Magnetic blue eyes, square jaw, steady gaze.

I liked it.

Not that Maria and I were short on male attention tonight. Right now, as we leaned on the bar, we were chatting with a slick guy in his late twenties who'd called us the most beautiful girls in Miami. A little over the top, but Maria was lapping it up.

I still couldn't believe we'd gotten into the Space, the newest hot spot in South Beach. The club was shaped like a giant, futuristic cube, with black-mirrored walls and two levels packed with people. Lucky for us, Maria's brother's friend worked the door and had accepted our fake IDs with a wink.

"Another round for the ladies," Raul said to the bartender. He wasn't my type, with the gold chains, chest hair, and fat gold rings. But Maria wasn't being picky tonight. She'd just been through an awful breakup. Her boyfriend had slept with her cousin—the type of betrayal you'd only hear about on a trashy talk show.

Maria gave me a nudge, and I knew she wanted a few minutes alone with Raul. If I had been brave, I'd have sent a drink over to Blue Eyes, who was sitting by himself near the dance floor. If I were even braver, I'd carry the drink over myself. But I wasn't brave, so I went to the bathroom instead.

I took my time, checking my appearance in the mirror, the curly black hair, dark eyes, red lips, white teeth, and lingering summer tan. I wore a little white dress with black zebra stripes up the sides. Totally chic, but who was I kidding? No one here would think I was twenty-one. I was three months shy of eighteen, and looked it.

When I left the bathroom, Blue Eyes was outside. He was taller than I'd thought, his broad shoulders blocking the cramped hallway. I wasn't sure if this was good or creepy, but I was definitely leaning toward good.

"Hey there," he said.

God, he was cute. Light brown hair. Mesmerizing eyes. A young Channing Tatum except for one thing—you could tell his nose had been broken.

"Hey." I gave him my best smile. "I'm Gabby."

He didn't return the smile. "That guy you're talking to. He's dangerous."

I frowned. "What do you mean?"

"I saw him slip roofies in your drinks. Your friend's already started drinking hers. You haven't. I'd keep it that way."

My jaw dropped. "Are you sure?"

"Yeah. He's gonna want you and your friend to leave with him. I wouldn't go if I were you."

"We won't." My anger surged. "We know one of the doormen. He'll throw his ass out of here." I started to move past him, anxious to get to Maria, but he put up a hand to stop me.

"No. Don't involve the bouncers, and don't confront him. You can't prove anything."

"I'll call the police, then. Maybe they can test the drinks."

He shook his head. "There's no way they'd do that. Best thing you can do is walk."

I was about to argue but stopped myself. This guy was on my side. If it hadn't been for him, I wouldn't have even known what was happening.

"Okay," I agreed. "Thanks for telling me."

A faint smile. "Glad to help."

I headed back to the bar, my feet faltering in my three-inch heels. Steadying myself, I observed Maria and Raul with new eyes. Maria was laughing at whatever he'd said, and his arm was locked around her waist. His game plan was so obvious now. Raul had targeted the youngest, most innocent-looking girls in the club, especially the vulnerable one whose sad eyes made her a prime target.

I continued across the room and slipped onto the barstool beside Maria. "Sorry to interrupt, guys," I said, touching Maria's arm. "My stomach isn't feeling so good. We'd better call it a night."

Raul snapped his fingers at the bartender. "Some water over here, please." He turned to me. "Slow it down, honey, you'll be fine. You probably need some food."

"It's not that." I made an ick face, putting a hand over my stomach. "I think it was a bad burrito."

Maria's mouth fell open, as if to say, *Are you kidding me?* "What burrito? We just had burgers."

"I had it for lunch, okay? I'm really not feeling well."

She scowled. "Fine. Just let me finish this." She took a long sip of her drink.

I wanted to snatch it from her, but if I did, Raul would realize I was onto him. Who knew how he'd react? "Sorry, but I can't wait. Let's get a cab."

"Forget a cab, I'll take you both home," Raul said, silky smooth. "I'm parked outside."

I didn't let go of her arm. "No thanks, we're good."

He glared at me. My insides turned cold.

That's what he wants, I realized. *To weaken me.*

No way. Not when my friend is in jeopardy.

I had to get Maria out of here. Now.

Unfortunately, she was on Raul's side. "Jesus, Gabby, let's take the ride."

"I'm worried I'll puke in his car." I put a hand on my stomach again and made a retching motion as if I was going to throw up any second.

Raul's nostrils flared, but he released Maria. Then he walked away—without saying good-bye, without asking for her phone number. He just left.

Maria turned on me. "Did you have to be so gross about it? You scared him off. He was a cool guy. He has a fucking Benz!"

"Let's just go, okay?"

I hustled her outside, glancing around to see if our bouncer friend was still manning the door. But he wasn't there, damn it.

Although cabs were all over the strip at this time of night, you had to be fast to snag one. And we weren't. Maria was going into slow motion, her speech slurring as she bitched at me. I held her arm, not wanting to risk leaving her for even a minute to run into traffic for a cab. If I did, she could pass out on the sidewalk. Or, worse, Raul might still be around, waiting to swoop in.

"I got you," said a male voice, startling me.

I turned to see Blue Eyes striding past me into the street. He raised a hand and stepped into the path of the next cab, directing it to the curb in front of us.

Relieved, I helped Maria into the backseat. Over the top of the cab, I said, "Thank you."

His eyes glittered. "No probs."

Then I got in.

Usually the sunlight spilling through my curtains and the blue sky outside my window wiped away whatever heaviness I carried from the night before.

Not today.

Even in sleep, Raul's stare hadn't released me. My mind played one scenario after another of what might've happened if Blue Eyes hadn't warned me about the roofies. My brain insisted on imagining every graphic detail.

But Blue Eyes *had* been there, thank God. And he'd watched over us until he was sure we were out of harm's way.

I wished I'd gotten his name, maybe even slipped him my number. If he'd been watching me so closely that he saw Raul drug our drinks, did that mean he was interested? He couldn't have been watching Maria, because she was obviously heavy into Raul. And yet when we'd spoken outside the bathrooms, he'd been all business.

There was no point in wondering about it now. I'd done the only thing I could do—I'd gotten Maria out of there. So why couldn't I shake the feeling that I'd missed out on something big?

I looked over at her, sprawled across my bed.

"Maria?"

"No." She threw an arm over her face. "I'm not awake yet."

"You can sleep in, but I have to get ready for church."

"Church? *Christ.*"

She rolled onto her stomach. I wished I could sleep some more, but missing church wasn't an option. It was part of the deal in my house. I grabbed a pale pink blouse from the closet and a beige pencil skirt.

"What happened last night?" Maria asked, her voice muffled against the pillow. "Tequila shots?"

"No. You had two screwdrivers but . . ."

"Two screwdrivers?" She sat up, a mess of tangled blond hair and dark roots. "I can handle two screwdrivers. Only tequila does this to me."

"What do you remember?"

"Nada." She shook her head. "It's like a black void."

"You were drugged. That guy we were talking to put roofies in our drinks." I gave her the quick version of the story as I pulled on my clothes.

"But you're okay."

"Yeah, because I never touched the drink. I was still buzzing from my first."

She was quiet for a while. "I only remember . . . gold chains. And a lot of rings."

"Yeah. That's Raul."

I heard my mom's sharp call from downstairs. "Gabriella!"

"Be right there!" I shouted back, my voice still hoarse from the club. "Gotta go. I know you feel like crap but . . . I'm glad you're okay. Lock the front door when you leave. I'll call you later."

"Cool." She brushed the hair out of her eyes. "And Gabby, thanks for saving my ass."

I smiled. "Nobody messes with my sista."

I took a couple of minutes to clean myself up in the bathroom, trying to tame my hair with some clips. But my hair had a mind of its own. As I left the bathroom, I felt curls pulling free, swirling in different directions.

Downstairs, Mom and Dad were at the kitchen table, finishing up their coffee.

"Maria's not coming down?" Mom frowned.

I'd known Maria since primary school, and Mom had never been a fan of the friendship. When I was a kid, I could never play at Maria's house—she always had to play at mine. I hadn't understood it at the time, but it probably had to do with Maria's mom's steady stream of boyfriends. Ever since

Maria had hit puberty, it was Maria herself that Mom didn't approve of. Her clothes were too little, her makeup too much, and she had—until recently—an older boyfriend. My parents had hoped we'd stop hanging out when we went to different high schools—me to St. Anthony's, and Maria to Rivera. But we were seniors now, and that hadn't happened.

"Maria's got a cold. I didn't want to rush her."

Mom and Dad exchanged a look. I could tell they were guessing Maria was hungover. But they wouldn't actually say it.

That was the big difference between me and my parents. They were below-the-surface people and I was an in-your-face person. If I had an opinion, I shared it. If I was pissed, I said it. My parents didn't operate like that. Forget the stereotype of hot-blooded, volatile Latinos—they were the cold-water kind.

Aunt Sarita said it was the way they'd grown up. My parents were the eldest kids of Cuban immigrants with strong work ethics and rigid Catholic values. They loved rules so much they became teachers. And when they had my brother, David, they thought they'd lucked out. In their eyes, he was the perfect little rule-follower. But I knew he was just good at covering his tracks. Then I came along—loud, messy, argumentative (their words, not mine). My parents didn't know what to make of me. Still don't.

Whatever. We'd made a deal, my parents and me. They

told me exactly what was expected of me: decent grades, church, family gatherings. And I told them what I needed: a midnight curfew, access to their beat-up Honda Civic, and the freedom to choose my own career path.

That was the hardest part for them. They didn't believe my interest in radio could turn into a career. And they didn't want it to. *Radio is dead*, Mom always said. *Ten years from now, local stations probably won't even exist.*

Dead or not, when I was on the air, I felt truly alive.

At eight thirty that night, I swiped my ID card and walked through the glass doors of WKTU Miami 5. Sleek and modern, the station took up half the ground floor of an office building on Miracle Mile. The foyer was splattered with hot pink Miami 5 logos and autographed shots of all the pop artists who'd visited the station over the years.

A shiver came over me. This radio station was where dreams were made—*my dreams,* anyway.

"Hey, Gabby!" Olive Mendez was in her early twenties, but she dressed like a pinup girl from the 1940s. Tonight's outfit was a floral Heidi dress, and her hair was done up with a big red bow. On Sunday nights Olive was both receptionist and assistant to DJ Caballero, screening calls and making coffee to keep him going.

"Ready for your show?" she asked with her usual bubbliness.

I nodded, despite my nerves. I was as ready as I'd ever be. And I had the feeling tonight's show would be the most important I'd ever done.

I found DJ Caballero spinning in his chair like a little kid, headphones on the desk next to the controls. He always did that when he was playing several songs in a row. That, or jumping jacks or push-ups. Anything to keep his energy up.

"Gabby, what's happenin'?"

"A lot, trust me."

He grinned. "It's gonna be good, ain't it?"

"Let's just say you'd better help Olive with the switchboard."

He clapped his hands together. "Snap!"

He'd taught me that—to talk confident. To take all tentative words out of my vocabulary, especially when I was on the air. He'd once told me that, in radio, it's "go big or go home." When you're live, you can't hesitate, can't sound uncertain. If you do, the listeners will pick up on it right away.

Caballero was a scrawny black-Hispanic guy with a big voice and an even bigger personality. For a decade, he had been a mainstay of Miami radio. Both on and off the air, he was impossible not to like. His charisma wasn't an act—it was just him. And despite the fame and VIP parties and celebrity elbow-rubbing, he was the most hardworking, down-to-earth guy you could ever meet.

Caballero said into the microphone, "Don't forget, at nine

o'clock the incredible Gabby Perez is going to take over Miami 5 and literally blow your mind. . . ."

My stomach flipped. *No pressure*. But I smiled and went to the lounge to read over my notes.

I had the lounge to myself, as Sunday nights it was only Olive, Caballero, and me at the station. With its hot pink walls and sleek white leather furniture, this was where the celebs chilled before going on the air. The fancy espresso machine was tempting, but caffeine was a no-no for me before the show. The natural boost of adrenaline from my nerves was more than enough to hype me up.

I took my notes from my handbag, smoothed them out on my lap, and began to read. Twenty minutes until showtime.

My show. It still didn't feel real.

I'd been volunteering at the station since January, doing anything that needed to be done—reception, paperwork, coffee, call screening. Like the other interns, I'd had dreams of being a DJ one day. The difference between me and them was that I started writing my own segments and recording them at night, when some of the equipment was free. Last spring, I'd finally worked up the courage to ask Caballero to listen to one of my segments—a sassy piece about a day in the life of a Miami Latina. I'd never forget seeing his face light up. *"We gotta get you on the air, mamacita!"*

And so here I was, the clock on the wall ticking. It was now

September, and after six months of doing this, the nerves were still there.

At one minute to nine, I entered the booth and Caballero passed me the headphones. Sitting down, I cleared my throat and listened as the current song faded out. I'd been told my voice was low and smoky and made for radio. Then again, that was from creepy male listeners who were looking for a date.

I leaned in.

"Hey, it's me, Gabby Perez and you're listening to *Light Up the Night* coming to you from the heart of Miami. I'm the yin to Caballero's yang, and I give you the female side. The real deal without sugar-coating or truth-tampering.

"Do me a favor, will ya? Get all your friends to hear this. I don't care where you are or what you're doing—tell everyone to shut up and listen. Something happened to me last night that you have to know about. Something really scary.

"I was with a girlfriend at this club. We were approached by a guy. You know the type: suave, full of compliments, lots of bling. His name was Raul and he said we were the most beautiful girls in Miami. He was hitting on my friend and she was loving it. I went to the ladies' room to give them a minute alone. When I came out, a guy was waiting for me. He told me he saw Raul slipping roofies into our drinks. I managed to get my friend out of there, and she passed out in the cab. This morning, she couldn't remember anything about last night."

I dared a glance through the glass. Caballero was wide-eyed. He mouthed, *Is it true?* and I nodded.

I lowered my voice, like I was talking intimately to a friend. "Here's the thing. Have you heard of roofies? You might know it as the date rape drug. It's super easy for a guy to slip it into your drink without you knowing, as I found out.

"Do you know what could've happened to us if Mystery Guy hadn't warned me? Do you have any idea?

"Mystery Guy, if you're listening, thanks for the heads-up. I owe you. To everybody out there, guys and girls, keep an eye on your drinks and those of the people around you. We've got to have each other's backs."

I gave Olive a nod, indicating that she could send a call through. "Thanks for calling into *Light Up the Night*. What's your name?"

"I don't wanna say." It was a shy female voice.

"No problem. That's some scary stuff I'm talking about, huh?"

"Yeah. I'm pretty sure someone did that to me. Put roofies in my drink."

I swallowed. "Tell me about it."

"It was at a frat party. I was a freshman. My friends thought I just got drunk and made a mistake, but I didn't even like the guy. He'd been hitting on me for weeks and I couldn't stand him. Then I wake up beside him the next morning."

That fucking asshole, I wanted to say. But this was live radio. "I'm so sorry. Did you confront him when you realized what had happened?"

"Yeah. He said I was into it, but I knew he was lying. I told him I was gonna call the cops, but I never did. I didn't think I could prove anything."

My fist curled around the microphone. "You did the best you could. I'm really sorry that happened to you. I'm sure every girl listening is going to guard her drink more closely from now on."

"I hope so."

"Thanks for sharing your story." I hung up. "That was brave of her. Who are these jerks who think they can drug us, anyway? I'm thinking they've gotta be the most insecure, cowardly turds out there. They must have"—I searched for a non-censorable word—"*man parts* so little they have to drug girls so we won't remember them. We've all got to be on the alert for guys like Raul—that gold-chained charmer could be out crawling the clubs even as I speak."

I took a few more calls. Ranted more. Played some music. Then ended the show at one second to ten, handing off to Caballero. There was no time to debrief, but his eyes said he was proud. It was a relief. I wasn't used to dealing with topics as serious as this, and I felt the weight of it on my shoulders.

When I walked into the control room, Olive looked up.

"You were fabulous, Gabby. We've never gotten so many calls. I wish your show was twice as long so I could've put more through."

"They liked the show?"

She grinned. "They want Raul's balls on a platter."

PRICE OF ADMISSION

THE NEXT MORNING I SAT in math class, calculating the hours until graduation. Since it was only the second week of September, that meant . . . 1,220 hours. Now *that* was the kind of calculation I was interested in.

"This is the most boring class ever," my friend Bree said with a sigh. She wrote on the scratched-up wooden desk, *Bordom is evil.*

Bree could never spell, but at least she was good at math. I had the opposite problem.

"Boring is right, but I need this friggin' class to graduate," I said, copying the equation off the board.

Unlike most of my classmates, I was turning eighteen soon. Since my birthday was in December, right after the cut-off date, I was one of the oldest students in the senior class.

Apparently December babies did better in school that way. All I knew was, if I'd been born a couple of weeks earlier, I'd be in college already.

"You'll pass the class, don't worry. Too bad you can't get JC to tutor you. He always gets As in math."

"Yeah, too bad." At the mention of my ex-boyfriend, I rolled my eyes. The breakup had happened four months ago, *before* summer vacation, and people still weren't over it. I should just be glad that Bree was still talking to me—she was the only one of my former group of friends who did. Breaking up with popular JC Suarez, it turned out, was the equivalent of social suicide at this school.

It had been a relief when Bree sat beside me on the first day of classes. I hadn't seen her—or any of that group—all summer. The trouble was, Bree was also a major distraction. Math wasn't a problem for her, so she didn't have to pay attention. Unfortunately, I did.

My parents would freak if I failed. *I* would freak.

Granted, I hadn't failed math last semester because I was bad at math. I *was* bad at math, but I could have pulled off a pass, at least. I'd failed because I'd started skipping class to avoid JC. Unfortunately, I hadn't realized that having over ten unjustified absences meant an automatic F. I'd had eleven.

As a consequence, my parents had grounded me for the first two weeks of summer, and I'd missed two weeks of mall and beach mayhem with Maria.

The bell rang. Saying bye to Bree, I headed to my locker.

St. Anthony's Catholic High School was in a tall, Gothic building that used to be a convent. Instead of hallways decked out with student art and antidrug posters, St. Anthony's hallways had paintings of Jesus, Mary, and the saints and framed photos of every pope since the 1930s. Not to mention a huge photo of Abbess Hildegard, who'd been the head nun here for forty years. Hildie, as we called her, glared down at us, as if to say, *Don't you dare, kiddies.*

A horde of freshmen boys blew by, almost trampling me. *I hate this school*, I thought for the millionth time. My parents had wanted me to go here instead of Rivera, where Mom taught chemistry and Dad taught geography. In eighth grade I'd gotten into some trouble—staying out past curfew, getting drunk once—none of it earth-shattering, but it was enough to make my parents clamp down. They figured Catholic school was the solution. The fact that it would separate me from my friends was a bonus.

I grabbed lunch from my locker and headed for the cafeteria. It had long wooden tables, the same ones the nuns used to sit at. You could just picture them in their habits, slurping soup and talking about God, or whatever nuns talked about.

Going to the caf was always a risk. If the girls I usually sat with weren't there, I was screwed and had to sit by myself.

I could never sit with Bree, because she inhabited the popular table—and the truth was that our friendship didn't extend beyond the classroom door. My eyes scanned for the girls, and luckily, there they were. The Paranormal Twins.

Adriana and Caroline dressed alike in drab, dark clothes and dabbled in anything occult they could find—tarot, tea leaves, aura reading, ghosts, aliens, zombies—the Paranormal Twins weren't picky.

I slid in next to Adriana. She had thick brown hair extending halfway to her butt, pretty hazel eyes, and a glittering nose ring. She might've been pudgy, but you could hardly tell underneath the layers of dark, voluminous clothing. Caroline, on the other hand, was thin and sandy-haired, with skin so white she'd probably burn just by thinking about the sun. Although the dark clothing did nothing for her coloring, at least her leopard-print glasses added some sass to her look.

"What's up, girls?" I asked, unpacking my lunch.

"Caro's uncle showed up on Friday night," Adriana said, like this was big news.

"Oh yeah? Where's he from?"

Caro gave me a *duh* look. "He's dead, Gabby. We channeled him."

"Channeled? Wow. So that technique you were talking about last week worked?"

"Sure did," Adriana said proudly. "We'll teach you if you

want. The key is to protect yourself with white light and only ask for helpful spirits to enter."

"I'll keep it in mind," I said between bites of sandwich. This paranormal stuff, at least, was a lot more interesting than dissecting the latest Kardashian crisis like my former friends did over lunch. "So what did your uncle say, Caro?"

"He said I'm going to find love soon. But I have to open myself up to it first."

I hoped her dead uncle was right, since Caro was desperate for a boyfriend. Problem was, dressing like the Wicked Witch of the West wasn't appealing to most guys.

At that moment, I spotted JC strolling into the cafeteria.

That was how he walked—he strolled. When you were so popular you practically owned the school, you could do that. JC and his best friend, Liam Murray, were headed our way, laughing and joking. I remembered how I used to get all nervous and tingly when JC came into a room. With his deliberately tousled dark hair, warm brown eyes, and genuine *glad to see you* smile, he was our school's most universal crush.

Then it happened—that second of eye contact, ending when JC looked away without acknowledging me. *Ouch.* It used to be that his expression would show hurt. Now he kept it neutral, as if he hadn't seen me at all. As if I were as much a ghost as Caro's uncle.

The Paranormal Twins noticed the snub.

"I hear they're all druggies now," Caro said. On the surface, she was shy and soft-spoken. But underneath, she was a Chihuahua who'd chew your arm off for a juicy bit of gossip.

She was trying to make me feel better. But I knew it wasn't true. JC's group of friends (formerly *my* friends) were pretty much on the straight and narrow, except for some booze and a little weed at parties. They were all from ultrainvolved middle-class families who expected their kids to get into college. The most rebellious thing they'd ever done was driving around the city late at night rearranging traffic cones.

No wonder my parents had thought JC was a positive influence on me. Me, who'd gotten drunk once in eighth grade and had never lived it down.

"I'd believe they're using," Adriana agreed. "Karina and Ellie meet in the girls' bathroom all the time and stay there way too long."

"They're both bulimic, that's why," I said.

The girls' eyes widened.

I waved a hand. "I'm kidding. I'm sure they just want to get out of class."

JC and his buddies sat down at their usual table—the one I'd sat at every day since we'd started dating in the spring of freshman year. Now I couldn't even walk by it without feeling icy stares. They hated me for breaking his heart.

JC was the type of guy who gave flowers and *Just Because*

notes. The type of guy who saw all the best parts of me and was ignorant to the rest. The type of guy whose family had welcomed me with open arms.

He had the same initials as Jesus Christ, for Christ's sake.

Even now, I wasn't sure I understood it. I just knew that the longer we were together, the less I wanted to be with him. And secretly, in the deep dark parts of me, I was annoyed by him. Something about him didn't feel . . . manly. Maybe it was that he was such a pushover when it came to his best friend, Liam. After screwing around in his classes last year, Liam had convinced JC to write two of his term papers for him. I couldn't respect that.

The breakup had gone badly. When I'd first told him I wasn't happy, I'd let him talk me out of it. But the end result was two months of emotional carnage.

All my mom's worries had been for JC. She'd pointed out that a guy like him might only come along once. She'd met my dad when they were only sixteen, and they'd married right after college. Didn't I want a guy who'd always be there for me, who'd adore me and our future kids, just like my dad?

She was right. But it wasn't enough.

JC was too good a person to go around hating on me. So everyone took care of that for him. The rumor was that I'd become a snob since I'd gotten my radio show. That I thought I was hot shit and could do better than JC Suarez.

Everyone was all too eager to assure him—and me—that I couldn't.

And the truth was, I believed it.

My brother, David, was watching TV in the living room when I got home from school, his feet propped up on the coffee table. Way to brighten my day.

His "hey" was more like a grunt.

I didn't ask why he was here. Once a week he came to pick up his laundry and have a home-cooked meal. Same deal for the whole three years he'd been in college. He might be pre-med, but doing laundry, cooking, and anything besides studying and applying expensive cologne weren't among his skills.

I thought the point in going away to college was to *go away*. But he'd chosen the University of Miami and lived a half-hour bus ride from here. I didn't see why my parents had agreed to pay his living expenses when he could live at home. But I was grateful, because it meant I didn't have to deal with him every day.

I went into the kitchen to get a soda.

"What's for dinner?" David shouted from the living room.

"Don't know." The casserole was in the fridge, but I wasn't going to inspect it for him.

I thought about going to sit with him for a few minutes,

but decided against it. Most of our conversations turned sour. They would start off pleasant enough, then he'd say something condescending, the old David snark, and I'd call him on it. Of course, Mom and Dad would see *me* pissed off and David as cool as a cucumber, and I'd get all the flack.

"Hey, Gab, come here!"

What did he want now? I figured I'd be civil and go in.

"So how's the party planning going?" he asked.

"Fine." Aunt Sarita and I had been planning my parents' twenty-fifth anniversary party since June, and David had never offered to pitch in.

"Let me know if you need any help."

I gave him a flat look. "Oh, come on. The party's next weekend. You're just offering because you know we've done everything already."

David bristled. "Hey, you had the spare time on your hands, not me. I did a summer hospital placement. You were at the mall."

"I put in a lot of hours at WKTU, too," I countered. "Okay, fine, why don't you come early to help set up?"

"All right, but Melody's coming with me, so I don't want to bring her too early."

Melody was the latest girlfriend—a petite blonde who studied nursing. She had a sweet disposition and never challenged David's opinions. She had all the makings of a future trophy wife *if* she could hang on to David, which was doubtful. He never stayed with girls more than a few months, since he always found some flaw that made them undateable. Not that I was one to talk after the sinking of the JC Suarez.

"Good show last night," David said, startling me.

He never listened to my show, and neither did my parents. In fact, my entire family—with the exception of Aunt Sarita— hoped I'd drop the radio dream and go into teaching or some other profession. Anything but radio. Too flaky.

But I'd come to count on them not listening—I could never be so open and comfortable on the air if I knew they were.

"I thought you never listened to the show."

"I don't. Melody told me about it. Was that true about the roofies?"

"Yeah, the story's true. You're not going to tell Mom and Dad, are you? They'd freak."

"'Course not." He looked offended.

That was the upside of David. I'd covered for him so many times he'd be insane to cross me.

"I don't want you to put yourself in a situation like that again, though, Gabby."

Did I detect a note of concern? "I didn't *put myself* in that situation, that scumbag did."

His eyes narrowed. "You shouldn't have been at the club.

Two underage girls would be a magnet for someone like that. You're lucky the other guy saw him do it. You dodged a bullet, Gabby."

"I know. Trust me, I know."

ON AIR

I WALKED INTO WKTU SUNDAY evening, hoping to catch a few minutes with Caballero before I went live. Although I'd stopped in a couple of times that week, as I usually do, I kept missing him.

Olive must've had the night off, because Sapphire was at the front desk instead, dressed in a bright blue minidress and heels. When I'd first met her, she'd been a shy college student named Stephen. Now she mostly came to the station as Sapphire, a six-foot-two hoochie mama.

Sapphire looked up and smiled. "We're still getting emails about your last show. Have you logged in to read them?"

"Yeah, I read through a bunch. I'll quote one or two on air. They're great." My stomach warbled. "Mostly."

She gave me a sympathetic look. "There's always ones like that. Don't let them get to you."

"I'm trying."

Nasty comments about my show were part of the game. But I hadn't been prepared for the *you don't know what you're talking about, bitch* ones. That was why I wanted to talk to Caballero before I went on the air. I knew that he wanted me to stay on the topic, but maybe it would be better to move into less volatile territory.

Sapphire handed me a sticky note. "Some guy keeps calling for you. Normally I wouldn't pass on his number, but he was really insistent. He claims to be the mystery guy you were talking about on the show. Says it's important that he talk to you."

I wanted to believe that it was Blue Eyes, but *anyone* could have said he was the guy who'd helped me at the club.

I glanced down at the phone number on the hot pink Post-it. It could be one of those haters who'd emailed. Or it could be Raul himself. I flashed back to that evil look in his eyes and shivered.

"Thanks, Sapphire." I shoved the note into my pocket and glanced at the glass doors, which had clicked shut behind me. Thank goodness we had solid security here. You needed to swipe your pass to enter the building; random people off the street couldn't just walk in.

I headed for Caballero's office, more convinced than ever that I should change the topic of tonight's show. But I also hated to disappoint him. He'd texted me last Sunday night:

You killed it. More on this next week!

I hovered in the doorway of the studio until he went to commercial. Then he swung his chair around. He looked super cozy in a red velvet smoking jacket. "Gabby! What a show last week. Bet you're more famous than ever at school."

I managed a smile. *Not exactly.* Caballero assumed that the radio show had made me into a school celebrity, and I'd been too embarrassed to correct him. Even when JC and I were still together, my radio show had been little more than a joke—it was *just Gabby trying to be big-time.* I'd learned that when you do something cool, something different, it doesn't make people like you. And since the breakup, my radio show was the number-one thing used against me. The consensus was that having a radio show had turned me into a diva.

"Did Sapphire tell you we've had a lot of feedback? Your story connected. That's what we want."

"I know. But for tonight I was thinking—"

His phone must've vibrated, because he looked down at it. "Aw, shit. Little Cabbie's got a fever." He pressed a button on his phone. "Can't wait for your show tonight, Gabby." Then he started talking to his wife.

I sighed. There was nothing to do but leave. I headed to the lounge to wait until it was my time.

A few minutes later, I went live. I took a deep breath, trying to channel the magic.

"Hey, everybody. It's Sunday night and you're listening to *Light Up the Night* with Gabby Perez, coming to you in style, the miracle child from Miracle Mile in Miami. How are you doing? Are you alone or curled up with a special someone? Thanks for all your feedback on last week's show. I'm glad the word's getting out about the dangers of roofies and the pervs who use them. One listener named Amber tweeted, 'Gabby, it's about time someone's talking about this. You effing rock.' Thanks, Amber. You effing rock too."

The phone lines had already lit up. On the other side of the glass, Sapphire and Caballero were holding up their index fingers, indicating that I should answer line one first.

"Hey, what's your name?"

"Call me Shanae. I've got something to say about your last show. You see, I *know* this Raul you was talking about."

My heart pounded. "So that's his real name?"

"Uh-huh. Raul's a daddy who got a dozen girls working the streets for him."

I swallowed my shock. "You're saying that Raul isn't your average sleazeball. You're saying he's a . . . pimp?"

"Mmm-hmm. That's Raul's MO. He drugs the girls up, then when it wears off, they've already turned a few tricks and they can't even remember what the hell happened."

Her words hit me like a fist in the gut. That could've been me and Maria. I glanced through the glass at Caballero. I wasn't sure I could handle this. But he was nodding and winding his hand, which meant to keep going.

"How do you know all this?" I asked.

"My little cousin. She was one of his girls until he traded her off a few months ago. She so messed up that even when we bring her home, she always go back to the streets."

"I'm sorry." I tried to think of what to say next, but I was reeling from what she'd told me.

My pause allowed Shanae to keep going. "Yeah, I'm sorry too. These girls so dumb, they think the blinged-up daddies is gonna help them. But they just using them. And once they in, it's like the daddies brainwash them. . . ." She kept going on. Caballero made an X sign with his hands. Time to cut her off.

"Thanks for calling in, Shanae. You've given us a look into the twisted minds of these predators." Before she could say more, I disconnected the call. I knew that I had to keep it together, but my mind was jumbled. Then I remembered Caballero's best ever advice: *Be real.*

"Holy crap," I said. "If Shanae is right, the guy my friend and I encountered last week is actually a pimp. And he was planning to add us to his lineup. I won't lie—I'm in shock right now. Even as I speak, I'm having flashbacks to that night. I can't help thinking about what might've happened if that guy hadn't warned me."

Sapphire kept sending calls my way. The callers wanted to talk more about pimps and prostitution and all the dangers out there. I rolled with it as best I could, and played songs in between calls. But I was miles out of my comfort zone, and sweating bullets. My ignorance of all this stuff came across, I was sure. But judging from the riveted looks on Caballero's and Sapphire's faces, it made for good radio.

When I handed off to Caballero at ten o'clock, it was a huge relief. He put a hand up for me to wait, so I did. After he'd done his intro and put on a song, he said, "That was awesome, Gabby. Amazing. Great job."

"Thanks."

"Who knows? You might've helped someone out there." He gave me the thumbs-up and put the headphones back on.

I walked by the control booth, poking in my head to thank Sapphire, then I went out into the parking lot.

The night cooled my cheeks. It had rained during the show, and the air held the soothing smell of palm trees. I drank it in, and felt my pulse finally start to slow down.

"Gabby."

I stopped in my tracks, gripping my keys. Then I spotted him. Blue Eyes. He was leaning against a gray car, his arms crossed over his chest.

He wore jeans, a white T-shirt, and scuffed sneakers. God, he was more achingly cute than I remembered. But his vibe was different than when I last saw him outside the club. There was a scowl between his brows, and he looked . . . pissed off.

"I didn't mean to scare you," he said. "You should've just called me back."

I bit my lip. "Sorry, I didn't know it was you. I don't take calls from listeners off the air."

"I wasn't a listener until I heard about your last show. You gave a lot of details about what happened Saturday night. Too many."

Was that what was bothering him? I didn't think I'd done anything to apologize for. I'd gone public with a story that could get *me* in trouble—thankfully my parents hadn't heard about it—because I'd wanted to warn people. "I was just giving everyone a heads-up about the danger."

His eyes locked with mine. "And giving Raul a heads-up too."

It was as if I'd broken some code I didn't understand. "What do you mean?"

"You need to stop talking about Raul on your show. The woman who called in tonight was right. Raul traffics girls."

So Raul really wasn't just some scumbag perv. He was a professional perv, a sex trafficker. And last Saturday night the girls in his crosshairs had been me and Maria.

"Don't you think I should be warning people about him? Isn't it my job as a radio host to do that?"

He came closer. The sudden movement startled me. "Tell me one thing, Gabby. Can I trust you?"

"Of course you can."

"So whatever I tell you will stay off the record? You won't go talking about it next week?"

"I won't."

He was standing right in front of me now. His nearness made me feel buzzed, magnetized. It was the same effect he'd had on me at the club. I had the urge to step back and step closer, all at the same time.

"I'm going to get Raul off the streets," he said. "That's why I was watching him that night."

Get him off the streets? But how could he . . . ?

Of course. I couldn't believe I hadn't realized it before. He must be an undercover cop. It explained why he'd told me not to call the police that night. He *was* the police, and he hadn't wanted me to interfere with his operation.

God, I felt stupid. I'd actually thought he'd been watching *me*—that he'd just happened to spot Raul slipping us the roofies. It hadn't even occurred to me that he'd been surveiling Raul.

I cursed under my breath. "Did I screw up your operation?" I asked, afraid of the answer.

"I don't know. As of last night, Raul was still doing what he does best. He probably didn't hear about last Sunday's show.

Fingers crossed one of his girls wasn't listening tonight."

I thought back to some of the emails we'd gotten about the show, and my stomach felt queasy. One of them could've been from Raul. "I won't mention him again, trust me."

"Good."

I'd actually tried to do the right thing by sharing the story, and it had backfired. "I'm sorry. If there's anything I can do to fix this . . ."

"Don't worry about it." His hard gaze softened. "You're good at what you do. Keep doing it."

I could tell he meant it. This guy's BS factor was zero.

He turned to get into his car. I didn't want to let him go. Somehow I knew he was going to haunt me.

"Hey, I didn't get your name."

He paused, turning around. "It's X."

"*X?*"

He shrugged. "It's just what I go by," he said, as if that were explanation enough. Obviously an undercover cop would use some sort of street name. X was definitely a unique one.

"I bet you're good at what you do too, X. When you get Raul, kick him in the balls for me, will ya?"

He laughed, and my heart did a somersault. "Count on it."

UNINVITED

FOR DAYS, X'S NUMBER SAT on the hot pink Post-it on my bed-side table, tormenting me.

I knew that I should throw it out. It would be beyond stupid to contact him. What would that accomplish other than making me into a total nuisance? I'd already compromised his operation.

The problem was, I couldn't stop thinking about him. The guy without a name. The blue eyes that pinned me to the spot. The serious face that had transformed when he laughed.

Curiosity was killing me. I wanted to know more about him—why he'd become a cop, how he planned to catch Raul. He looked too young to be a cop, and yet he had a toughness to him, a jaded look in his eyes, as if he'd seen it all. As if nothing he encountered on the streets could faze him.

Okay, so it was more than curiosity. He was the cutest guy I'd ever seen—even the broken nose gave him a sexy edge. Just the thought of him made a wave of heat crash over me.

It was ridiculous. I had to stop thinking about him. My parents' anniversary party was coming up Saturday night, and I'd be screwed if it didn't go well. That's what I needed to focus on.

Luckily, I had Aunt Sarita's help.

On Saturday morning, I drove to her place. Sarita lived in a pretty bungalow surrounded by exotic, brightly colored flowers and wild rosebushes. We sat on her back patio, drinking virgin mimosas and eating buttery pastries. The morning sun warmed my skin and reflected off my sunglasses. I smiled to myself. My favorite place in the world.

"Did you sell out your show yet?" I asked her.

"Sold the last two paintings this week." She refilled my glass with more ginger ale and orange juice. "You're gonna love this. One of the buyers is from Texas. She's the wife of a beef industry CEO."

"No way. And you let her buy it?"

"Eventually. Once she promised to talk to her husband about industry ethics."

I laughed, but I didn't doubt a word. Sarita treated her paintings like a litter of puppies—she only let them go to good homes. Mom thought it was ridiculous that someone who lived "painting to paycheck" dared to ask questions about the buyers. Sarita had no pension, no benefits, and worst of all, no husband. I was sure Mom's greatest fear was that I'd end up like her.

Of all my aunts and uncles, I was the closest to Sarita. Ever since I was a little girl, she'd made me feel special. We even had the same untameable curly hair, though hers was currently dyed a deep garnet red. And she had the coolest peekaboo tattoos, including a tiny scorpion between two fingers and a blue butterfly behind her left ear.

"Are we all set for tonight?" she asked.

I nodded. "The food should be there at six. Hopefully that'll be enough time to set it up before the guests arrive—I don't want it to get cold. David says he'll come a little early to help out, but I'm not holding my breath."

She gave a careless wave. "We don't need him. We'll be fine."

"Knowing him, he'll make it look like he did everything."

"Don't worry, Gabby. I won't let him steal the credit. I'll make sure your parents know how much work you've put into this."

Another reason I loved Sarita: she was always on my side. Maybe it was because she'd grown up as the oddball—the daughter whose choices made my grandparents cross themselves and go to confession. She knew what it was like to be me.

"But no matter what I say to your parents, it won't be enough, Gabby. You know that, right?"

I sighed. "I know."

Sarita didn't need to get more specific—we practically talked in code these days. One party wasn't going to fix my relationship with my parents. One party wasn't going to make them suddenly approve of my decision to break up with JC, or support my radio career, or stop worrying about my future.

But it was something.

They were pleased. *Hell to the yeah.*

A little Esperanza Spalding played softly in the background. Fancy food was spread out over the dining room table. I'd even splurged on Dead Sea hand soap for the downstairs bathroom. What more could they ask for?

It was seven o'clock, and the first guests would arrive any second. I had changed at the last minute into a knee-length gray skirt and a short-sleeved black blouse. Even more important, my hair was tamed with lots of hairspray and a hundred pins. Neat, neat, neat, just as Mom liked it. I saw the flicker of approval in her eyes.

"Don't stress, you're doing great," Sarita whispered to me as guests started to arrive. She was a walking work of art, her floor-length yellow sundress setting off her red hair.

"Thanks. When's your boyfriend coming?"

"Boyfriend? Oh, Mike and I broke up last week. I have a date later, though. Hopefully I can ghost outta here by ten."

I grinned. Sarita was the best.

Around eight, I took over answering the door, since my parents were deep in conversation with some old friends. The house was becoming pleasantly packed, with a few guests drinking cocktails on the patio. Eventually I had a couple minutes to sit down and have something to eat, but then a colleague of my dad's sat down next to me and started talking politics. After ten minutes of nodding, the doorbell rang again, saving me.

Or maybe not. I opened the door and came face-to-face with JC and his parents. I'd been expecting the Suarezes—they'd been church friends with my parents for years—but JC? What was that about?

"Hello!" I tried my best to sound enthusiastic. "I hope you're all hungry. We've got plenty of food. And there's wine and champagne and . . ." I waved my hands.

All politeness, the Suarezes smiled and came in. They were good at pretending not to hate me. JC didn't bother with a smile. As he walked past me into the living room, I caught a whiff of his trademark deodorant spray. I flashed back to a time when my heart would skip a beat when he came to the door. When he was all shiny and eager and sweet, and I'd been so flattered that, of all the girls at St. Anthony's, he'd chosen me.

JC slid me a pained look that said he didn't want to be here. And I gave a shrug that said, *Then why are you?*

Of course, his parents had made him come, and he was the ever dutiful son. But they weren't doing anyone a favor.

To avoid the living room, I gathered up dirty plates and brought them into the kitchen. The front door opened again, and it was David and his girlfriend. A little late to help with the setup, but I didn't care. At least JC would now have people to talk to, instead of just standing there watching my every move. He and David had always gotten along.

Melody was adorable. She was petite enough and pretty enough to get away with the blond pixie haircut. She gave me a hug, even while I held a dirty plate in each hand. "I'm so into your show, Gabby!"

I had to admit, it boosted my mood. "Thanks."

Melody's good nature didn't seem to be an act. I wondered if she'd have the sense to dump David before he dumped her.

Dad started dinging his wineglass, and everyone hushed.

"Thanks so much for coming tonight," Dad said, using his teacher voice. He slid his arm around Mom's waist. "What a wonderful thing to look around and see the people we care about. We'd like to thank our children, Gabby and David, for organizing this party." I forced a smile. Dad must know that David had done squat; maybe he was only saying it for show. "And thanks also to my sister-in-law, Sarita."

Sarita gave a gracious royal wave.

Mom took over. "Twenty-five years. Can you believe it? We've been together since high school." Wait a minute, was that Mom getting misty-eyed? That was so *not* my mom. "A few people have asked me what our secret is. But there's really no secret. Every partnership has its rough patches. The key is knowing that, underneath it all, you are cherished. I'm so lucky."

To my surprise, I started getting teary-eyed too. My parents were not super affectionate with each other—at least, not in front of me. They didn't fight much, but they weren't all kissy-kissy either. I figured they loved each other, but it was strange hearing them say it.

I felt eyes on me. JC's eyes. He was demanding that I look at him. When I finally did, I saw an expression that wasn't love, wasn't longing. It was resentment.

When the applause started, I slipped upstairs to my bedroom. To escape. I had to be away from it all—especially JC.

I sprawled on my bed, heaving a sigh. Why did he have to show up and make everything so damned awkward? I bet he wouldn't have come if I'd had a boyfriend. An image of X surfaced in my mind, all serious and sexy. I couldn't shake him.

For some reason, the electric charge I'd felt in his presence still lingered.

There was a knock at my door. "Yes?"

"It's me." JC pushed open the door. "Can we talk?"

I nodded reluctantly. I didn't see what he could possibly want to talk about. As far as our relationship was concerned, I was all talked out months ago.

He sat down at the foot of the bed, keeping his distance. "I'm sorry."

"For what?"

"For coming."

I sighed. "Ah, don't worry about it. I'm sure your parents didn't give you a choice."

"Actually, they did." His brown eyes stared into mine. "I wanted to see you."

Oh, God. Where was this going?

"I see how alone you are at school."

"It's not a big deal. I mostly hang out with Adriana and Caro."

He cocked a grin. "The paranormal freaks, huh? Guess you have no choice."

I couldn't deny that Adriana and Caro hadn't been my first pick of friends, but they were actually really cool. "They're not freaks. They're my friends."

"Whatever you say. Look, Gabby, I'm sorry I can't pretend

everything's okay with us. I know it would make things easier for you. It's just that you turned my whole life upside down. I never expected to be single in senior year."

It took a lot of willpower not to roll my eyes. "Girls love you, JC. You know that. Take your pick."

"I choose you."

I closed my eyes. We'd had this conversation so many times. Guess it was time for my old line: *You could do so much better than me.* But I was tired of saying that, tired of putting myself down so he could feel better.

He must've misread my pause, because something sparked in his eyes. "Maybe we could get to know each other again as friends. Hang out, the group of us. And then . . . see where things go."

No freaking way. I knew what he was saying. He was saying that if I hung out with him again, he'd let me back into his circle of friends.

The sad part was, I could almost buy into it.

Almost.

I saw the hope in his eyes, saw a glint of something else . . . triumph? He knew my weak spot and was using it to reel me back in.

"I can't." I got up and walked over to my dresser, pretending to arrange things in my jewelry box.

"Gabby, I *saw* your face when your mom was talking. Don't

you want that to be us? Every relationship has its rough patches; your mom said it herself. Do you want to throw away—"

That was when I lost it.

My head whipped around. "It's not gonna happen, okay? Let it go."

He got to his feet. "*Me* let it go? You're the one looking at me with those puppy dog eyes like you're desperate to have me back!"

My mouth fell open. "What are you talking about?"

"Oh, come on. You're always staring at me at school. This is all a game, isn't it? To make me want you."

Had I been staring at him? I didn't think so. I mean, I looked at him when he passed me in the hallway, but . . .

He was doing it again. He was making me second-guess myself.

"It's not *my* fault no one wants to hang out with you," he said. "I've always tried to help you. Tried to give you friends, give you a life. But if you want to be a loser, that's your call."

I couldn't believe it. Was JC Suarez, supposedly the nicest guy at St. Anthony's, calling me a loser now? Had the breakup turned him into an asshole?

"You're speechless," he said, standing over me. "Finally Gabby Perez is speechless. It's about fucking time."

I wished I could slap the smirk off his face. "Get out of my room! Go!"

He opened his mouth to retaliate, but then his lip quivered. "I'm sorry. I didn't mean it. I—" He reached out his hand.

"Don't touch me!" I sidestepped him, slamming into my mom, who was standing in the doorway.

Her eyes were huge. It dawned on me that they could probably hear us fighting downstairs. Hear *me*.

"Be quiet, Gabby," Mom whispered. "I don't know what this is about, but this is *not* the time. You're embarrassing us." She looked at JC. "I'm so sorry, JC."

"It's okay, Mrs. Perez," he said, hanging his head. "It's my fault . . . I shouldn't have come."

Mom's sympathy for JC tore me up. Forget that I had any feelings, that I needed her on my side. She'd heard me shouting and assumed I'd started the argument.

I knew that if I stood here one more second, I was going to tell her exactly what I thought of her. So I pushed past her, ran down the stairs and out the door. And kept on running.

It felt good to run. Tears streamed down my cheeks. I didn't care—it was dark out; no one would see. I ran all the way to Aunt Sarita's, the place I'd been running to ever since I was a kid. But it was dark, of course. She was still at the party, or maybe she'd ghosted by now and was out on her date.

Letting myself into her backyard, I went over to the swing and rocked back and forth until I had calmed down. It was all so clear. JC had been using guilt to try and control me ever since we broke up. He'd used people's sympathy for him to make them isolate me, and now he was trying to manipulate me into giving him another chance. I wasn't going to play his game one second longer.

He might be able to influence everybody at school, and even my own parents. But not me, not anymore.

Fuck him. Fuck the so-called nicest guy in school.

I was done.

I opened my eyes at 9:47 a.m. This was odd—my parents hadn't woken me up for church. I went downstairs. Dad was at the kitchen table with a cup of coffee, still in his pajamas, his black-gray hair uncombed for once.

"We're not going to church today?" I asked.

"No."

"Is this because of last night?"

"Ask your mother."

"C'mon, Dad. Just tell me."

"Things didn't end well last night after you left." He spoke in typical Dad style—factual, like he was reporting a dry piece of news. "JC's parents were upset about the things you said to him."

"The things *I* said?" I told myself not to lose it, not to let JC keep doing this to me. "What did I supposedly say?"

He shrugged uncomfortably. "They didn't elaborate."

"Dad, I'm so sorry your party was ruined. I feel horrible about it. But it's not my fault. JC was trying to—"

Dad put up a hand. "No need to get into it. It's over now. I'd prefer to move past it."

In Dad's defense, he looked more worn out by the whole thing than angry. Emotionally sticky stuff took a lot out of him.

Then Mom walked in, wearing her bathrobe. "You might as well go back to bed, Gabby." Her tone was more along the lines of *get out of my sight*. She crossed the kitchen to pour herself some coffee.

I stood my ground. "Can I please tell you guys what happened?"

"Fine," Mom said tightly. "I'd love to hear why you felt you could treat a guest that way."

The intensity of her anger jolted me.

I sat down at the table. "Maybe you didn't notice, but I lost all my friends when I broke up with JC. Everybody hates me now. And then at your party he has the b—I mean, the nerve to say to me that if I give him another chance, he'll let me have my friends back. He was manipulating me. When I refused, he called me a loser."

Dad frowned. "Really?"

"Really."

Mom's lips flattened. "You could try to be understanding of him, Gabby. He was deeply hurt by the breakup."

"Trust me, Mom, JC's been making sure nobody lets me off the hook for breaking up with him." Couldn't she, just once, try to see this through my eyes? "Think about it. JC doesn't speak to me for months, then shows up at your anniversary party with some crazy strategy to convince me to start seeing him again. He came into *my* room. Called my new friends freaks. Called me a loser. And then you come upstairs and just assume that I'm the one who started it? That's total bull."

Mom put a hand to her forehead. "Look, I don't know what happened in there. All I know is that when I came in, JC was very upset. Whatever he might've said, it's up to you to keep hold of your temper, Gabby."

"So he gets a pass, then?" I shook my head in disgust. "He crashes your party and I get blamed. That's what I'm hearing."

Mom gave me the *I'm so disappointed in you* look I knew too well. "You should treat him with special care. Teenage boys are extremely vulnerable. His—" She broke off, as if debating whether to continue. "His mother told me he sees a psychiatrist. He's been depressed."

A psychiatrist? That threw me off. Whenever I saw him at school, he didn't seem depressed at all. He and Liam were always laughing their asses off. Was I supposed to buy that he was laughing on the outside but crying on the inside?

My mom went on. "Now do you see why you have to be careful with him? Why you can't let your temper control you? JC was crushed last night, Gabby. You can't take the name-calling seriously. He's clearly feeling desperate. I'm going over to the Suarezes' this afternoon to apologize. They left so quickly I didn't have the chance to do it properly. I'd like it if you came with me."

After everything I'd just said, she wanted *me* to apologize? "No. Way."

Mom looked deflated. "Well, if you change your mind . . ."

"I won't change my mind. But feel free to give JC a message for me. Tell him to man up and leave me the hell alone. Thanks."

And I walked out of the room.

THE CLUB

THERE WERE WORSE WAYS TO spend Tuesday lunch hour than at a meeting of the Revelations Club. Started by Adriana and Caro, the club was supposed to study the Book of Revelations, but it was really a cover for the Zombie Apocalypse Survival Club. Thankfully, no staff member had stuck around long enough to suspect our real purpose.

We met in the basement chapel that the nuns had once used for early-morning and late-night prayers. Containing an altar and four pews, it was piled high with desks, boxes of old textbooks, and random school junk. Adriana had asked to use this room, claiming religious significance. The truth was, she wanted it because it was private, almost devoid of natural light, and overall fit the zombie apocalypse mood.

Adriana started the meeting with an update of the latest

zombie sightings. One in Maryland, one in upstate New York, one in California.

"That last one needs further investigation," Alistair Zellin said. "I hope the CDC is collecting tissue samples." Tall and reed thin, he looked a bit zombie-like himself. Alistair was new to school this year. Though his inventions had won him the state Engineering Olympics, they didn't help with social acceptance. The poor guy had tried to find friends among the senior boys, only to get atomic wedgied by Liam Murray in the locker room. After several more humiliations, he'd stopped trying. He'd wound up in Adriana and Caro's orbit, as I had. It turned out he was a natural fit for the zombie club.

"So what do we do if the shit hits the fan?" Adriana asked. *The shit hits the fan*, I'd learned, was basic doomsday prepper terminology. "How will we find each other?"

"We could meet here in the chapel," Rory Kovick answered between crunches of Doritos. "It's central. We could all walk here if we had to. Or steal a car."

Rory took this apocalypse stuff way too seriously. It shouldn't be surprising. This was a guy whose online persona was Roar, God of Gaming.

"Then we'd better stockpile some supplies," Alistair said. "Nonperishable food, for starters."

"I'm sure we could hide supplies in here without anyone knowing," Adriana said. "But we'll have to remove them next summer in case they finally clean it out."

"It's getting the stuff in here that could be the problem," Caro pointed out.

"I can smuggle in some boxes under the guise of engineering equipment," Alistair said.

Rory pumped his fist. "Great! We'll need weapons too. I'll bring my knife collection, a Taser, and my dad's vintage Colt 45."

Uh-oh. That's all I needed—to be part of a group hiding an arsenal of weapons in the school basement. My parents would so not approve.

"Don't bring in any weaponry," Alistair cautioned him. "There's too high a chance an enemy could access our stash and use our weapons against us. Keep everything at home under lock and key."

"Okay, cool," Rory said.

I caught Alistair's eye, and gave him a nod. Rather than tell Rory he was insane to suggest bringing weapons to school, he'd talked him down in just the right way.

"Now, for the demonstration." Rory got up from a pew, hoisted his army pants around his chubby middle, and grabbed a long metal serving spoon from his bag. "Who wants to help me? Gabby?"

"Sure, pretend *I'm* the zombie." I got up and did a jittery zombie walk, making the others laugh.

"Here's how to impale a zombie with any household object.

Saw this technique on YouTube." Rory came at me with the spoon, pretending to impale my stomach with the handle. I bent over, making the appropriate moaning noises. "Now that she's bent over, you finish her off. Go for the head." He pretended to bonk me several times on the head. I sank to the ground dramatically.

The others clapped.

"Good job, Zombiegirl," Rory said.

"Anytime." I dusted myself off and sat down again. I wondered what X would think if he saw me participating in this stuff. He'd probably laugh that gorgeous laugh of his. No matter what I was doing, he was always there, in the back of my mind. I should get over him already.

"It's your turn next week," Adriana told me, bringing me back to reality. "What are you going to do?"

"Um." I was still thinking about X, and my senses were taking a while to return.

"Since you're into radio, maybe you could research radio communications during the apocalypse," Alistair suggested. "Staying in touch with other survivors is going to be crucial."

"Sure, I'll put something together for that." Maybe I'd ask Caballero his thoughts on the matter. I was sure he'd crack up.

"I'm starving," Caro said. "Let's go to the caf."

They all agreed. I'd been hoping to avoid the caf again today, since the dirty looks I'd been receiving since JC had spread his version of Saturday night's events were worse than usual. But I was enjoying myself with these guys, and I didn't feel like spending the rest of lunch hour by myself.

The five of us went upstairs and found a table near the concession. I was careful not to look in JC's direction. God forbid he accuse me of staring at him.

We all bought slices of pizza. I wasn't picky about pizza— thick or thin, oven or delivery, meat or veggie—but today's was downright disturbing. It was white, flat, and tasted like the flavor had been surgically removed.

"How'd your parents' party go last weekend?" Alistair asked.

Unfortunately, he was probably the only senior at school who hadn't heard about it.

"Drah-ma." Adriana did a mock shiver.

"JC showed up," I said. "There was a bit of an argument."

"Sorry to hear that. JC's an asshole. All those guys are." Alistair's face darkened. He was probably remembering the atomic wedgie.

Had JC been a part of that? I'd never known him to be a bully—he was just the opposite, always going out of his way to help people. But after the way he'd been acting lately, it wouldn't surprise me.

"Yeah, he's a total asshole," Rory agreed, turning to me. "JC was telling everybody in the locker room yesterday that you're frigid. I even said, *Really? Gabby?* And he was like, *Yeah.*"

"Rory." Alistair gave him a look of disgust, while Adriana and Caro had stopped mid-chew, ready for my reaction.

I put down my pizza, my hand curling into a fist. That was a brand-new low for JC. I wanted to jump out of my seat and go tell him he'd earned the title of Douchebag of the Year.

But I remembered that Mom had said he was seeing a psychiatrist. If he was in a funk of some kind, I should probably leave it alone. And if Mom heard I'd confronted him at school, she would freak.

I lifted my chin. "I'm not even gonna respond to that."

Everybody looked at one another as if this was a very un-Gabby-like response.

"*I* know why he's lashing out," Adriana said. "The breakup messed with his manhood. He couldn't handle that you rejected him sexually, so he's going to insult *you* sexually."

"True that," Rory said, nodding eagerly. "He talked like you're not interested in guys at all. Like he suspects you're a lesbian. Personally, I see nothing wrong with lesbians. I think they're sexy."

Under other circumstances, I might've laughed. "Picture that, huh? If I'm gay, then JC wasted way too long trying to convert me."

"No one thinks you're gay," Alistair said, "especially if they listen to your radio show. I really enjoyed it Sunday night."

So much that the mention of it made him blush, I could see.

Good thing I hadn't chosen to rant about bad breakups and unsupportive families. After Saturday night's disaster, it had been very tempting. But instead I'd talked about what it was like to be captivated by someone. To be unable to get that person out of your head. And my listeners had responded with stories of love at first sight and crazy hot attractions.

I couldn't help but wonder if X had been listening. He'd been all over my mind during the show. Maybe he'd tuned in just to make sure I wasn't talking about Raul again. Would he have clued in that he had inspired the show?

"I didn't hear it," Rory said. "I was in a Call of Duty tournament. What'd I miss?"

"It was about crushes," Alistair informed him. "Essentially, it was about the phenomenon of finding ourselves captivated by someone before we even know them."

"Is it available on iTunes? As a podcast?" Rory wanted to know.

"Sorry," I said.

"I heard it too." Caro's eyebrows went up. "Sounded to me like you're crushing on someone, Gabby."

"Maybe. Maybe not." I smiled a little. Unfortunately, since the crush was all in my head, there was nothing more I could say. It wasn't like I expected to ever see him again.

"So guys, who else is pumped for Friday night?" Adriana drummed on the table. "It's gonna be incredible!"

"What's Friday night?" I asked.

Adriana and Caro glared at me. "The psychic fair," they said simultaneously.

"Oh, right." In a moment of duress, I'd agreed to go. It was the most important event of the year for them, so not going would be like skipping out on Thanksgiving dinner.

"Sorry, can't go," Rory said apologetically. "Finish gaming tournament."

I didn't know if he meant he had to finish a gaming tournament, or had a gaming tournament with Finnish people. It really didn't matter.

"Are you coming?" Caro asked Alistair.

"I'll think about it. Are these psychics any good?"

"Depends which one you get," Caro said. "I'm going to be seeing Miss Lisa. She's a medium, a channeler, clairvoyant, clairaudient—I'm probably missing something. I had to book the slot months in advance."

"She did a reading for me last year and it was right on," Adriana said. "I'm talking, every detail." She turned to me. "Don't forget to bring money for cover. It's twenty bucks."

"Twenty bucks?" That was steep. I still had some money saved up from my two years at Target, but I had to be careful.

My internship at WKTU was unpaid.

Our table shook, jostling our lunch trays and spilling our drinks. I looked up. Ellie, Karina, and Bree were quickly walking away, giggling. My former friends. JC's entourage.

Oh no you didn't. This wasn't just an insult to me, it was an insult to my new friends too. JC admitted he thought of us as freaks.

I would've expected this from Ellie and Karina, but not Bree. I thought we were cool.

I stood up. "Excuse *you.*"

The girls glanced back. Ellie and Karina's eyes were smug. Bree mouthed awkwardly, *Sorry, Gabby.*

Fine. Maybe I could give Bree a pass, but not Ellie and Karina. I stared them down. They were muttering to each other, and I could imagine what they were saying.

JC's right. She's such a bitch.

Of course, JC and Liam were watching the whole thing, laughing.

This wasn't the JC I used to know. He'd never been the *take pleasure in another person's pain* type. He'd never been the type to kick someone when they were down.

Maybe I never knew him at all.

Breakfast these days was a very quick thing. I avoided spending time in my parents' presence as much as possible. I was sick of that look from my mom. Sick of her talking at me between tight, angry lips.

As I was eating some toast, Mom came into the kitchen, already dressed for work. She loomed over me, freshly coiffed and teacherly. "It's time you got a job, Gabby."

"I have a job." WKTU was my job. She knew that. That was why I'd quit Target.

"Technically, you're volunteering."

"Interning," I corrected her. "Most people would kill for this opportunity. I can't ask to be paid—the operating budget's too small to pay anyone else. The receptionists are making minimum wage as it is, and the DJs don't make that much."

"Exactly my point." Mom's eyes lit with satisfaction. "If you want to earn a good living one day, you should train for something more practical. That doesn't mean you can't DJ as a side job."

"I don't have to make a lot of money, Mom. I'll settle for a decent living. And I could always branch out into TV broadcasting if I want."

I knew she had more respect for TV than radio. Maybe that could help bring her around.

"If you ever want a career in TV, you'd better watch yourself, Gabby. I hear they have you talking about prostitution and pimps now. It could come back to haunt you."

I glanced at her, trying to gauge what she knew. "How

would you know what I've been talking about? Have your students been talking about the show, then?"

"They have," she admitted. "And I wasn't too happy about your choice of topic."

It sounded like she hadn't heard specifics about what had happened that night at the club, which was a small mercy. The last thing I needed was to be grounded right now.

"It's a timely topic, Mom. I was trying to warn people about the dangers out there."

"I understand that. And believe it or not, I'm not asking you to quit your show. But you should get another job as well. And yes, it would mean spending less time at WKTU."

How could she ask me to spend less time at WKTU when she knew how much that place meant to me? "You're just mad at me about the party."

She glared at me. She hated when I did that—when I talked about what was really going on.

"You never made David get a real-world job. He never had any job at all."

Mom took a breath. "Don't compare yourself to David."

"Right, David got straight As, so he had a different set of rules." I raised a finger. "But don't forget, David has an unhealthy sense of entitlement. *I* don't have that. I'll settle for fairness."

Mom was exasperated. I saw Dad creeping by the kitchen.

I waved him in. "You want me to get a second job too?"

He came in reluctantly, clearly not wanting to get in the middle of this. "We think it's a good idea," he said gently. "College tuition is going up every year."

"I'm going to Miami-Dade for radio and TV. It'll be super cheap compared to what you're paying for David."

"We're helping David because he has a lot of schooling ahead of him and he couldn't do it without our help," Mom said.

Wow, that was a blindside. I'd assumed that because they were paying for David, they'd pay for me. Guess I'd been wrong.

"I just want to get this straight," I said. "If I don't study what you want, you won't pay."

"Oh, Gabby, don't make it sound like a punishment," Dad said, patting my hand. "We're not saying we won't help you out with expenses. But if we invest in your education, we want to make sure we're investing in a viable career for you."

"Sarita went to Miami-Dade. She's doing great."

It was the surest way to get an eye roll from them. "If she's doing so well, why don't you ask her for a loan?" Mom said. "Think she could afford it?"

"Maybe not, but she supports me in the ways that count." I got up. "Have a happy day."

THE PSYCHIC FAIR

WHAT THE HELL AM I doing here?

I kept asking myself that as I walked around the psychic fair with the Paranormal Twins and Alistair on Friday night.

Maria had called me last-minute to see if I'd go to a Rivera party with her, but I'd had to say no. I was already regretting that decision. I loved Rivera parties. They were a chance to see old friends and catch up on new gossip. The Rivera crew knew about my radio show and actually thought it was cool. The best part was that they didn't worship JC Suarez or give a shit what he said about me.

But instead of partying with Rivera kids, I was at a psychic fair, my nostrils assailed by a thousand dizzying scents.

We were in a massive room at the Miami Convention Center. There had to be five hundred people here. We'd been inside all of ten seconds when we joined a group crowding around a black woman with gaudy makeup.

"What's she—" I started to ask, but Adriana shushed me.

"She's a voodoo priestess!" Adriana whispered. "She's channeling a restless spirit."

Everybody gasped as the woman started seizing violently, shouting that she was reliving death by electrocution. But when it was over, I wasn't sold.

"I want my twenty bucks back," I muttered to Alistair, who stifled a laugh.

For girls who claimed to have psychic tendencies, the Paranormal Twins were oblivious to my boredom. They walked around excitedly, stopping at almost every booth.

"Hey, this lady sees auras!" Adriana said, yanking us over to see a little old lady with long white braids and a heavily wrinkled face. "What color is mine?"

The woman looked past Adriana, beside her, then above her. "Pink."

Adriana's mouth fell open. "Pink? Seriously?"

Caro stepped forward, as if coming to her friend's defense. "What shade of pink are we talking about?"

"Pink, you know, like bubblegum," the lady said with an Eastern European accent. "Don't worry, it's sign of a nice person. Loving person. Is good thing." She turned to Caro. "Yours is yellow. Bright and happy like sunshine."

Alistair and I looked at each other. So the Paranormal Twins with their dark clothes and dark interests actually had pink and yellow auras. Classic.

"And you, young man, are dark—a blue. Very serious man." She smiled at him. "All business, as they say."

Alistair seemed satisfied with that. I was hoping to slink away before she saw me, but the woman's eyes landed on me. "Purple. Yours is purple."

"Doesn't that represent sexual frustration?" I asked, only half kidding. With the amount I was thinking about X, it would be true.

But she wasn't laughing. "No. It's a . . . how you say . . . wise color. Intuitive person. Artist maybe. Very sensitive."

I couldn't disagree with any of that. We stuffed dollars into the jar on her table, and moved on.

"Where's that music coming from?" Alistair asked, scanning the crowd.

We followed the drumbeats to the far corner of the room. A large cardboard sign said "Soul Dance" and a group of alternative-looking people were dancing around, shaking their bodies with abandon.

To my shock, Alistair jumped into the mix. His body was like a wiggly worm, and he closed his eyes and gave himself up to the music, his arms flowing around him like he was shadowboxing with the wind. It was a beautiful thing to see him letting go like that. In fact, soon we were all dancing, jumping, and jiggling, like kids bouncing on a bed.

When it was over, we bought some ice-cold passionflower drinks and sat down on the carpeted floor, tired but happy.

"The dancing alone was worth my twenty bucks," I said. "Got my cardio for the day."

"'Soul Dancing, trademark, is a form of meditation aimed at reducing stress and freeing us from our inner captivity,'" Caro said, reading from a pamphlet. "It says 'patent pending.' I didn't know you could patent dancing." She checked her phone. "It's almost nine! Who wants to watch my reading with Miss Lisa?"

The "Miss Lisa" Caro and Adriana had been talking about wasn't what I'd pictured—she looked like a forty-year-old soccer mom with good highlights. She wore white linen pants, a white blouse, and gold-rimmed Dolce and Gabbana glasses.

"That's her?" I muttered to Alistair.

"Indeed," he said, obviously thinking the same thing.

Caro marched right up to her. "I'm Caroline Hanlon, nine o'clock."

Miss Lisa shook her hand. "Nice to meet you. Come back here and we'll get started." Miss Lisa indicated a small curtained-off area behind her booth.

"Can my friends watch?"

"That's up to you. I'll be getting very personal. If other

people come in, I have to warn you—their energies can some-times interfere with a reading."

"No worries," Caro said cheerfully. "Come on, guys."

We followed them into the space between the curtains. As we stood on the sidelines, Caro and Lisa sat down. Lisa's feet were flat on the floor, and she sat up straight, palms facing upward. I glanced at the others. We were all holding our breath, waiting for her to begin.

"One of your spirit guides is stepping forward," Miss Lisa said, closing her eyes. "I ask that this guide provide information that is in highest good. And so it is."

In the next fifteen minutes, I learned more about Caro than I ever knew before. Everything from the death of her grandmother when she was five, to the shock of her parents' divorce, to her search for love.

"Will I find love?" Caro asked, her voice full of hope.

Lisa paused, then said, "In the twilight of the apocalypse, you will find true love."

Huh? Up until that point, I'd been ready to say Lisa was legit. Now I wasn't so sure.

"But when'll that be?" Caro pressed.

"If it's going to happen after the apocalypse, hopefully not soon," I whispered to the others.

"I can't say when." Lisa splayed her hands. "That is all the angels were willing to tell me."

When the reading was over, we left the curtained-off room. Caro seemed mystified by the last question, and I was eager to get more of that passionflower punch. That's when Miss Lisa touched my arm. "Excuse me, dear. I'm compelled to tell you something."

I froze. "What?"

"Someone needs your help. This person . . . they're in a place of darkness, but they don't know it. You can help them break free."

I swallowed. Before I could ask a question, Miss Lisa's next client came up and introduced herself. Lisa simply smiled and said to me, "Angels be with you."

I left the area with my friends. My stomach was in knots. Someone needed my help. But who?

Maria. The psychic must have been talking about Maria.

She texted me the next morning, asking to meet at the mall. That was my first clue that something was wrong—she'd been avoiding the mall lately, not wanting to get into any more debt. But the faded mascara streaks beneath her eyes were a dead giveaway.

I hugged her and sat down. We were on a bench in the middle of the mall, our favorite guy-watching spot. It was surprising our butt prints weren't carved into the bench after how much time we'd spent here this past summer.

"You're not pregnant, are you?" I blurted out.

"Pregnant? God, no."

What a relief. Maria had had several scares over the two years she'd been with Renaldo. If she were to find out she was pregnant now that they'd broken up, it would be horrible.

"Then why so low?"

Maria struggled to get the words out. "I'm not pregnant but . . . Elisa is."

Elisa. Maria's cousin, the one who'd "stolen" her boyfriend. I preferred to think of her as having done Maria a favor by taking him off her hands.

I wasn't going to react the way Maria wanted me to. "Be glad it isn't *you* carrying his baby."

"It was supposed to be me," she said tearfully.

I sighed. When I'd seen Maria last, the night of the roofies incident, she'd been in the *fuck him, I'm moving on* phase. But she'd regressed. Today it was the Maria who kept asking herself what she'd done to make her man stray.

"Don't wish it were you. Think of it: Elisa's going to be bogged down with a baby while you're out partying. Odds are he's going to leave her before the baby's two. I'm telling you."

I could never understand why some girls thought that having a baby was the best way to keep a guy, when it was actually the best way to lose him. My radio callers complained about absentee dads constantly. Guys who didn't want to be tied down. And yet so many girls believed that pregnancy would lead to marriage and a picture-perfect little family.

Yeah, right.

"I bet my mom will expect me to go to her baby shower," Maria said, sipping whipped cream off her latte. "I can't. I don't ever want to see that bitch again."

"Don't worry about that. Your mom's probably doing a happy dance that it's Elisa and not you. Am I right?"

"I guess so."

"I'll be honest with you, Maria. I'm doing a happy dance too. See?" I grooved on the bench, waving my hands in the air. "I'm dancing, girl."

Maria managed a smile.

One thing never changed when it came to me and Maria. In our friendship, I was the counselor. I was the one who tried to boost her confidence. The one who gave her the good advice she never followed. I was the one who'd seen her through three pregnancy scares, took her to a clinic to get the Pill, then put an app on her phone to remind her to take it.

Hell, I'd even discouraged her from dating Renaldo in the first place. The guy was in his early twenties, jobless, goalless, and living with his mama. But somehow his lazy grin and wannabe gangster persona had sucked her in.

"I called him last night." Maria glanced at me, biting her

lip. Before I could open my mouth, she raised a hand to shut me down. "I know you said not to call him, but I had to. I have the right to know how it started with Elisa, don't I?"

"And? Did he give you any answers?"

"Not really. He said he'll always love me and that there's a part of his heart she can never have."

I gagged. "You're fucking kidding me. Did you tell him to stick it up his ass?"

"I told him it was bullshit."

"Thank you."

"And that if he really loved me, he wouldn't still be with her."

My eyes bulged. "That makes it sound like you want him back!"

"I don't. But it's obvious she got pregnant so he wouldn't go back to me."

Crap. I felt sorry for Maria. Not because Renaldo had cheated and dumped her—that was the universe smiling on her, even if she couldn't see it yet—but because the situation had brought out all her insecurities. I thought of the parallel with JC. Was he upset because he'd lost *me*, because I was so damned special? Or was it because he couldn't handle the thought that someone didn't want him?

"Look at that guy over there, outside Mexx," I said. "In the blue T-shirt."

"He's cute. But he's with a girl."

"Exactly. And he's holding her shopping bags. Isn't that what you want? A cute sweetie who'll hold your bags? And it wouldn't hurt to have a guy who actually has a job so he doesn't have to mooch off you all the time, wouldn't it?"

"Great guys are an urban myth, like that charmer with the roofies."

"Oh, come on."

"Seriously. Name one great guy."

I thought about saying my dad, but that would be weird. "DJ Caballero. He adores his wife and kids. Girls flirt with him all the time, but he doesn't flirt back."

"Caballero's like forty-five, isn't he? He's too old and tired to play around. Look at JC. He was supposedly one of the good ones, right? But when you broke up with him he went all bitchy on you. Made everybody shun you like you were an Amish girl or something. Is that a nice guy?"

She'd hit the mark. "All I'm saying is, don't give up hope. Don't imagine every guy's like Renaldo because if that's what you believe, that's what you'll attract." Hearing myself, I realized the Paranormal Twins must've had an impact on me. They were always talking about the laws of attraction. Visualize it, and it will come to you.

Oh, I was visualizing what I wanted, all right. I was visualizing a gorgeous, six-foot-tall undercover cop named X. A bad boy who was working for good. What I wouldn't do to have him walk by us right now.

Sigh.

"Remember one thing, Gabby. You can't ever trust a guy. Ever." She downed her latte, a glob of whipped cream sticking to her upper lip. "Put *that* in your radio show."

ABSENT

WHEN I WALKED INTO MATH class on Monday morning, last week's test sat on my desk. 70%. Nice.

Bree hadn't shown up yet, but her test was on her desk. 86%. With a mark like that, she should be tutoring me. Or I should at least be copying her work. Unfortunately, my years of Sunday school and sin talk wouldn't let me.

The bell rang, and the last of the students hurried in before Ms. Saikaley closed the door.

"You'll find your tests on your desks," Ms. Saikaley said. She wasn't a popular teacher, partly because she taught the most universally hated subject, and partly because she had this condescending way of looking at you above her reading glasses, as if to say, *You really don't get it, do you?*

"Only half of you managed to pass the test," she announced.

"The concept of binomials didn't quite get through, people." Her gaze passed over each one of us. "So guess what? We're going to revisit it again before the midterm next month."

We all groaned.

"Miss?" Paul Clifton's hand shot up.

Her eyes zeroed in on the cell phone sitting on his desk. "It's one point off your mark every time you have your phone out, Paul."

"Yeah, but did you hear about Bree O'Connor?"

The class went eerily quiet. I felt something twist in my stomach.

Ms. Saikaley frowned. "What about Bree? Did something happen?"

"She went missing," Paul said. "Saw it on the news this morning."

"Are you serious?" I asked, but I could see that he was. Even jokester Paul wouldn't joke about that.

The seat beside me suddenly felt very empty.

"Yep," Paul said with an eager nod. "We were all at Jeff Given's party Friday night. She told people she was gonna get a cab home, but she never got there. No one knows what happened to her after she left. She wasn't that drunk or anything."

"Thank you for informing us, Paul." I could tell that Ms. Saikaley was as stunned as the rest of us. "Now, why don't you all take a few minutes to look over your tests, and come up and see me if you have any questions?" Then she scooted behind her desk and went on her computer.

Everybody was whispering and checking their phones. I googled the name Brianna O'Connor, and saw the missing person report Paul was talking about.

Police have asked for help from the public in locating a missing seventeen-year-old girl.

Brianna O'Connor went missing from the Coral Gables area.

Brianna is described as:

120 lbs

5'5"

Slim build

Green eyes

Long straight blond hair

She was last seen wearing a pink tank top and a short black skirt.

It was unbelievable.

I'd known Bree since ninth grade, and she wasn't the type to run away. She didn't clash with her mom and stepdad the way I did with my parents. Didn't push the boundaries. Her only complaint was being forced to spend a month of her summer vacation in boring Iowa with her dad and his new wife.

I'd been to many parties at Jeff's house. There was the usual mix of bad behaviors—the weed, the booze, the ill-thought-out hookups. But they weren't the kind of parties where people got so trashed they didn't make it home.

Ms. Saikaley got up and wrote on the board: *Probability and Statistics.* Dear Mother of God, was she actually going to proceed with the lesson?

Yes, she was.

Since Ms. Saikaley had a rule that you couldn't ask for the bathroom pass in the first ten minutes of class, I made sure I was the first to raise my hand after that. In the bathroom, I hid away in the end stall, took out my phone, and went to Bree's Instagram. Although I'd been worried the cops might've shut it down, it was still up, and had already been flooded with emotional comments from friends wishing she'd come home.

Bree hadn't posted since early the previous week, when she'd put up a picture of herself in a white cami in front of the bathroom mirror, pouting for the camera. It was a typical Bree selfie. I scrolled down to see the previous posts. They were all quotes about love—about the roller-coaster ride of love, the thrill of it. One quote, written as if in blood, caught my eye.

Would you die for him? If you hesitated, then it isn't true love.

Did Bree have a crush? Or a secret boyfriend? Maybe she was just yearning for one. She hadn't had a boyfriend since her short relationship with Liam last year. And with an idiot like Liam, the word *relationship* was a stretch.

I downloaded the quote onto my phone. It felt important.

Some people came into the bathroom. When they started talking, I knew immediately that it was Ellie and Karina.

"I'm so freaking out right now," Ellie said. Through the crack in the door I saw that she'd stopped in front of the mirror, inspecting her face for breakthrough freckles. Although Ellie was universally considered pretty, all she saw were her flaws.

"What the hell happened to her? This is so fucked up." Black-haired, with Slavic bones and a dancer's body, Karina was the opposite of Ellie—she saw nothing in the mirror but perfection.

"I'd told her to wait an hour and I'd give her a ride. I don't know why she didn't just stick around. This is literally making my stomach sick. Do you think she got kidnapped or something?"

"I don't know. She was wearing those crazy high heels." Spotting some freckles, Ellie grabbed her compact and covered them up. "She could've accepted a ride from a stranger because her feet were killing her."

Ellie gave a snort. "She would *never* get in a car with a stranger. The girl won't even share her mascara, for God's sake."

"Maybe she wasn't so careful that night. She didn't get high, did she?"

"She seemed fine to me. I wouldn't have let her leave by herself if she was all screwed up. I don't think she was taking Blings. Maybe I'm wrong."

I frowned. *Taking Blings? What are Blings?*

"Were you with her all night?"

"No. Hello, Drew and I were hooking up. Were you with her?"

"No."

They were talking in circles. Time was going by, and I figured I'd better flush myself out before Ms. Saikaley sent a search party. When I came out of the stall, they seemed startled.

"Hey," I said. "Scary about Bree, huh?"

They glanced at each other, as if deciding whether to talk to me or not.

"Yeah, it sucks," Ellie said, not taking her eyes off her reflection.

"She's probably with that guy," I said casually, washing my hands. "If you know what I mean."

They looked confused. *"What guy?"* they both asked.

That was interesting. Whoever Bree was referring to on her Instagram page, her friends didn't know about him. "Oh, I thought she had a boyfriend. You know, because she posted all those love quotes."

"A boyfriend? Bree?" Karina made a face. "Uh, no."

"We'd know if she did," Ellie added.

"Oh, I guess I'm wrong," I said, grabbing for some paper towels and discovering there were none.

I went back to class. Thankfully, Ms. Saikaley was mid-lesson and hadn't noticed that I'd been gone for fifteen minutes.

I sat down, glancing at the empty seat next to me. Had Bree been using the Blings the girls were talking about, then encountered someone who'd hurt her?

I slipped out my phone and brought up X's number. I'd put him into my contacts on one of the many occasions I'd been tempted to call him.

Hi, it's Gabby. My friend Brianna O'Connor is missing. Left a party Friday night and never made it home. Please keep an eye out. I sent him a picture of her.

Two minutes later, X's reply came. Heard about it. I checked out her pages. She's probably with an older BF. Will be on the lookout.

So X had thought of that possibility too. Hopefully that's all it was—hopefully she was on a romantic bender with a secret boyfriend, and would return home soon, all apologies.

But I wasn't so sure.

A week went by. Bree's face was all over the news. The school picture, blond and sweet. The sexy selfies. Although the police chief said they were getting hundreds of tips every day, the investigation clearly wasn't getting anywhere. The beads of sweat on his bald head said it all.

It was surreal. The girl I'd been friends with since freshman year was now the missing person in the photo. The girl who might end up on a milk carton.

Everybody at school had a theory. Crazed cults, drug-induced fugues, amnesia—nothing was off the table. Any of those theories was better than the more realistic one—that she'd been the victim of a killer. I couldn't bear it.

The only thing people agreed on was that the longer she was gone, the less likely it was she'd turn up alive.

Sunday it rained, which fit perfectly with my mood. Church mass was the longest ever, and I was pretty sure Mrs. Suarez was giving me the evil eye. That evening, the rain escalated to torrential, which made for a white-knuckled drive to WKTU. But it also meant more people would be listening.

I'd thought the roofies show was the most important one I'd ever do. Not anymore.

Caballero pushed back his headphones and smiled. "Hey, Gabby girl. What's up?" The guy never seemed to be in a bad mood, even on a dreary night like tonight.

"I'm going to talk about the missing girl, Bree O'Connor. She's a friend of mine. I think our listeners might be able to help."

He nodded solemnly. "Good idea. Make sure you give the

number of the cops' tip line. We don't want any tips being directed here and getting missed."

"Okay. I emailed Olive a picture of Bree for our website. She's going to tweet it during the show."

"Excellent idea. You're using your show to make a difference, Gabby. I'm proud of you. You're a natural at this. Our Sunday night ratings are awesome, thanks to your show."

"That's good to hear." Caballero was one of the few people I'd met who could give a compliment and mean it. Because he was confident in who he was, it didn't diminish him to boost others up. I wanted to be like that someday.

I headed to the lounge, where I read over my notes, did some vocal exercises, and drank decaf green tea.

Less than an hour later, I went live.

"This is Gabby Perez with *Light Up the Night* coming to you on a rainy night from the miracle street of Miracle Mile. Straight like an arrow and sharp as a tack, I'm gonna get serious with you tonight. I'm sure you've all heard about the missing girl Brianna O'Connor. Bree's what her friends call her. I know because I'm one of them. And her disappearance has shaken me up.

"If you don't know who I'm talking about, Bree is the blond Catholic schoolgirl you've been seeing on the news. She went missing last weekend. She left a party planning to take a cab home, but she never arrived. There's no evidence that she even got into a cab. No one knows what happened to her. It's as if she vanished into thin air.

"But people don't vanish, especially people like Bree. She's responsible. She always let her parents know where she was and when she was coming home.

"I don't know what happened to Bree. But I'm scared for her. She might've trusted the wrong guy to take her home. Or someone might've grabbed her off the street."

I took a second to breathe. Caballero and Olive looked at me anxiously through the glass.

"If you have any clue what happened to her, please call the police tip line at five-five-five, three-five-four-three. You don't have to tell them your name. Whatever you do, don't give up on Bree. Her friends and family won't give up either. Ever.

"Tonight I'm going to play songs that Bree loves. She's a huge fan of Pitbull, so I'll start with 'Red Wine.' Hope you're listening, Bree."

I was relieved to go to music, because I was on the verge of tears. But I was going to keep it together. I had to.

It was a hard show to get through, but I made it. I talked more about Bree, gave some funny anecdotes about her. Then I talked about violence against women. About how all women needed to plan for their own safety. I ended with, "It's a beautiful, ugly world out there. This is Gabby Perez wishing you a good, safe night."

Caballero actually gave me a hug before I handed off to him. I went into the control room, where Olive said, "They're retweeting Bree's picture like crazy."

"Good." That was something, at least.

But I worried that it wouldn't be enough.

There he was.

Through the faint, misty rain, I saw X leaning against my car as I left the station. Something inside me lit up.

He wore a black shirt under a black leather jacket, blue jeans, and sneakers. Tough, sexy, at home in his own skin. I had been aching to see him.

"Good job putting the word out," X said, bypassing small talk.

"Tried my best. I hope it didn't seem random, texting you about Bree. But if you're out there anyway, I figured it was worth a shot."

"Don't worry. I get it."

That put me at ease, and I managed a smile. "How've you been? Did you ever catch up with our buddy Raul?"

"I'm almost there." He cleared his throat, slipping his hands into his pockets. I felt the weight of his pause, and I knew that something bad was coming. "It's not going to be easy for you to hear this."

My gut tensed. "Hear what?"

"One of my guys saw Bree around a few times."

"*What?* He saw her? When?"

"A month ago, before she went missing. He saw her hanging out at clubs with a guy he was keeping tabs on, a pimp named Milo. She was new to his entourage and looked underage. He's sure it's the missing girl on TV."

I struggled to process this. Bree was hanging out with a *pimp?* It didn't make any sense. "It must've been another girl. I'm sure a lot of girls look like her."

"True. But I trust his eye."

"He didn't take pictures of them, did he?" I asked, hopeful.

"No. If only it were that easy."

"So what do you think is happening?"

"You know her, Gabby. I don't. Why do *you* think she'd be hanging around with a pimp?"

I fumbled for an explanation. "Bree might not know he's a pimp. Or—" I bit my lip, not wanting to say it. "She might be with him against her will. Maybe she was drugged."

I saw a flicker of doubt in his eyes, and hurried on. "Bree's from a good family. I just can't picture her running off with some pimp. It doesn't add up."

"You saw her page. All those posts about love. Could be she's fallen for Milo. It's too soon to call this one, Gabby. We'll find her, but we have to do it right. Take it slow."

"Slow?" It was the last thing I wanted to hear. "If it's actually her . . . she could be going through hell right now. He could be forcing her to turn tricks. Maybe if you could get a picture of this Milo guy, the press would circulate it."

X shook his head. "It wouldn't help. Pimps are very mobile. We know for a fact that Milo has connections all over the country. If he smells the cops, he'll skip town. He could send Bree off to another city or trade her with another pimp. We'd probably never see her again."

Send Bree away? Trade her off? My head was spinning. I reminded myself that we didn't know for sure that it was her. We didn't know anything for sure.

His expression was gentle. "You gotta keep it in perspective, Gabby. Bree is probably alive. If my guy hadn't spotted her with that pimp, we'd have no reason to believe that. More likely she'd be lying in an unmarked grave."

I hoped X was right that she was alive—even if it meant she was with a pimp. But we needed to get her away from him as fast as possible. "What if this Milo decides to kill her because of all the press she's getting?"

"Milo won't kill her. She's worth too much to him, and

money's his bottom line. That's how pimps operate. Swans like her can pull in thousands a week for him."

"Swans?"

"White girls. Especially the blondes. They're valuable. Milo will do everything he can to hold on to her."

X took out his keys. But instead of moving, he looked me in the eye. "I heard you talk about Bree on your show. Heard what people are saying about her on the news. Everybody's painting a picture of this perfect little sweetheart. But nobody's really like that. Tell me something else about her. Something that isn't so sweet."

It was a strange thing to ask. I thought about it. "A couple of weeks ago, her friends deliberately bumped my table in the cafeteria—they were just being idiots. When they were walking away, Bree looked back and mouthed that she was sorry. She's a nice girl, but she can be . . . kind of a sheep. She goes along with the crowd."

I hated criticizing Bree. I even felt guilty that I'd been upset with her over the table-bumping incident. It wasn't her fault that Ellie and Karina had gone all *Mean Girls* on me.

X nodded and thanked me, as if what I said was actually helpful.

Before he could turn away, I caught his arm. "I want to help you find her. I could talk to her. No matter what situation she's in . . . I could help."

He seemed to consider this. "Got a decent fake ID?"

I hesitated, reminding myself that he was a cop. But I was sure my fake ID was the last of his concerns. "Yeah, I've got one."

"Good. You'll hear from me soon."

THE KISS

"I BET ZOMBIES GOT BREE O'CONNOR," Rory said the following Tuesday. "She could be huddled in an alley munching on some roadkill."

The rest of us looked at one another in disgust. Zombie club or not, it wasn't acceptable to talk about Bree that way. As seriously as we pretended to take the zombie thing, it was mostly a joke. And Bree's disappearance was anything but.

I was about to tell Rory to shut it, but Alistair did it first. "Bree's off-limits."

"But—"

"Off. Limits."

Rory sighed. "Fine."

"I think poor Bree was kidnapped," Adriana said. "Somebody could've dragged her into a car and . . ." She didn't dare fill in the blank. "Afterward, he could've dumped her some-where. You hear about cases like that."

I'd hoped, selfishly maybe, that the zombie club wouldn't talk about Bree today. I couldn't sit in class or walk through the hallway without hearing her name. Then my thoughts would go spinning out of control. Had she been lured in by that pimp? Was he keeping her by force? Was she suffering at this moment?

Everyone at school was upset, but I could tell that JC was especially shaken up. His usual laughter was gone, replaced by a sullen sadness. He'd grown up a block away from Bree, and they'd known each other since kindergarten. He drove past her house every day, and often crossed paths with her parents. Despite the way JC had treated me, I couldn't help but feel bad for him.

"I'm not so sure she was kidnapped," Caro said. "My mom and I joined the search this weekend. There had to be two hundred of us out there. No one found anything. Not one lit-tle thing. If somebody grabbed her off the street, you'd think she might've dropped something."

Rory snorted. "Yeah, and it's hard to picture her being grabbed off the street anywhere near Jeff's house. Coral Gables isn't exactly crime central."

"A lot of people who get kidnapped go with the assailant willingly," Alistair pointed out. "They accept a ride from a stranger, get into a cab—or what they *think* is a cab."

"We could do a séance," Adriana said. "In case she's . . ." Once again, she wouldn't finish the sentence.

Nobody said anything.

Caro chewed her bottom lip. "I wish I'd known about this when I saw Miss Lisa."

"Is she that psychic you were talking about?" Rory asked. "Sounds like the name of a kindergarten teacher."

Caro ignored him. "I figure if Miss Lisa knows something, she'll contact the police. She's helped with investigations before."

"By looking into her crystal ball?" Rory said, crossing his eyes like an idiot.

Adriana turned on him. "I don't get you. You believe in zombies, but you don't believe in psychics? That makes no sense."

Rory put up his hands. "Don't shoot the messenger, baby. The zombie phenomenon is scientific fact. Just google 'zombie virus' and you'll see."

As they argued, something inside me stilled. I remembered the words Miss Lisa had said to me as I walked out. *Somebody needs your help.* I'd assumed that person was Maria. But now I realized it must have been Bree. It made perfect sense, and it explained the intensity of Miss Lisa's message. *If* she was legit. The jury was still out on that one.

Adriana was looking at me. "Did you research telecommunications during a zombie apocalypse?"

"Sorry, I didn't get to it. Should we head?"

We tossed our lunch bags and went up two floors to our lockers. My locker, formerly right next to JC's in the cool part of the grad hallway, was now next to Rory's. A cheerleader named Meagan had gladly switched with me in the first week of school. It was a win-win for her; she'd landed a locker in the cool section, and had spared herself from the funky odor emanating from Rory's locker.

We turned a corner and stopped in our tracks. Three cops, one principal, and a German shepherd. A row of lockers was wide open, and the dog was sticking his nose in each one before moving to the next.

The lockers belonged to JC and his friends.

A crowd of students had assembled, watching the spectacle. Liam grinned like it was all a joke.

A drug raid. Although the school admin threatened raids all the time, I'd never seen it happen until now. The timing probably wasn't a coincidence. The cops must know by now that people had been doing Blings at the party where Bree was last seen. Blings, from what I'd gathered, were a psychedelic drug, kind of like acid, that gave a wicked high, not to mention the occasional wild hallucination.

JC went pale when the dog barked in front of his locker.

We watched as the cops took everything out of it—every book, pencil, item of clothing. Then a cop unceremoniously dumped the contents of JC's backpack on the floor. JC's expression turned to disgust as the dog's wet nose burrowed in his stuff.

"Told you they're all drug fiends now," Adriana murmured.

"They won't get caught," Alistair said dismally. "They might be stupid enough to use, but they're not stupid enough to keep anything incriminating in their lockers."

The dog gave a final sniff of JC's belongings, then bypassed the next locker. Three lockers down, he paused again to nose through Liam's stuff, his tail wagging madly.

Liam just laughed. When the dog finally moved on from his locker, he gave an exaggerated "Phewf!" and wiped his forehead with the back of his hand.

"What a shame," Alistair muttered.

Thursday afternoon, Olive and I were in the mailroom at WKTU. Unlike the fashionable lobby or lounge, the room was musty and crammed with old flyers and stacks of mail. The presence of mousetraps in every corner (thankfully empty, at the moment) didn't help.

Olive looked like a living doll in a white doily sundress and ballet flats. "I can't believe people still send letters. They're such a pain to reply to." Olive used a letter opener to pry one open. She scanned it. "Some old man doesn't want Caballero using the word *pissed*. Talk about having too much time on your hands."

I frowned. "What's an old guy doing listening to WKTU, anyway?"

"Damned if I know. Some people need a cause." She shrugged, her glossy side pigtails bouncing. "Should we recycle it?"

I was tempted, but I shook my head. "Put it in my pile. I'll answer it."

My phone vibrated.

I glanced down, my heart skipping a beat. It was X.

If you still want to help me find Bree, meet me tonight at 9. Wear casual street clothes. I'll text you later with the location. No pressure to do this.

My pulse sped up. I answered: I'm in.

Olive had a knowing look in her eyes. *"Somebody has a date,"* she sang.

"I wish." I couldn't deny the thrill of receiving a text from X, but this was far from a date. "You know, I don't think I've ever been on a real date. With my ex, we never really dated. We just, sort of, got together." I pondered that. "Maybe if there'd been some sort of trial period, I'd have realized sooner that we were better off as friends."

"Hindsight's great like that, isn't it?" Olive said wryly. "You're so right—most people don't even date anymore. It's hook up, hang out, then break up. What a shame. I like to make a guy work for it. Andrew takes me on a date once a week. I'm talking dinner and a movie, the whole shebang. And I make him pay."

"Hey, with my cash flow, if a guy wants to pay, no argument here."

"What can I say?" She grinned. "I'm an old-fashioned girl."

At eight thirty that night, I stood in my bedroom, pulling on jeans, old sneakers, and a gray hoodie. I took a deep breath, staring into the mirror.

We're gonna find her.

We have to find her.

Downstairs, I zipped up my hoodie. "Going to a movie with Adriana and Caro," I said to my parents on my way out. "Later."

Traffic on the expressway was lighter than I expected, and I made it downtown in twenty minutes. I loved downtown Miami at night. The city lights were like glow sticks against the dark sky. It was a place of endless excitement and possibility, where the party didn't start until half the city was already in bed.

The GPS guided me through a few turns, and before I knew it, I was heading up Flagler Street. It was a student ghetto where dive bars with flashing neon signs advertised two-for-one drinks, ladies' nights, and starving student specials.

Although I was a few minutes early, I figured I'd get out and look around. Across the street, a group of young people was hanging out. They were street kids, the kind with piercings in their cheeks, gauges in their ears, and crude tattoos across their knuckles. Several were sitting cross-legged on the sidewalk playing bongo drums. A street artist in a knit cap was drawing something while others gathered around him.

Pulling up my hood against the breeze, I tapped my feet to the rhythm of the drums. I'd only been standing there a couple of minutes when someone called from across the street. "Hey, Gabby! Over here!"

I scanned the area, then I did a double take. It was X. He was the street artist.

Seriously?

He was standing now, holding the sketch under his arm. In a long, beat-up cargo jacket, baggy jeans, and ratty old boots, he looked every bit the young street artist.

Holy shit. This must be his cover.

I hesitated only a beat before crossing the street to join him. I couldn't believe how at home he looked among the street kids, how he blended in perfectly. X held open his arms and hugged me, pulling me against his chest and whispering, "Just go with it." As if I'd object. It felt so delicious to have those arms around me. When he released me, his blue eyes were twinkling. "Look what I drew."

It was a black chalk drawing of a girl in a hoodie standing on a sidewalk. It was me. The picture was incredible, and yet he must've sketched it in two minutes flat.

"Holy, it's good."

"Good enough for twenty bucks?" X said, and some of the others laughed. "Kidding." He tucked the sketchbook into his backpack, slinging it over his shoulder. "Let's get a drink, okay? There's a McDick's around the corner."

He slipped an arm around my waist, said bye to the others, and we walked north on Flagler. When we were a short distance away, he said, "I thought you'd have seen me right away."

"I saw you, but it didn't register. So this is your cover. You're a street artist."

"Yeah. Best way to keep tabs is to be on the ground."

"Your talent isn't fake, that's for sure." I glanced at him. "Are you trained?"

"Self-trained. Does that count?"

"Well, if you ever need a second career . . . talent like that could make you a shitload of money."

He turned to me. "Who says art should have a price tag?"

"I do." I smiled. "My aunt's Sarita Lima, a painter. You might've heard of her. If she didn't sell her paintings, she'd still be working in retail, and *that* would be a crime. She used to talk customers out of buying anything made in China, which was most of the inventory at her store."

At McDonald's, we were met by the scent of fried food and the beeping of the registers. "Coffee?" he asked.

"Hot chocolate," I said. "Or else I'll be up all night."

"Coffee for me. I plan to be."

We didn't have to wait long. X paid with three scrunched dollar bills, then we sat in an isolated corner.

"You must work crazy hours." I sipped the hot chocolate.

He shrugged. "Night's when it all goes down."

I couldn't help but study him, the way he held his cup, the way his blue eyes surveyed the place. X was a chameleon if I'd ever seen one. He looked as much at ease in the role of street artist as he had when I'd first seen him, dressed slick for a nightclub. But he looked younger now, nothing like the jaded cop he was.

"I spotted Bree last night," X said.

I practically jumped out of my seat. "Seriously?"

"Yeah. And she was with him."

My stomach dropped. *Him.* Milo. The pimp.

"I followed her until she got into a car. That's why I wanted you here tonight. She could be out again. If we spot her, a familiar face could help."

"Definitely." If Bree saw me, I had to believe she'd want to reach out, no matter what kind of situation she was in. But if Milo was with her, finding a way to talk to her could be next to impossible.

At X's cue, we carried our drinks outside. He simply said, "I'll take you to places where I think she could be."

He knew the neighborhood well, that much was obvious. The places, the people. He said hello to even the shadiest-looking characters we passed, and gave several of them money from his pocket. I wondered if my instinct that he'd had a rough life was true. Maybe it had trained him for this sort of work.

"You're a pro out here," I said.

"Just being myself, mostly."

"Are you from Miami?"

"Yeah. You?"

"Coral Gables all the way."

"Pretty sweet. So how'd you get the radio gig?"

I tried not to show my surprise. For once, he was asking about me. "I've always been interested in radio. Always been a talker. My parents would say I'm a loudmouth." I glanced over at him, and we both smiled. My heart flipped over, because how could it not when he looked at me like that?

"So last year, I visited WKTU and offered to help out, do whatever needed doing. Eventually I started recording little segments. I got DJ Caballero to listen to them, and he gave me a chance to go on the air."

"Were you nervous the first time, knowing thousands of people were listening? Or does that stuff not faze you?"

"I was a freaking mess." I shuddered at the memory. My stomach had been sick for days before—not that I'd admit to that particular detail. "My biggest fear was freezing up. If you have even a second or two of dead air, your audience is changing the station. I knew that Caballero was going out on a limb to let me go on, and if I screwed up, it was his audience I'd be losing."

X bit his lip, like he felt for me. "Talk about pressure. It went okay, though?"

"No, it was terrible. I was so afraid of freezing up that I wrote out an entire script. The second I went on the air, I started reading it, going way too fast. It was god-awful. I burned through half my script in fifteen minutes. And I saw the look on Caballero's face—he was trying to smile, but . . . I knew I was done. I actually said out loud: *this isn't working.*"

"Whoa." X seemed fascinated. "So what'd you do next?"

"I tore up the script. The listeners could hear me doing it. I said I was boring myself to tears and that it was time to get real. Time to talk about what was *really* bugging me."

His brow lifted. "Oh yeah? What was really bugging you?"

"Guys. Well, it was specifically my boyfriend, but I didn't want to embarrass him. So I just started ranting about guys and the annoying things they do."

"What was it your boyfriend did?"

"It's more what he didn't do. His best friend walked all over him, but my boyfriend never called him on it."

"You don't like it when people don't stand up for themselves," X said thoughtfully.

"Exactly. It's so unattractive. It's not . . . manly."

"Manly." That made him smirk. "I like that. You want a manly man, huh?"

"Go ahead, laugh. I'm not saying I want some caveman guy, but you have to be confident in who you are, you know? Anyway, what was I saying? Oh, right. So I asked the listeners their biggest pet peeves about guys, and the calls flooded in."

X laughed. "That's some story. So dissing the male sex helped you connect with your audience."

"Pretty much."

"I take it you got rid of the boyfriend. Did you ever find what you were looking for?"

God, did my cheeks have to fill up with blood right then? "Um, no. Not yet."

He didn't seem to have noticed my sudden fluster. "My

little brother's into radio. He wants to be a DJ someday." He gave a shrug, like he wouldn't hold his breath. "Your people must be proud of you."

My people? I guess he meant my family. "My parents want me to do something more practical. They're both teachers. But I'm going to Miami-Dade next year for TV, radio, and broadcasting, whether they like it or not."

"Sounds like you know what you want. That's a good thing." He sipped his coffee. "So your aunt is Sarita Lima, huh?"

He knew who she was! "Coolest person ever—and yeah, I'm biased. You should meet her." But the moment I said it, I caught myself. Somehow, our walk had started to feel like a date, and now I was acting like it.

And then it hit me that there was no way X didn't have a girlfriend. He was a cop and he was gorgeous and he probably had Miss Miami waiting for him back at his apartment right now. The thought made my chest ache.

Who knew a crush could actually be painful? Maybe that's why it was called a *crush*.

I looked at him, caught the chiseled profile of his face against the street light, and realized something with startling clarity.

X was going to break my heart.

At that moment, his hand closed around mine—but only

because he was leading me across a busy intersection. "This is where I saw her. Right here, where we're standing."

And suddenly I was back in reality. Miss Lisa's words came to mind. *Someone needs your help. They're in a place of darkness. . . .*

I sighed. "I wish I were psychic. I wish I could just go to her. Bring her home."

"Me too." His hand tightened on mine.

"I figure you've got a curfew," he said an hour later. "With teachers as parents and all."

It was around eleven, and we were back at my car. I would never admit it, but my legs felt heavy from walking so much.

"My curfew's midnight. We could go a little longer." As exhausted as I was, I didn't want to call it a night. What if Bree was right around the corner?

"It's okay. I have other things to take care of tonight."

"Another . . . operation?"

He nodded.

We stared at each other for a few moments, his eyes lingering on my face. I wondered if he felt some of what I was feeling. This pull between us.

"Thanks for letting me come along," I said. "Whenever you're able to go looking for her, count me in."

"Tomorrow night, I'll be out again."

"Then me too."

I reached out to hug him—I couldn't help it. Not only did he not resist, he pulled me against him. I knew right then that our connection was real, that he must feel close to me too. My nostrils caught the scent of smoke and musk. I wasn't going to be the first to let go. I'd been craving his arms around me, and I wouldn't end it one second before I had to.

"Gabby . . ." He took a small step back. He looked down into my face, his eyes questioning.

Oh my God. He's going to kiss me.

Please do it. Please.

My knees faltered as he bent his head toward me. His lips were white hot on mine, and we opened our mouths to each other with a scary, almost maddening need. I couldn't think or breathe or do anything but kiss him back.

My body was glued against his. He pulled back for a split second, as if attempting to stop what was happening, but then we were lost again.

At some point, he ended it, but we were still holding each other, our chests rising and falling together.

"Sorry," he said, clearing his throat. "Got caught up."

How should I respond to that? I wasn't sorry at all.

I saw the frown between his eyes. There were probably rules against stuff like this, I realized. Or maybe I'd been right that he had a girl waiting for him at home.

"You're not with someone, are you?"

"No, I'm not. I just don't want to mislead you."

I understood what he meant. He couldn't promise me any-thing, not when he was working undercover. "It's okay," I said cheerfully. "I get it."

"Cool." But his eyes glittered with skepticism, like he wasn't sure that I did.

LOST

"I WAS HOPING I COULD stay over tonight." It was the next day after school, and I sat in Sarita's kitchen drinking jasmine green tea.

She hadn't been expecting me. She'd answered the door in her painting gear, a light blue muumuu flecked with every color of the spectrum. "You're always welcome, Gabby. Spare room's yours. But I'll be out late with Ben, so maybe tomorrow night?"

"Well, the thing is . . . I plan to be out late too."

"Ah." Her eyes glittered. "Wanna bypass curfew, huh? Be my guest. But you'd better tell me the details if I'm going to be coconspirator."

"I will, but you have to promise not to tell my parents."

"I'm like a therapist. Total confidentiality is guaranteed

unless someone's life is in imminent danger." She held up a paint-stained pinky. "Pinky swear."

I laughed. We'd been doing that since I was a kid, when I'd come to her with the things I didn't want to tell my parents. Sarita knew about every disappointment, every schoolyard bully, every crush. She knew about the roofies incident several weeks ago, and all about my relationship with JC—the good, the bad, and the ugly. She'd been the only one who'd coached me to listen to my own heart rather than the noise around me.

Mom was probably jealous of our relationship, but I figured that, deep down, she was glad I had an adult I could talk to.

"You know that missing girl from my school, Bree O'Connor? I've been helping an undercover cop look for her."

Not a lot shocked Aunt Sarita, but her mouth dropped open. "Really? How'd this come about?"

"Remember when that jerk slipped Maria and me roofies? The guy who warned me is the undercover cop. Goes by the name of X, and his cover's a street artist. He's trying to bust pimps who are targeting underage girls. He thinks Bree's in one of those prostitution rings."

"Oh, God. That's terrible." Sarita gave her head a quick shake, as if she couldn't bear to think about it. "How are you supposed to help him find her?"

"It's not so much that I can help him find her. X knows the

streets and the club scene better than I ever will. It's that if we *do* spot her, I can talk to her, hopefully convince her to make a break for it."

She sipped her tea, quiet for too long. "It's admirable that you're trying to help."

I was waiting for the *but*.

"But if anything were to happen to you . . ." A shadow passed over her face. "I don't know about all of this, Gabby. It makes me nervous."

"I'll be with a cop. He can protect me. If anyone got near me, he'd totally flatten them."

She caught the look in my eye. "You're into this cop, huh? I can't blame you. I spent a whole decade dating men in uniform."

"Oh yeah? You never told me that."

"Military guys, cops, firefighters . . . at heart, those guys are pretty traditional. They're looking for a conventional life and a conventional wife. That was never me."

"Me neither." I was tempted to tell her about the kiss, but I stopped myself. She might not approve—not just because he was an undercover cop, but because she was always cautioning me about older guys. I figured she'd gotten involved with an older guy when she was my age and had lived to regret it.

Instead I told her about Miss Lisa's prediction at the psychic fair. "She said the person I was supposed to help was in a place of darkness, but I could help them break free. That was the same night Bree went missing. It can't be a coincidence."

"My thoughts exactly." Unlike my mom, Sarita wouldn't automatically dismiss the words of a psychic. "All right, Gabby. I'll give you a key."

I smiled. Tonight was a go.

Ten o'clock. The Phoenix.

Posh and exclusive, the Phoenix was a go-to for celebs coming to Miami. Although the club was notorious for brawls between hip-hop artists, the violence only made the place more popular.

Turns out the club was a favorite among high-rollin' pimps too.

I'd left the car at Sarita's and taken a short bus ride downtown. Parking was almost impossible to find around here, and anyway, I hoped X would drive me home. With any luck, we'd be bringing Bree home too.

I met him outside the club. The sight of him blew me away. He was dressed *GQ*—pinstripe blue shirt, low-rise jeans, brown leather shoes. He was clean-shaven, and had used a touch of product in his close-cropped brown hair. I knew before I got near him that he'd smell of some sexy cologne, and God, did he ever.

I wished that I could step right into his arms, pull his face down to mine, and transport us back to last night's incredible kiss. But his body language—hands in pockets, keeping his distance—told me not to. I reminded myself that this was his job. And getting involved with a minor would be against the rules.

X took my hand and we walked up to one of the doormen. I was holding my fake ID, but the doorman didn't bother with it. He pounded knuckles with X, lifted the velvet rope, and waved us in. I wondered if he knew that X was undercover, or if he knew him some other way.

X took my ID from me and studied it. "Carlita Gonza-lez, twenty-two. Guess I'm with an older woman tonight." He examined the picture. "Close enough."

I paused. Older woman? He must mean that his cover was supposed to be younger than twenty-two. He couldn't possibly be a cop and be twenty-one, could he?

"My friend Maria's sister," I explained. "She gives us all her old IDs."

"My big brothers weren't so generous. I had to steal theirs."

So he had older brothers too, not just a younger one. I wanted to ask more about his family, but I didn't have the chance. He led me forward into the crowded darkness.

Unlike the tourist trap that was the Space, this club was long and narrow, a maze of connecting rooms. I had the sudden memory of going into a haunted house when I was thirteen, and freaking out as creatures emerged from all sides. The décor was black and red wine, from the velvet couches to the curtains lining alcoves. As we walked through the different rooms, I counted six bars, manned by half-naked female bartenders who looked like supermodels.

X ushered me to a cozy corner table where a tall, tattooed guy was chilling. The guy didn't look like a cop; most of the exposed area of his body was inked.

"Hey hey!" He bumped fists with X.

"Manny, meet Gabby."

"Hola, chica." Manny smiled appreciatively, eyes drifting over me. I pulled down the hem of my dress, which had ridden up as I sat down. Like X, I was done up for the club scene—short black dress, faux-leather jacket, big, glossy curls, and dark, chic makeup.

"So, *Gabriella*," Manny said, rolling his *r* and rubbing his goatee. "What are we drinking? Soda? Juice box?"

I could see that he was playing with me. "Club soda with lime."

"Fancy. I'll go get it. Shitty table service 'round here." He bounced out of his seat and went up to the bar.

X spoke close to my ear. "Milo was seen here last Friday night, but Bree wasn't with him." The feel of his breath on my neck made me shiver. "If we see her, I'll find a way for you to talk to her. You won't have a lot of time. You should have ready what you're going to say."

I nodded. "I know Bree. She'll talk to me."

I glimpsed the doubt in his eyes. "You'll need to convince her to go somewhere with you, somewhere safe, where you can talk more. Don't say anything about involving the police or her parents. Nothing that could faze her."

X could be wrong. From what I'd seen of Bree's family, they were warm, supportive people. But I guess if Bree had been through a lot of trauma since her disappearance, the thought of her parents could overwhelm her.

"Our exit route?"

"The back door of the club. Past that Exit sign." He pointed down a dark hallway. "From there, we'd take her back to my place."

"Okay, makes sense."

"Whatever you do, don't talk to Milo or anyone with him, male or female," X warned. "If things go wrong, stay near me or Manny. We won't let anything happen to you."

Manny returned with three drinks. X took his Coke from him. "I'll be back in a little while. Hang with Manny." And with that, he disappeared into the club.

"Guess it's just you and me, sweetie pie." Manny lifted his drink. "Cheers to that."

"Cheers. Lot of ink you've got there, buddy."

Manny ran his hands down his arms with fake sensuality.

"What can I say? I'm a canvas of artistic beauty. You got any?"

"No. My parents would freak. And I can't think of anything that would be meaningful enough that I'd want to keep it on me forever."

"I got a love/hate relationship with them, you know? These tats saved my life a few times. And they've almost gotten me killed too. So I guess it evens out."

X slid in beside me then. "Milo's here."

A chill went through me. "Bree?"

"I couldn't tell. I want you to walk by his table. He's got some girls with him. None of them look like Bree to me, but I can't be sure. If she's going out, she'd probably make herself look different."

My pulse kicked up. "Where is he?"

"In the next room." He nudged his chin in the direction he'd come from. "He's in a booth with two big guys and three girls. He's Hispanic, twenty-five, black collared shirt. Looks like a college athlete. Doesn't look like what he is. Make sure you don't stare, don't draw his attention."

I nodded, and got up.

X put a hand on my arm. "If she's there, don't stop, and don't make eye contact. Just come back this way and let me know."

"All right."

Taking a breath, I slowly walked into the other room,

sipping my soda as I went. The room was packed with people, and X's description of Milo was pretty generic. But then I saw him.

Doesn't look like what he is. Milo looked like a rich college boy, not a pimp. It made sense—he wouldn't have been able to lure Bree if he were decked out in fur and covered in bling. He was clean-cut, dressed sharp. In fact, he looked like an older, more polished version of JC. Maybe that was part of the appeal, I thought dismally. Bree had always had a sweet spot for JC.

One thing was clear—Bree wasn't with him. The three girls at Milo's table were heavily made up, but I would've recognized Bree immediately.

"Then where is she?" I asked X once I got back to the table.

"He must be worried someone will spot her. Guess he's gonna keep her in hiding for a while." He sighed. "I know you're disappointed, Gabby. This is what we deal with all the time. You think you're making progress, then the pimps switch it up."

I gritted my teeth. "What about the other girls with him? Maybe I could talk to one of them if they go to the bathroom. Find out where Bree is."

X shook his head. "No way. Milo's girls are loyal to him."

Manny gave me a sympathetic look. "Pimps have got PhDs

in manipulation. That's how they do what they do."

"But—it makes no sense!" It was hard to believe that Milo's girls were so devoted to him when he was selling them for sex. Who would put up with that?

"They see him as their protector," X said, putting a firm hand on my arm. He probably didn't trust me not to do something stupid.

My fists tightened. I wanted to march right up to Milo's table and punch him in the face. I wanted to demand that those girls tell me where the fuck Bree was.

X must've sensed my mood. "We'd better go now. I'll drive you home."

I didn't argue. If I stayed here much longer, I really might do something stupid. I got up. "Bye, Manny."

Manny gave a somber wave. "Bye, chica."

Outside, we headed for his car. I was so frustrated I wanted to scream. With every step we took away from the club, I was getting farther and farther away from the answers I needed.

X opened the door for me, then got in. He started to drive, heading south. "I'm staying at my aunt's tonight on Twenty-Seventh Street."

"Sure."

I didn't trust myself to say more. I'd probably take my frustrations out on him, and he didn't deserve it.

"Manny's gonna tail him tonight," he assured me. "If we

can find out where he stays, or where his girls are staying, that'll help."

"That's good. Whatever has to be done—do it. I know you've got different operations going on, and you're probably under a lot of pressure, but don't give up on Bree."

"I won't."

"Tell me one thing, though." I paused, trying to think of a rational way to say it, then decided I didn't care. "Can't you just fucking arrest Milo? I mean, you spotted him with Bree. Isn't that enough to bring him in? Maybe you could, I don't know, break his knuckles and make him talk."

X looked at me sharply, then he turned back to the road, saying nothing.

Of course. What could he say? He couldn't bring Milo in and rough him up. And even if he did arrest him, Milo would probably send Bree far away where no one could find her. But still. The powerlessness was driving me crazy.

He turned off at the next exit, but instead of continuing on toward Coral Gables, he pulled into the nearest parking lot and cut the engine.

Anticipation slid through me, taking the edge off my anger. What was this about?

The air in the car crackled with tension. He shifted in his seat, as if he was working up the courage to say something. As far as I was concerned, he didn't have to say a thing. I popped some gum into my mouth.

He looked over at me. "Gabby . . ."

I leaned in toward the gearshift, giving him the green light to get closer.

"You think I'm a cop."

I sat upright, as if I'd been splashed with cold water. "Of course I do. Sorry, but it's pretty obvious."

"I'm not a cop."

I sighed. "Look. I know you can't confirm it. I probably shouldn't have even mentioned it, but I'm frustrated that it's taking so long to find Bree."

"I'm not a cop, Gabby."

I searched his eyes, not knowing what to believe. "So what are you, then? A street artist named X? You admitted that was a cover."

"It is, basically."

Then I realized what he was doing. My little outburst had made him think I was volatile—volatile enough to break my promise and talk about all of this on my radio show.

"I would never do anything to jeopardize your operation. I'll never talk about it on the air, or to anyone." Even as I said it, I remembered that I'd already mentioned it to Sarita. But it would go no further than that.

"You're not hearing me, Gabby. I'm not a cop. I never said I was."

"What was I supposed to think? That you follow around pimps and track missing girls as a hobby?"

"It's not a hobby to me. It's . . ." A light came into his eyes. "It's a calling."

Something inside me stilled. He was telling the truth. And it made absolutely no sense. "Are you an informant, then? You help the police?"

He shook his head. "Nothing like it. I prefer to avoid the cops altogether. They're no help at all."

I was mystified. "So if you're not a cop, then what are you?"

"I'm part of a group. We help girls caught in sex trafficking."

"Like, a citizens' group?"

His mouth lifted at the corner. "You could say that. We're called the Destinos."

My jaw dropped. *The Destinos?*

Everyone knew about the Destinos. They were a badass street gang. Last year they'd gained a reputation for taking down Los Reyes, a brutal gang that had dominated the Miami drug and sex trades.

"You've obviously heard of us."

"I know of a *gang* called the Destinos. Is that the one?"

"Yeah." His mouth crooked. "You've probably heard that we stir shit up. We do. But we hyped that reputation to scare Salazar and the Reyes gang. Once they were dealt with, we went underground. That's how we work best. We like to sneak up on the bad guys."

I didn't know how to react. So the Destinos were about *helping* people? Anyone who knew about them would think they were just another street gang. Sure, they were responsible for taking down Los Reyes, but that was because they were involved in a turf war. Or so I'd thought.

"I never tried to deceive you, Gabby," he said regretfully. "I hope you know that."

Did I? Why couldn't he have told me he was a Destino?

To think I'd walked the streets with a gang member believing he was a cop. I'd felt so safe with him, so sure that he could protect me. But as a member of one of Miami's most notorious street gangs, he was more likely to be a target of a rival gang than my protector.

And yet . . . X didn't seem like a manipulator. He might not have revealed much to me, but what he had revealed was the truth. I was the one who'd assumed he was a cop, I reminded myself. That wasn't his doing.

I didn't know what to say, so I said nothing. X turned on the ignition and pulled back onto the road. We didn't speak as he drove to Twenty-Seventh Street. When we got there, I pointed out Sarita's house. He parked in the driveway.

Unbuckling my seat belt, I hesitated. Part of me wanted to stay with him, wanted to not leave the car until he'd answered every single one of my questions. Another part of me warned that I needed to be alone to process all of this.

I decided to be smart, for once, and get out of the car.

"Gabby," he said, leaning over my seat.

"Yeah?"

"If we get a lead on Bree, I'll let you know."

I nodded. "Do that."

NO MORE ILLUSIONS

WHEN I WOKE THE NEXT morning, it took several seconds to orient myself. Saturday, 11:02 a.m. Sarita's little white guest room. Wispy curtains. Pastel blue furniture. This room had been my home away from home since she'd moved here when I was in junior high. Some of my old tween books were still on the bookshelf.

Directly across from me was a painting of a toddler on a beach, holding a pail and shovel, gazing down at a smushed sand castle. I was sure Sarita could have sold it for thousands, but she'd refused. Not because she'd gotten attached to it, but because she'd said it was flawed. *The water's too blue to be real.* But it was a flaw only Sarita could see.

Last night's revelations washed over me. I'd actually mistaken a member of a street gang for one of Miami's finest.

That was a mistake for the record books. *Way to go, Gabby.*

But the more I thought about it, the more I realized I shouldn't be too hard on myself for thinking he was a cop. He'd used words like "cover" and "tailing," hadn't he? And when I'd met him, he'd been surveiling Raul. What other conclusion could I have come to?

My initial instincts about X had been right. He looked dangerous because he *was* dangerous. I couldn't slot him into the safe cop category anymore.

It didn't matter, I told myself. Cop or gang member, I didn't care who was helping Bree as long as they were helping her. The Destinos could do things the police wouldn't do. Cross lines the police wouldn't cross.

Saving Bree was all that mattered.

It was a little strange to shuffle into the kitchen and run into Sarita's shirtless, sleep-rumpled boyfriend.

"Gabby, this is Ben. Ben, Gabby," Sarita said without a hint of embarrassment. She looked adorable in a polka-dotted dress and strappy sandals.

"Hey." I gave a little wave.

"Hey," he said uncomfortably, focusing on his coffee.

So this was the Ben she'd been talking about. Auburn hair, morning stubble, undeniably cute, and barely thirty years old. I couldn't remember what she'd said he did for a living. Who cares? Maybe it was his age, but I doubted he was a keeper. I bet he was a lot of fun, though.

I slid Sarita a *way to go* look. With a serene smile, she held open a small box. "Pain au chocolat?"

"Sure," I said, selecting a still-warm croissant. "I'd better get going. I'm heading over to WKTU later."

Driving home, I realized how lucky I was that Ben had been there. Otherwise Sarita would've asked me about last night's search, and I'd have had no choice but to tell her that X wasn't a cop. Sarita might not react too well. She'd always had a flair for the dramatic, especially when it came to my safety. She might even tell my parents what I'd been up to.

When I got in, Mom was in the living room, knitting, with an e-book reader propped up on her legs. Mom always had to be doing two things at once. Over the years she must've knit a hundred scarves, but since she didn't know anyone who needed them, she always donated them to the church.

"How was your sleepover?" she asked.

"It was good." She probably imagined we'd stayed up late chatting in our jammies, like we might've done when I was twelve.

"Are you volunteering at the station today?"

I tried not to twitch at the word *volunteering*. "Yeah, I'll go over for a couple of hours. Then I'll hit the streets with some CVs." The last thing I wanted to think about right now was finding another job, but I couldn't risk not having enough money for next year's tuition.

"I wanted to talk to you about that." She put the knitting and e-reader aside. "Sit for a minute."

I sat down, wondering what this was about and how long it was going to take. Before she could speak, I put up a hand, thinking I'd save her the time. "I've thought about it, and you're right. I shouldn't have taken for granted that you guys would pay my tuition next year. That was bratty of me."

"I never said it was *bratty*." She frowned. "We want you to find a viable career, that's all."

"I'm going to get another job as soon as possible. I was thinking I could work ten or fifteen hours a week, so I can still go to WKTU, then full-time in the summer. By the fall, I should have enough money. I'll be fine." I got off the couch.

She put up a hand. "Sit down, please, Gabby."

I sighed, sitting down again.

"Your father and I were talking about it, and we don't want you to rush out and find a job. The main thing is that you focus on your schoolwork for now. I don't think it would be easy to find a job until closer to the holidays, anyway."

This was a one-eighty from our last conversation. Then it dawned on me. This was about Bree. For all Mom knew, there was a serial killer out there snatching girls off the street. Apparently the thought of me job searching had freaked her out.

"I heard that you talked about Bree O'Connor on your show last week," Mom said, confirming my suspicion. "It was a good way to use your platform. Your father and I are proud of you for that."

They were proud of me? I wanted to believe it. To *feel* it. But I was so used to tuning out my mom's criticism that my instinct was to tune out her praise, too. "Thanks, Mom."

"JC's very upset about Bree, you know. Camila says he's not handling it well. He's known her since they were little."

"Yeah, I know."

So Mom and Mrs. Suarez were still talking to each other. After what happened at the anniversary party, I wasn't sure. For once, the mention of JC didn't get my back up. I'd seen the signs of his distress myself.

"How are you coping with it?" Mom asked.

The question took me by surprise. She wasn't the type of Mom who regularly checked in on my emotional state; I figured she didn't want to know. But I answered her truthfully. "I'm sad for her."

"I'm sad too." Mom pursed her lips. She did that when she was trying to keep her emotions in check.

I wished I could tell her what I knew. But maybe I could,

at least, offer some comfort. "I'm pretty sure they'll find her, Mom. She'll be coming home."

God, I'd missed the beach.

At quarter to five that afternoon, I took off my sandals, digging my toes into the warm sand. It was a perfect blue-skied day with just enough breeze to toss my hair around my shoulders. Closing my eyes, I breathed in the salty wind.

When I opened them, X was beside me. My brown eyes met his blue ones. I was amazed, as always, by the connection I felt whenever I saw him. The revelation that he was in a gang had changed nothing.

"You're early," I said.

"So are you." In a white tank and cutoffs, he was so handsome it hurt. He had tanned, muscled arms that I ached to have wrapped around me. Sweat glistened above his collarbone, which somehow made him even more tempting.

"Thanks for meeting me."

"I'm down for the beach anytime."

"Sorry if I was a bit freaked out last night. The gang thing threw me off."

"You made no secret of that." His mouth twitched with amusement. "I still can't believe you thought I was a cop. I'm not sure if that's a compliment or an insult."

"It's neither. Last night . . . you probably thought I judged you. I wasn't trying to. I was in shock."

He shrugged one shoulder. "I don't see why judging somebody gets a bad rap. Smart girl like you would be better off judging me."

His amused smile was gone. He was dead serious.

"Why's that?"

"Just what you said. I'm in a gang."

My stomach felt uneasy. "But a good gang, right? I mean, you're not going after innocent people or hurting anybody for no reason."

"Right, but I'm sure any gang member would be able to assure you of that. Every gang's got a cause. Mine happens to be about helping girls get out of bad situations. Most gangs are all about helping themselves."

"Well, I want you to know that as long as the Destinos are looking for Bree, that's what matters to me. I don't care what you guys have to do or how you do it."

He smiled, and I felt it all the way down to my toes. "I knew there was a badass in you. Am I right?"

I nodded, and his smile widened.

He glanced over at a middle-aged couple who were setting down their towels a few feet away. "Let's walk."

Shoes in hand, we headed down the beach, close enough to the water that the tide stretched out to nip our toes.

"How did you end up with the Destinos?" I asked.

"It's simple. I got to know some guys. We became a pack. We were looking for a fight, and we found one."

"That's the vaguest explanation I've ever heard."

He slanted me a look. "Everything I say is off the record, Gabby. You don't talk about it on the air, to your best friend, your parents, your dog—nobody. Does anyone know where you are right now?"

"No, no one."

"Good."

"So are you going to tell me how your gang got into rescuing girls?"

"If you really want to know, our leader's sister was kidnapped by sex traffickers a couple years before we started up." A shadow passed over his face. "She didn't make it. But there were others like her, girls we could help."

A wave of sadness came over me for this girl I didn't know.

"Why are you against working with the cops? Couldn't you help each other?"

"Hey, if the cops could help us, I'd be fine with it. But they've only ever screwed things up for us." With a swift movement, he caught a beach ball hurtling at his head, and tossed it back to a kid. "There was a girl from California, fourteen, whose pimp brought her here. We spotted her a few times but could never get to her. She was in a bad situation, this girl. I was so damned determined to get to her fast, I got the cops involved. Told them where she'd been spotted, who the pimp was—I gave them everything. And I came up with a plan for us to get to her. But they didn't go along with it. They moved in on the pimp right away and took him into custody before we could figure out her location. The pimp's guys put their plan B into effect—they sent her out of town, probably traded her with another pimp across the country. Nobody's seen her since."

I felt heartsick. "God, that's awful."

"Yeah. That's why we don't give anything to the cops. When you work with the cops, they run the show. Besides, their system's ass-backward. It's set up to treat the girls like criminals. They round up prostitutes and what do they do? They put them in jail first, ask questions later. Pimps and sex traffickers, the cops hardly go after them. A lot of the time, they don't even know how. And don't get me started on the johns. Even if they get charged with solicitation, they usually get off with counseling."

"Seriously?" I couldn't believe the system was so messed up. "So you don't think we should let the cops know that we think Bree's alive?" It felt weird, *wrong*, to have this information and not share it with the police. Her poor family was going nuts. They were on the news almost daily, sobbing, begging people to help them find their daughter.

"If I thought it would help Bree's situation, I wouldn't

hesitate to call the cops," he said. "But our best bet is to reach her ourselves. Trust me, Gabby. If Bree wants out, we'll find a way to get her out."

If Bree wants out? Did he even need to say that? "Okay, I understand. I know the Destinos can handle it."

"Right. We do what has to be done. Like with Mr. Roofies."

My eyes widened. "You tracked Raul down?"

A smug smile.

"You kick him in the balls for me?"

"Among other things."

"Like what?"

"You don't need to know the details. We handled him. I doubt you'll be seeing him at the Space anytime soon."

"Screw that! I want to know."

X laughed. "Fine. We fucked him up. Dropped him off at his mama's place in Jacksonville with the word *pimp* tattooed on his forehead."

I shuddered. "For real?"

"For real." His face sobered. "So yeah, we hurt people. We have to. And if we ever find out Raul's back in business, we'll take it up a notch. But I'm pretty sure he got the message."

"What about the girls?"

"They're at a shelter for girls getting out of the sex trade. The staff knows what we do, and they don't ask questions."

I'd never heard of a place like that, but that must be the point. They wouldn't want pimps banging down their doors.

"You mentioned your leader," I said. "Did he ever get justice for his sister?"

"Yeah, he did. Then he up and left the gang." X scowled. "He wasn't in it for the long haul."

"And you are?"

He nodded. "When he left, I took charge."

"You?" I repeated, swallowing that information. So he wasn't just in a gang. He was the *leader* of a gang. My stomach quivered. Knowing he was the leader of the Destinos made this all, somehow, scarier. Trying to cover my nerves, I asked, "So, um, what's the former leader doing now?"

X stopped walking. "Who cares? He's not a Destino anymore." He looked down at his phone. "We'd better head back. I gotta be somewhere."

"Oh. All right." It was the topic of their former leader—it had rattled him. Too bad I hadn't left it alone.

The walk back was mostly silent. We put on our shoes and went to the lot where we'd both parked.

As we approached my car, I slowed my pace. "Where are you going now? Anything I can help with?"

"Nah. I'm taking my little brother out for dinner."

"That's cool. How old is he?"

"Sixteen. He lives in a group home." He dug into his pocket for his keys. "It's a shitty place to live. So I take him out as much as I can."

I felt for him. It must be horrible to see your kid brother living in a place like that. "Maybe you could get guardianship of him."

"I'd never be able to be his guardian, not with my record."

"Oh." Fighting to conceal my surprise, I gave a shrug like it was no big deal. "Did you steal something?"

He took a step closer to me, his eyes both kind and exasperated. "No, Gabby, I didn't steal anything."

There was so much about him I didn't know. So much about him I probably couldn't imagine. And it was driving me crazy.

I pressed closer to him, so close my chin touched his chest. "Well, we all make mistakes," I said softly.

He searched my eyes, and I saw what he wanted.

He trapped my mouth underneath his and kissed me. A hot, open-mouthed kiss. And we went to that place again. That place of need, of lust, of *I need you so much*. His kiss was sensual, generous, and yet I knew he was offering me nothing—not a relationship, not a promise. Not even his name.

I moaned against his mouth, and heard his answering groan. In the back of my mind, I thought of how JC had called me frigid. But X exposed that as a lie. I wanted him with my body, heart, and soul. I wanted him more than I'd ever wanted anyone.

As we kissed, it hit me: No more illusions. X wasn't a cop. He was in a gang, and he had a criminal record. I should probably be running from him at top speed. But I was doing the exact opposite.

There was no fighting how I felt about X. Wherever this took me, I would go.

"Hey, girl. Ready to par-tay?" Maria asked, sliding into the passenger seat later that night. A wave of perfume hit me. The car would probably smell of it for days.

"Aw yeah." I pumped up the music.

Her call about the Rivera party was a godsend. I so needed to get out. Since X's kiss several hours ago, I'd done nothing but relive those intense moments. Was kissing another art form for him, like his drawing?

When the kiss had ended, he'd left me standing next to my car, melting in the sun. Wanting more.

It was pure insanity.

I sniffed the air. "The new Chanel?"

"Damn right, baby."

That was something Maria and I had in common. Screw scent-free environments, we both loved to smell good. I just hoped I didn't ever overdo it like Maria had tonight.

Remembering how X had smelled today—of hot-blooded man and minty aftershave—I suppressed a groan.

When was I going to see him again? When?

Within ten minutes, we'd arrived at Chris Gerber's house, home to the most legendary of Rivera parties. Drinking, smoking, hooking up, and melting down, it all happened here, while pictures of the mayhem were snapped and posted online to make others jealous.

When we walked up, Chris, Marco, and Pete were smoking on the porch. They were what Maria and I called PJs—party jocks. Guys whose lives were all about sports, parties, and not much else.

"Hey, Gabby," Chris said with a grin. "What's up, Buttercup?"

We'd had a flirtation going since the sixth grade. But we'd never gotten together, because a hookup with a PJ was not on my to-do list.

"Last-minute party, huh?"

"Yeah." He took a drag and turned his head to blow smoke. "Parents went out of town. Told me five minutes before they left so I wouldn't have time to organize anything. I called my man Pete, and inside an hour, we've got it going."

Maria and I went inside. Blasting music. The smell of beer. Walls thumping as if they had a heartbeat of their own.

Maria headed straight for the drink table in the kitchen, pouring herself a screwdriver. Judging by the amount of vodka she put in, I'd be carrying her out of here later.

"Gabby's here!" someone shouted, and then I was being hugged by my old friends Alicia and Becca. Both tall brunettes, they had been my besties in junior high, along with Maria. These days, we were social media friends and occasional party friends. They were the ones I'd gotten drunk with in eighth grade, resulting in my banishment to St. Anthony's.

"Tell us about the missing girl!" Becca said. "I loved that show you did about her. I cried my eyes out."

"So did I," Alicia said. "Sounds like you knew her really well. What do you think happened to her?"

I was aware that a group of people were now listening.

"She probably trusted the wrong person. But I think she'll come home. I really do." I wouldn't say more than that. There was no way I'd jeopardize what the Destinos were doing to find Bree.

"Wow." The girls looked awed, like I'd imparted some great wisdom.

Then we danced.

After dancing for a while, we plunked down on the couch, and caught up on the latest happenings. Becca and Alicia were single, but both had their sights set on certain guys, and shared their plans for reeling them in.

Alicia turned to me. "Have you got a new boyfriend, Gabby? I bet you meet all sorts of hot prospects at the radio station."

"There are zero single guys there. I'm not with anyone right now." It felt like a lie, and yet it wasn't. X and I weren't together. For some guys, a kiss sealed the deal. It meant you were going out, or at least seeing each other. But I was sure X didn't play by those little high school rules.

"JC is here, you know," Becca said.

"Really?" That was a surprise. "I didn't realize he hung out with anybody at Rivera."

Maria looked sheepish. "He does, sometimes. Sorry, Gabby. I was worried if I said anything, you might not want to come."

"That wouldn't stop me. I see him every day at school. It's not a big deal."

I couldn't help thinking it was odd that JC was hanging around with Rivera kids. When we were together, he'd never been interested in them. And he was friends with practically every senior at St. Anthony's. How many friends did he need?

"Well, if he bothers you, we'll leave," Maria said.

"No worries." If JC was here, fine. I doubted he'd come after me the way he had at the anniversary party. He probably wouldn't speak to me at all. Besides, these days, JC and his friends were too torn up about Bree's disappearance to bother with the icy stares and hallway jabs.

The conversation then moved on to Maria's ex, Renaldo, and she dove into a rant I'd heard many times before. I figured it was a good time to get something to drink.

The kitchen counters were stacked with all types of booze. Unfortunately a guy with a sleazy grin was now the gatekeeper. "Five bucks for whatever you like, sexy lady."

A cash bar at a party—was he serious? "I just want a Diet Coke."

"Whatever you say. One buck, baby."

I gave him a dollar, watching carefully as he poured the Diet Coke into a plastic cup. After the roofies incident, I was going to be forever paranoid.

Back in the living room, Maria was having a meltdown. It wasn't a surprise. A little booze plus the topic of her cheating ex was enough to reduce her to a sobbing mess.

"Let's go talk in private." I took her hand and we left the living room, heading for the small den at the back of the house. Glazed eyes watched us enter. It might have been drug central, but it was a lot quieter in there.

We found a corner, and I gave Maria the usual pep talk. *He's not good enough for you and never was. You should be thankful that he's gone.* But she wasn't listening. She never listened. So I just put an arm around her and let her cry.

"You wanna go home?"

She wiped away her tears, careful not to smear her mascara. "Are you kidding me? No way. It's only ten thirty."

That was a good sign. Her spirit might be bruised, but her will to party was unbroken.

Glancing past her, I saw JC enter the room. He looked a bit on the scruffy side in baggy pants, an old T-shirt, and a ball cap. He slapped hands with some guys chilling on a couch near the door. Then he took a couple of baggies out of his pocket and exchanged them for cash.

"What are you staring at?" Maria said. "Oh, him."

JC must've heard her, because he turned our way. He didn't seem surprised to see me. He gave me a vague *who cares* shrug and left the room.

"I'll be right back," I told Maria, scrambling to my feet.

I caught up with him in the hallway. "JC—wait."

He turned, his expression switching from apathy to anger. "What do you want?"

"I saw what you were doing in there. Are you out of your mind? You could get charged!"

He scoffed. "You think I'm a drug dealer? Now that's an interesting accusation. The dumpee becomes the dealer. What a great way to turn people against me, Gabby. Go tell everyone at school on Monday and see what happens. Better yet, talk about it on your show. I'm sure the ratings will go sky-high."

I noticed the sweat beads on his forehead, and the glazed, dead look in his eyes. He wasn't just dealing, I realized. "You're using, too." I stared at him in disbelief. When we were together, JC had never used drugs—he'd been anti all that stuff. And now?

He didn't deny it. Maybe he wanted me to know.

JC put a hand to his chest. "I'm touched that you care so much. Really I am. And if you want to rat me out to my parents, go right ahead. They already know."

Maybe they did, I realized. That could be the real reason he'd been going to counseling.

"I'm not trying to get in your business," I said. "I was just trying to help."

"Help? You're a past life to me, Gabby. Over now."

JC stalked off.

An uneasy feeling swept through me. I didn't know who could help JC, but he was right about one thing—that person wasn't me.

PUSH

"LOOKING SPIFFY," I SAID TO Caballero the next night at WKTU.

When Caballero went to an event, he did it in style. He reminded me of Prince in a purple suit with a white silk scarf around his neck.

"Red carpet tonight. The wife and I are going to a movie premiere."

"What's the movie?"

He swiveled in his chair and picked up the invitation off his desk. "*Jugular*."

"I'm guessing it's horror."

"You bet your ass it is. They're calling it *Saw* meets *Paranormal Activity*. Get this, if we don't lose our appetites from all the gore, there's a buffet at the Marriott afterward, catered by some *MasterChef* winner."

"Sounds awesome."

"Hey, you gotta take the perks where you get 'em. I'm hoping the movie will scare the pants off my wife. That woman can scream." He held up his phone. "I'm gonna record her and play it on the air tomorrow."

I laughed. "You're so evil!"

"'Course I am." He grinned, glancing at the digital clock above the controls. "Ten minutes."

Ten minutes couldn't come soon enough. I needed my on-air fix.

I'd spent most of the day dwelling on last night's confrontation with JC. Had our breakup been the trigger that made him use drugs? I couldn't help but think that it was—that maybe, if I'd handled it differently, this wouldn't have happened. But I knew it was pointless to think that way. If JC wanted to be self-destructive, that was his choice.

It was a relief when I went live. I tipped my chin toward the microphone, entering into my own little world.

"Hey, everybody, I'm Gabby Perez with *Light Up the Night*. Yeah, I missed you too. I want to thank all of you who've been praying for my friend Bree O'Connor and who've been on the lookout for her. Let's not stop until we get her back." I swallowed. "As you all know, I love to talk about relationships. Especially about cheaters. The people who deceive us. But one thing we haven't talked about is when we deceive ourselves.

Tell me, have you ever met someone you knew was bad news, but you went out with them anyway? Have you ever been in a relationship that you knew wouldn't work, but you stayed in it? Have you ever known the right thing to do, the smart thing to do, and done the exact opposite? Tell me about it."

Within seconds, the phones lit up, and we were off.

When my hour was done, I handed off to Caballero's replacement, DJ Sandro Track, and went back to my car. I turned on my phone, hoping there was something from X. But there was nothing.

Maybe it was up to me to make the next move, to show him that I wanted to be in his life. What type of person did I want to be, anyway? The type who goes after what she wants, or the type to sit around and wait?

I texted: Where are you? Wanna hang out? Then I sent it before I could stop myself.

There, I'd done it. I wondered how he'd react to my message. It obviously had nothing to do with Bree—it was about us. He couldn't read it any other way.

I waited, holding my breath. X always had his phone on him. If he didn't respond within five minutes, that would be my answer.

Then his response came up.

I'm at home. Come over. I'll meet you outside. He gave his address.

Oh my God.

* * *

In fifteen minutes, I was there. Could've made it in ten, if I hadn't been driving so erratically and made several wrong turns.

I parked at the curb and got out of the car. He was standing outside his building in flip-flops, jeans, and a black paint-stained T-shirt. As I walked up to him, I was aware that I didn't know exactly what I was doing here. The faint smile on his lips told me he was aware of it too.

"Come on in."

X lived on the second floor of an outside walk-up. When I entered the apartment, I stopped and stared. His living room was an art studio. One entire wall was a work in progress. It was a Miami cityscape painted in stark colors—black, blue, yellow. His art supplies were scattered as if he'd been painting when I called. Music with a hard bass thumped.

"Your landlord lets you do this?" I approached the wall. Every person in the painting was so real, every building perfectly symmetrical.

"I'll paint over it when I leave."

"But how could you ever paint over this? It's amazing."

"It's just for fun." Picking up a wide brush, he added some yellow touches to a black, looming building. "Painting has a way of keeping me grounded. Some people meditate, I paint. It's the same with your radio show, isn't it? You can block out the world and just be."

He was right; going on air was totally consuming—it took me over, put me right in the zone. "It's funny. When I sign off, I'm always relieved that the show is over, but I also feel let down *because* the show is over. Does that make sense?"

He nodded. "Perfect sense. You turn off the show and turn on the world. And sometimes the world sucks."

I walked up to the wall, my finger hovering above it, but not touching. "It's so vivid. If you had this on canvas, you could sell it for a wackload of cash. Oh, wait—you don't want to make money off your talent, right?"

He shrugged. "Ideally, maybe. But my art pays the rent. If I've got some talent, I try not to take it for granted."

The song on the radio ended, and DJ Sandro Track's smooth voice filled the apartment. X had been listening to WKTU, I realized. To my show.

He was so close to me that his leg brushed against my hip. I shivered. *What are you doing here, Gabby?* I asked myself.

Suddenly nervous, I went over to where several canvases were leaning against the wall. Each one was signed with a distinctive X in the right-hand corner. "How much do you sell these for?"

"Fifty bucks, mostly. Twenty-five for the small ones, a hundred for the big ones."

I couldn't believe it. Didn't he have any idea what his talent was worth? Sarita sold paintings for thousands. I was no art critic, but I could see X's work was extraordinary.

"So tell me something, Gabby."

"What?"

His hands came down on my shoulders. "Why are you here?"

I took a slight step away from him. What did he expect me to say?

"I didn't feel like going home after the show. Needed to burn off some energy."

He raised a brow, and I saw the heat in his eyes. "And you think there's something I can do about that?"

The air was heavy between us. I felt like a coil about to spring. "Did you, um, have fun with your brother last night?"

His eyes told me that he knew what I was doing, but he went with it. "It was all right." He went over to the sound system and turned it down, then sat on the couch, putting his feet up on the battered wood coffee table. "He's close to getting expelled from his third high school. I can't get through to him."

I sat down on the couch, leaving some space between us. "You're doing what you can. I hope he wakes up before he gets expelled again."

"Me too. I wanna shake the kid, you know? He's still got

time to turn it around, but he doesn't care."

"What's his name?"

"Kaden."

"What's *your* name?" I couldn't resist.

He didn't look amused. His blue eyes went shuttered. "My name's got baggage."

"Can't blame me for trying. You're a mystery to me, X. I want to know more."

I inched closer to him on the couch, and looked up into his eyes. I was laying my cards on the table. When I reached out to touch his arm, he caught my hand underneath his.

"You're an amazing girl, Gabby. You never try to be something you're not. You're . . . unshakeable."

My heart filled up. I'd had no idea he thought of me that way. "I don't know anything—that's all I know."

He smiled. "That's Socrates."

I nodded, surprised. "Only thing I remember from last year's history exam. When'd you read Socrates?"

"In juvie. I finished high school while I was locked up. With a 3.9." He paused. "My mother always said I was the smart one. She thought it was because she was so sick when she was pregnant with me that she couldn't keep down the vodka."

"Oh. That's . . . horrible." I realized that he'd been

deliberately trying to shock me. It had worked. But I wasn't going to let him scare me away. I could see through his hard exterior to the person beneath.

"Sounds like you've had a tough go," I said, choosing my words carefully.

"You could put it that way." For a split second, I might've spotted vulnerability in his eyes, but then his expression turned cool. "I can't give you what you want, Gabby."

I frowned, not sure what he was getting at. "What do I want?"

His faint smile softened the hard lines of his face. "Whatever it is good girls want. I can't give it."

That got my back up. Did he think I wanted some picture-perfect boyfriend to bring me candy and flowers? I'd already had that. "I was with a guy for two years, and it sucked. He tried to be Mr. Perfect, but I couldn't stand it. I broke up with him last spring, but I should've done it a year before that."

"I'm surprised. You don't seem like the type to suffer in silence."

I decided to take that as a compliment. "I let other people influence me too much. And I didn't want to hurt him. Anyway, the point is, I'm not looking for anything serious right now. I'm not asking you to be my boyfriend. I just want to hang out with you."

There. I'd said it. We could hang out, maybe make out, no strings attached.

He watched me closely. "What does that mean? You want to be my friend? Or you want to hook up with me? The bedroom's down the hall. There's nothing I want more." His eyes were electric blue, and I saw that he meant every word. I couldn't help but glance down, seeing the strong effect my closeness was having on him. He turned away, gritting his teeth. "But you don't really want that, do you?"

My throat went dry. I was still reeling from his invitation to the bedroom.

"You could never be with someone like me, Gabby. Your parents wouldn't even let me in the front door. And you know what? They shouldn't."

"Why the hell not?" I wasn't going to stand for him putting himself down.

"Because I'm not like you. I never had your type of life, with the nice home and loving parents. That stuff makes you who you are. If you don't have it, you become something else. Someone else."

"So just because our families are different, we can't spend time together?" I shook my head, disgusted. "That's such a cliché. If you don't want me, just say it."

"What I'm saying is, I don't want what you want. Someone like you—"

I cut him off. "Someone like me? You make it sound like I'm from some perfect world, but I'm not. I mean, yeah, my family has enough money, but it's not like we're rich. And I don't have the best parents, trust me. They'd do anything to see me give up the radio gig."

X stared at me. "Is that your criteria? They don't agree with you on something, so they suck? You're the luckiest person in the world, Gabby. My mother never gave a shit about me and my brothers. I don't even know who my father is, but he sure must've been fucked up to leave me with my mom." He shook his head, as if he shouldn't bother, because I'd never understand. "You don't know what it's like to be scared every fucking day. Scared that there's not gonna be food when you get home. Scared your mom's boyfriends are gonna make you their personal punching bag. Scared that social services is gonna come and take you and your little brother away. Scared that they *won't* take you away."

I dropped my eyes. There I was, complaining about my parents when he hadn't even had true parents. I wished I could take back what I said. Because deep down, I knew how lucky I was. For all our conflicts, I knew my parents loved me.

And that was X's point. He was saying he couldn't love me. He didn't even know how. And he was convinced that's what I wanted.

As I gazed into his blue eyes, all my arguments fell away. He was right. I wanted him to love me. Because I was falling for him.

Somehow, X knew me better than I knew myself. I guess that was his specialty—reading people.

I got up. "I'd better go."

I wanted him to stop me, to ask me to stay for a while longer. But he was already heading for the door. "I'll walk you down."

"Don't bother." I closed the door behind me, harder than I'd intended. I hurried down the stairs, determined not to cry until I'd started driving.

When I got to the car, I glanced back and saw him standing in the window. We stared at each other for a long moment, frozen in time.

Then I got into the car and drove away.

Two weeks passed, two agonizing weeks. X sent me an occasional businesslike text updating me on the search for Bree. But he didn't ask me to help find her, and he didn't suggest we meet up.

I should never have gone over to his apartment that night. He'd sensed how I felt about him and sent me packing. At least he'd been honest with me. He could've tried to take advantage of my feelings for him. He could've said a few choice words and stripped me down, literally. But he hadn't. He'd done the right thing.

The gang leader was a gentleman.

Which made me want him even more.

I should've waited for us to get to know each other better before pushing him for more. Maybe, over time, he'd have come to care about me too. Maybe he'd have realized that he could care for me despite his horrible childhood. I refused to believe that he wasn't capable of loving someone. Not when I could feel his passion for helping people, and his devotion to his brother. No, X was perfectly capable of love. He just didn't want to love *me*.

I told myself to put aside the romantic fantasy and get over him. That's what I'd told so many girls on my radio show. *If he can't give you what you want, say thankyouverymuch and move on.*

So why couldn't I?

X had said I was unshakeable, but he was wrong about that. My feelings for him had shaken me to the core.

Every time I got a call, some part of me sparked, hoping it was him ready to smooth things over between us. Hoping he'd even want to meet for coffee. But he didn't do that. And I might as well accept that he never would. He was probably relieved that I'd backed off.

I couldn't trace how it happened, how I'd come to fall for

him. I just knew that from the moment I'd seen him watching me that night at the bar—the night he'd saved Maria and me from Raul—I'd been hooked on him.

Hooked on a guy who wouldn't even tell me his real name. Gotta love it.

"You're out of it today," Adriana said Monday in the cafeteria.

"I'm just tired." The truth was that heartsickness had taken my sleep and my appetite. But I didn't feel like admitting it.

Rory's pimply face zoomed in close to mine. "Gabby might've contracted the zombie plague. Look, she's not even blinking!"

"Very funny," I said, pushing his face away. "I told you, I'm exhausted. No need to drive a stake through my skull."

"I still say that's what happened to Bree," Rory said. "According to ZombieSighting.com, undead activity in Miami has spiked recently."

Alistair glared at him. "We told you not to joke about Bree."

Rory looked offended. "I wasn't joking. And even if I was, why is everyone acting like she was a saint? Remember when she bumped our table? Do you think my mom could get the Coke stain out of my pants? Noooo."

"Bree didn't bump our table," I said. "Ellie and Karina did."

Rory shook his head adamantly. "No way. I saw her do it."

I wanted to knock Rory's Coke over his current pair of pants, but Alistair gave me a look that said not to bother.

"Guess what's coming to town on Halloween," Alistair said, changing the topic. "It's going to blow your minds."

Rory's eyes bulged. "But I thought it wasn't coming to Miami!"

Alistair grinned. "They added a Miami date due to popular demand. I saw it on the website last night."

Adriana and Caro did a *Squee!*

I looked left and right. "Is anybody gonna fill me in?"

Alistair turned to me. "Have you ever dreamed of spending Halloween trapped in a mall full of zombies?"

"Um, not really. Have you?"

"Indeed I have. And my dream is about to come true. It's called ZombieMall. It's a chance for people like us to test our skills. To see if we can really survive."

"Holy." A shiver went through me. I couldn't tell if it was excitement or nerves.

"It's kind of like a fire drill, but with zombies," Rory said cheerfully. "It's gonna be awesome! The only thing is they don't let you bring weapons of any kind—not even wooden or plastic ones. So it's just you, your bare hands, and a horde of hungry zombies."

"We should start strategizing," Alistair said. "I'll print out the schematics of the mall so we can prepare."

Once we'd finished eating, we went upstairs to grab our books from our lockers, then parted to go to our classes. My teacher launched into a lesson about the Boer War, but I sat there, in a different world. For the thousandth time, I thought about texting X to apologize for coming over that night. But what good could it do? He'd think I was pathetic.

I was jolted back to the present when I heard shouting and commotion outside the classroom. My first thought was *Zombie attack!* but I shook the silliness out of my head. I was spending way too much time with Rory. It was probably just a fight.

Our teacher rushed out of the class, and a bunch of us flooded into the hallway to see what was happening. I heard the words *ambulance* and *seizure* shouted back and forth between teachers.

I took several steps forward, straining to see inside the crowd. My hand covered my mouth. JC was on the ground, bucking uncontrollably.

Oh my God. What was happening to him?

EMTs arrived within minutes. By that time, the seizure had stopped, and JC was wheeled away on a gurney with a teacher by his side.

"It was a grand mal seizure," Mom told us at dinner. She'd just gotten off the phone with Father Juan, who was at the hospital with JC's parents. "They did a CT scan, and there hasn't been any brain damage. He's awake and talking normally."

"Thank God," my dad said. "I wonder what would bring that on. Did Father Juan say?"

Mom shook her head. "He asked for our prayers, and said there would be several weeks of recovery."

"Several weeks?" Dad frowned. "But if he's doing so well . . ."

"That's code for rehab," I said, figuring there was no use in keeping the secret anymore. Even if JC's parents hadn't known about his drug use, they'd know now.

Dad's mouth fell open. "JC is using? I know he's had some depression, but I never would've expected this. Are you sure?"

"Yeah, I'm sure. He says his parents know about it."

"Poor Camila." Mom put her head in her hands. "How long has this been going on?"

"A few months." *Since the breakup,* I didn't add.

"What's he on?" Dad asked.

"There's this new psychedelic drug out there called Blings. I don't know much about it except that it's really addictive."

Dad nodded grimly. "It's a major problem at our school too. You haven't tried it, have you?"

"Of course not." I tried not to take offense at the question. He and mom were both shaken up. And probably not half as shaken up as I was. I kept seeing JC shaking uncontrollably, his mouth wide open, his limbs thrashing.

"Well, this explains his behavior at our party." Dad looked pointedly at my mom. "Gabby did say he'd been behaving erratically."

"Yes, I suppose that explains it." Mom slid me an apologetic look, but I just shrugged. I didn't need something like this to prove my point.

ALL HALLOWS' EVE

TONIGHT WAS THE NIGHT WE'D been waiting for. Halloween. We would prove our skills as zombie survivalists—or go down in a free-for-all of clawing hands and gnashing teeth.

I was hoping that being with my friends tonight would bring me out of my funk. With every day that passed, the pain of missing X hadn't gone away. It sat there, like a dead weight on my chest. No matter what I did, it was there.

I tried to accept that we weren't meant to be a couple, that we were meant to learn from each other and be better people for it. At least, that was the sort of thing the Paranormal Twins would say if they knew. Which they didn't.

And then there was Bree. No matter how much I worried about her, it didn't change a thing. She was still out of reach.

I needed to get out of my routine, to do something

different. Hopefully, dodging zombies was just what I was looking for. It didn't hurt that, since yesterday was Alistair's birthday, we went to Adriana's pre-ZombieMall to eat cake. After ZombieMall, Caro and I would be returning to Adriana's for a sleepover. The plan: horror movies till dawn.

"Happy Birthday to you! Happy Birthday to you! Happy Birthday dear Alis-tair, Happy Birthday to youuuuuu!"

Alistair's gaunt cheeks had a faint flush as we sang. Then he blew out all but one candle.

"Ha, one girlfriend!" Rory said. When we all looked at him, he explained sheepishly, "That's just something my family says."

I saw Alistair subtly glance over at Caro. Interesting. Was a romance brewing?

This was my first time at Adriana's house. It was a sprawling ranch-style bungalow in an exclusive area of Coral Gables. Her family had a live-in housekeeper who stalked us throughout the house, cleaning any dirt our shoes left on the pristine floors. Adriana had never mentioned what her parents did for a living, but she'd said they were workaholics. Clearly their workaholism had paid off nicely.

Adriana's massive kitchen was like something out of a home makeover show, with state-of-the-art everything. We sat on barstools around the granite island, digging into the two-tiered chocolate cake that Adriana and Caro had cut school that afternoon to make. As we ate and licked icing off our fingers, it hit me that these people were really my friends now, not just my default friends. They had stuck by me, even when everybody said I was the worst kind of snob.

Rory put his hands to his temples. "Holy simultaneous sugar rush and carb coma! Roar, God of Gaming, dangerously vulnerable to attack." He sprawled out on the couch.

"This is excellent cake," Alistair said, a small blob of chocolate icing sticking to the corner of his mouth. Caro reached up with a napkin to wipe it off, and he blushed.

Adriana leaned back in her chair. "I wish we could dress up in zombie makeup tonight. But we're supposed to be the innocent victims."

"Don't worry, I'm sure we'll be covered in fake blood by the time we get out of there," Caro said.

"Hope not." I was wearing my favorite black pants, black boots, and a purple Guess shirt.

Once we were finished with the cake, we cleared away the dishes, and Alistair spread out a map of the mall. "Let's take one more look at the mall schematics. Rory, are you paying attention?"

"Yep. Go ahead."

"The first few minutes will undoubtedly be a feeding frenzy—from what I've read, a third of participants are bitten in the first five minutes."

"A third?" Rory said from the couch. "Screw that. Not for my thirty bucks."

"We all need to head here," Alistair slammed a finger down on the map, "to the north escalator, as quickly as possible. That gives us several potential hiding places, and a number of escape routes. Those who stay in the mall lobby won't survive for long."

"What about the lower-floor bathroom?" Adriana asked, studying the map. "Maybe we could hide in there during the initial frenzy."

"Each bathroom has only one exit," Alistair replied. "It's more likely to become your tomb."

"I'll take that as a no," Adriana said.

Soon after, we piled into my car and headed downtown. I parked in the underground lot, then we followed a crowd of people into the mall. Everybody was lining up near the Gap.

Anticipation rippled through the crowd. Several people dressed as movie ushers came by to take our tickets and give us waivers to sign.

"What the hell?" I said, flipping through the pages. "Some people get PTSD from this?"

Rory examined the waiver. "Check out the top of page three. It gives a list of possible reactions to extreme fear. Panic attacks. Uncontrollable outbursts of laughter or crying. Spontaneous bowel release."

"Spontaneous bowel release?" I repeated. "That, I cannot handle."

"Your bowels will be fine," Alistair assured me. "You're a cool cucumber, Gabby." He looked pointedly at Caro. "When in doubt, clench your buttocks and count to ten."

Caro smacked his arm playfully. "Worry about your own ass, not mine!"

Alistair laughed.

"The safe word is *apple*," Adriana said. "Apple. Remember that."

That made me no less nervous. "A safe word? I thought that was for S&M."

"There's a whole subculture of zombie sadomasochism, you know," Alistair said thoughtfully. "We should explore that at our next meeting." His face heated up. "I mean, in theory."

We broke into laughter, but smothered it when we noticed that everyone around us had gone quiet. Ushers were locking the mall doors with heavy clicks behind us. Was it to keep the crowd outside from coming in, or to prevent the participants from getting out?

A cute usher with an eyebrow ring stood in front of the crowd. "Welcome, shoppers! Please go about your shopping as usual. That report you heard on the news about zombies being on the loose is, I assure you, totally—" Before he could finish, a zombie jumped out from behind him and tore into his neck.

Blood sprayed out of his neck, drenching anyone within five feet of him, like it was shot out of a ketchup-filled cannon.

Everybody screamed. The blonde beside me practically deafened me.

The feeding frenzy had begun.

The crowd dispersed in all directions. Zombies were emerging from everywhere, limping toward their victims.

"Stay close together," Alistair cautioned us. "This way!"

We quickly moved toward the downward escalator. We were almost there when a zombie popped out of a garbage can next to us. Rory gave a shriek, scrambling away from the threat. The zombie went after him, and Rory took off.

"Rory!" Alistair shouted. "Come back this way!"

The zombie chasing Rory wasn't very fast, but then, neither was Rory. He kept tripping over victims, falling to the floor, then picking himself up and narrowly escaping with his life. The zombie chasing him broke character once and started laughing, then made a horrible groan and kept pursuing him.

"Why isn't he circling back?" Caro said, exasperated. "We don't have much time before ..." We saw two zombies heading our way.

"If we leave Rory, he's a goner," Adriana said tragically. "But we can't stay here. Let's go!"

We hurried down the escalator. Once we got to the bottom, we heard an odd, bloodcurdling scream.

"That sounded like Rory," I said.

"We shouldn't have left him." Caro was clinging to Alistair's arm. "We might've been able to save him."

"It's survival of the fittest," Alistair told her gravely. "In a situation like this, death is inevitable." He looked past her. "Run!"

A chunky zombie who made a show of eating his own entrails was dragging toward us. We darted under the escalators, huddling together like a football team.

I turned to Alistair. "What's our next move?" I knew this was make-believe, but it was freaking me out. I could tell that Adriana and Caro felt the same. But Alistair was thriving under the pressure.

"We head for the food court," he said. "With all of the tables, it'll be harder for the zombies to touch us. Remember, we're faster than they are. And we're strongest when we stay together. Let's go!"

We jogged toward the food court. A quick scan told us that three zombies were there, but that was still better that the screaming chaos upstairs. There were six guys in basketball jerseys, obviously with the same idea, fending off the zombies.

"Should we try to make an alliance?" Caro asked Alistair. "There's strength in numbers."

"No. Never. They could use us as zombie fodder. We can

only trust ourselves. Wait a minute." He blinked. "Is that zombie *Rory?*"

We stared in disbelief. Yes, it was Rory. He must've grabbed someone's messy black wig and smeared blood all over his army fatigues.

Caro gasped. "Oh my God, Rory's been turned!"

Alistair shook his head. "He turned himself. What he did was against ZombieMall rules. Only the actors are allowed to play zombies. It's a liability issue."

I shrugged. "He wanted to get his money's worth."

My phone rang. I took it out of my pocket to turn it off, but then my heart slammed against my ribs. It was X.

I could feel the others looking at me disapprovingly, but I had to answer it. "Hello?"

"Gabby, Bree is here," X said.

With all the screaming going on, I could hardly hear him. Did he just say Bree was there?

"*What?* I can't hear you." I cupped a hand over my other ear and distanced myself from the group. "You see Bree?"

"I'm looking at her right now."

"Oh my God, where are you?"

"At the Phoenix. Get here right away. I'll meet you outside."

"I'm there. Ten minutes." I hung up.

Finally, after all this time, a Bree sighting!

I ran back to the group. "Friend in crisis. I've gotta go. Sorry, guys. If you need a ride—"

"Don't worry about it," Adriana said, her eyes focused on the action behind me. "We'll get a cab. Watch out!"

They broke into a run.

I turned around, finding myself face-to-face with a stringy-haired zombie. Half of her face was a mangled mess. Whoever had done her makeup clearly had talent. She advanced on me, backing me into a corner and grabbing my arm.

"No, please, I don't have time. I have to go."

Zombiegirl had no intention of backing down. "Rawr," she gurgled, barfing out what looked like spaghetti.

Then I remembered. "Apple!"

Zombiegirl sighed and moved aside. "Whatever."

I hurried to the basement parking garage. Slipping into my car, I paid the attendant and drove out of the lot. There was a crowd of people blocking the street and sidewalk, waiting for the ten o'clock ZombieMall experience. I honked my horn until they let me through.

Then I headed for Bree.

As I drove, my mind was working a mile a minute. What would I say to her? Would she even listen to me? I'd figure it out. I couldn't lose this chance.

I slowed the car as I drove past the Phoenix. I couldn't see anywhere to park, so I pulled over in front of a fire hydrant and figured I'd pay the ticket.

X was waiting for me outside the club. The sight of him pulled at my heart, but I couldn't think about that now.

He put his hands on my shoulders. "Take a breath and calm down before we go in. Bree's not going anywhere."

Nodding, I tried to catch my breath. "She's with Milo?"

"Yeah, they're both in costume, sitting at a booth. She's wearing a red wig and a butterfly mask, which she sometimes takes off. Manny's watching her right now. I'm hoping she'll go to the bathroom at some point. You can talk to her there."

"What if she doesn't?"

"Then we'll go to plan B. In the meantime, we wait. Come with me."

Pounding fists with the bouncer, X led me to a corner booth in one of the front rooms. It gave us a clear view to the ladies' bathroom.

"When Manny gives the word, you'll go in." X set his phone down on the table. "Try to convince her to leave with you. Manny and I will be waiting for you outside the bathroom. If Bree agrees, we'll take you through the back exit and drive you to my place."

"What if Milo . . ."

"Don't worry about him. Your job is to convince Bree to go with you."

"Okay."

It took several minutes for my breathing to steady again. This was it, do-or-die time. Milo had let her emerge on Halloween, when she could wear a disguise. I wondered if X had predicted this, if that's why he was here tonight.

X was watching me. I tried not to think of how good it felt to be near him again, or how amazing he smelled, or how sad I was about what had happened between us.

"You got here pretty fast."

"It wasn't easy. I was trapped in a mall full of zombies."

An eyebrow shot up. "Oh yeah? I heard about that. ZombieMall, right? Fun times."

"I'm not sure I'd call it fun. Entertaining, yes. My fight-or-flight instincts definitely kicked in."

The conversation went nowhere from there. Our last meeting hung between us. And I was too focused on what I'd say to Bree to attempt to make small talk.

Then X's phone buzzed. A text from Manny came up.

On her way.

X put a hand on my arm. "Once she's inside the bathroom, you can go in."

I saw the girl then, with the butterfly mask and blood-red wig. She wore a short sparkly black dress and ankle booties, and her physique was very much like Bree's.

"Now go," X said. "Remember, I'll be right outside."

I walked across the room and entered the bathroom. There were two girls at the mirror, touching up their makeup. Bree had gone into a stall. I slipped into the next one, waiting for her to come out.

I heard her pee. When she flushed, I left the stall and went over to the sink to wash my hands. The other girls had gone, thank God. It would be just us.

The stall door opened, and there she was. She had pulled her mask up, revealing her face.

Bree.

I knew her immediately, despite the dark smoky eyes, glittery fake eyelashes, bright red lips, pink cheeks. Her green eyes flickered when she saw me. She quickly pulled down the mask and went over to the sink.

I came up next to her. "Bree, it's me. I'm here to help."

For several seconds, she didn't respond. I wondered if I should repeat what I'd said. Then she turned around, pulling back the mask. "Don't. Don't get involved in this, Gabby."

"I can help you get away from him."

She turned on the taps and scrubbed her hands. "I didn't ask for your help."

"Listen to me, Bree. There are two guys waiting for us in the hallway. They'll get us out through the back door. Then we'll go somewhere safe where we can talk."

"There's nothing to talk about. I'm fine. I don't need to be rescued."

When I didn't budge, her head snapped around. "You have no idea how dangerous this is."

"Please. Just come with me, and we'll talk. Then, if you want to go back to him—"

She pressed on the hand dryer, drowning me out. She rubbed her hands together, waiting for me to go away.

But I wasn't going anywhere.

When she finally turned around again, I reached for her hand. She yanked it back. "Don't!"

"Sorry."

The intensity in her eyes frightened me. "You'd better run while you can, Gabby. In a few seconds he'll come in here looking for me. I'd hate to see you get hurt." She took a step closer to me. "It would be a mistake to tell anyone you saw me. A big mistake."

She pushed past me and walked out. I was tempted to go after her, but I knew better. So I waited a few seconds to give her space, then left the bathroom. Manny and X were standing in the dark, narrow corridor, their eyes questioning. I shook my head.

"What happened in there?" X asked.

"I'm not sure. She said she didn't want my help. Said it was too dangerous."

Something inside me cracked, and I put my hands over my face, sobbing. X's arms encircled me. I'd been so close, so close! And I couldn't convince her to come with me.

After a few moments, I lifted my head. "We should call the police. Tell them where—" I broke off.

In the corner of my vision, I saw two guys coming toward us. One black, one white, both over three hundred pounds. I knew right away that they were Milo's goons. And they didn't look happy.

"The fuck were you doing talking to one of Milo's girls?" the white guy demanded, looming over us. He had the long greasy hair of a pro wrestler.

"They're off-limits," the black guy said, crossing massive arms over his chest.

X gave a shrug. "What girl are you talking about?" As he spoke, he moved between me and the goons. His hand dug into my hip, nudging me out of the way. I noticed the red Exit sign down the hall.

"You mean the redheaded chick?" Manny said, playing dumb. "Sorry, bros, she ain't my style. Not a big fan of bone racks, you know what I'm saying?"

X turned to me, eyes intent. *"Go."*

But there wasn't time. At that moment, Milo's goons rushed us. The white guy slammed his full body weight into us, shoving X and me to the ground. Then there was another impact, and I heard X grunt in pain. Oh my God. Had he been stabbed?

But I must've been wrong about that, because X swiftly rolled off me and jumped to his feet. X slammed a fist into the goon's belly, winding him, then he rushed him like a tidal wave, battering his face, chest, and smashing a side kick into his knee, making him scream in agony.

I scrambled to my feet, flattening myself against the brick wall. Manny's body was at my feet, and I heard him groaning as the black guy kicked him. I thought about jumping on the back of Manny's attacker, but I knew it wouldn't do any good.

"Go!" X shouted to me again, then he took a punch in the jaw. But I couldn't go; I was blocked by the fighting.

Manny managed to crawl toward the guys' bathroom and grab a beer bottle off the floor. He smashed it against the brick wall, then leaped to his feet and slashed at the massive guy, narrowly missing him. They circled each other in the cramped space. Manny went on the attack, slashing once, twice, until he'd ripped the jagged bottle down the goon's bare arm. He howled in pain, blood pouring from the gash.

Four bouncers rushed into the corridor to break up the fight. The diversion was just what X and Manny needed to disentangle themselves, and the three of us slipped out the back exit.

We ran down the block to X's car. He tossed me the keys. "Could you drive?"

"Sure." I didn't question it. He must be hurt, exhausted. I climbed into the driver's seat, while X took shotgun and Manny got into the back. I drove off quickly.

X said over his shoulder, "You okay back there, Manny?"

"I'm fine. Those fucking motherfucks!"

X looked at me. "You okay?"

I nodded. "You?"

"I'm all right." His jaw was clenched. "I'm losing a bit of blood, though, so we should probably stop in at the hospital. There's one a couple miles up."

"What?" My eyes widened in alarm. He was taking slow, ragged breaths.

Oh my God. My instinct had been right—he *had* been stabbed when Milo's guys had first attacked us. And yet he'd gotten up and fought like a fiend afterward.

A wave of hysteria threatened, but I forced myself to stay calm. I had to get him to the hospital as quickly as possible. X sat there quietly, pressing a bunched-up hoodie against his side.

I was worried he'd pass out, go into shock. But he stayed conscious the whole way to the hospital. I stopped the car in front of the automatic doors, and Manny helped him inside, shouting, "We got a stab wound here! *Andale*, people!"

Two nurses came up on either side of X, leading him through another set of automatic doors. Manny went in with him, but came out seconds later.

"They won't let me stay to hold his hand, not even when I said I was his brother from another mother. We have to wait out here."

We found chairs in the crowded waiting room, full of miserable-looking people and coughing kids. I'd always hated hospitals. Whatever problem you came in with, you were likely to leave with something worse. But right now, all I could think about was X.

"How bad do you think it is?" I asked Manny, who was texting someone.

"No idea. If it were bad, X wouldn't let on. Now, if I'd been stabbed, I'd be howling like a bitch."

"You're not comforting me."

"Don't worry, they're taking care of him. X won't let a couple of bloated bullies bring him down, trust me."

I looked him over. He was a patchwork of blood and bruises. "You should get checked out too."

"Why bother? There's nothing they can do for broken ribs. It's happened to me before. But I'll go clean myself up. Back in a minute."

He got up and went over to the bathroom. I stared down at my shaking hands.

You have no idea how dangerous this is, Bree had said.

She was right.

* * *

Minutes turned into an hour, and there was no update on X.

A dangerous-looking guy entered through the sliding doors of the ER. I stiffened in my seat. He had a scar snaking down his left cheek—a face you wouldn't mess with. His eyes scanned the waiting room, coming to rest on Manny and me.

I shook Manny awake.

"Huh?" Manny looked up. "Don't worry, he's one of us. I texted him." He knocked fists with the guy. "Matador."

"How's X?"

"Nobody's saying nothing."

"I fucking told him the girl was a lost cause," Matador said between gritted teeth. "Milo's girls worship him."

Tears flooded my eyes. Is that what the Destinos thought—that Bree was a lost cause? That she worshipped Milo? No way. She must be terrified of him. That had to be the reason she had warned me to stay away.

"Easy, Mat," Manny said, putting a protective arm around me. "This is her friend here."

"So?" Matador looked down at me with a shrug. "I'm gonna see what's happening." He approached the desk and started talking to a nurse. Although she shook her head, saying she had no information, he didn't budge. His plan was to stand in that exact spot until she had an update.

It worked. Eventually she was uncomfortable enough to leave her post, go through a set of automatic doors, then come back with news.

Matador returned to us. "Superficial stab wound. Stitches, no surgery. They're sending him home soon."

I could finally breathe. Superficial was good.

Within minutes, X appeared, his left hand cradling his side. "Nothing serious. They'll send me the bill."

Matador offered to take his arm, but X waved him away. "I'm fine. Jacked up on pain meds. You should get back to what you were doing."

"Who's gonna drive?" Matador asked.

"I will," I said.

Manny turned to the scarred Destino. "Drop me off?"

"Sure."

As I drove X's car back to his place, I was so relieved, I could cry.

X moved slowly up the stairs to his apartment, but refused to let me help him. The first thing he did was take off his blood-stained shirt. His torso was gorgeous, ripped, and I had to make an effort not to stare. There was a gauze bandage on his left side, covering the stitches.

I noticed that X had several old scars—a long red scar running down his collarbone, a faded pink one circling the width of his left shoulder. He'd been stabbed, slashed before.

Maybe it was part of the deal when you were a Destino. Or maybe he'd gotten them during his messed-up childhood. The thought made my heart hurt for him.

I grabbed two bottles of water from the fridge, and handed him one.

"Thanks," he said, settling on the couch. "I'll call you a cab." He looked at his phone. "It's two a.m. Did you get in touch with your parents?"

Incredible that after all we'd been through tonight, he was concerned about me getting in trouble. "They think I'm sleeping over at a friend's. If I go home now, I'll have a lot of explaining to do."

"Sure. Bedroom's yours."

He closed his eyes, breathing deeply. After several seconds, I realized he had fallen asleep.

I went down the hall and grabbed a couple of blankets from the closet. Back in the living room, I dimmed the lights and draped a blanket over him. He caught my wrist and his eyes opened. "You're a sweetheart."

It's because I love you. I would never say it out loud, of course. But even if I did, he was probably too drugged up to remember it tomorrow. I sat down beside him. "I'm sorry you got hurt. It's my fault. I'm the one who wanted us to find Bree." I was trying to hold back tears, but doing a terrible job of it.

"Shhh, don't cry. It's not your fault. Come here."

He guided my face to his and kissed me. Maybe he meant to soothe me, to comfort me. But the slow kiss was agony, and soon spiraled out of control. He threaded a hand through my hair and pulled me closer, pressing me against his wounded side. He groaned but didn't stop kissing me.

I curled up against him, hearing the unsteadiness of his breath as he deepened the kiss.

"God, Gabby. You don't know what you do to me."

"I'm probably . . . hurting you."

"I'm feeling pretty high right now."

Of course he was high. That's what this kiss was about. And yet I couldn't stop. It seemed to go on and on, and I was completely lost.

At some point I finally mustered up the strength to pull back. His eyes were half closed, his breathing erratic. "Gabby . . ."

"You need to rest."

"I can't with you so close. You feel too good." He gathered me against him, my heat next to his heat. Eventually, I could feel the steady rise and fall of his chest, and knew that he was asleep again.

I had no intention of moving out of his arms. This was probably the last time I'd be so close to him, and I would savor every minute of it. I laid my head against his chest, lulled by the beat of his heart.

MORNING SUN

I WOKE UP TO FEEL X sliding away from me. Light flooded through the thin living room curtains. I didn't know what time it was, but I guessed late morning.

"Sorry," he whispered. "Go back to sleep."

I rubbed my eyes. X was standing, shirtless, his jeans falling dangerously low over his butt. Desire curled in my belly. What a sight to wake up to.

"You want coffee?" he asked.

"Sure." My eyes followed him around the kitchen as he made the coffee. He was moving slowly but pretty well for someone who'd been stabbed the night before.

I went to the bathroom to freshen up, then returned to find X sitting at the kitchen table, sipping coffee. He'd poured me a cup.

"Sorry, I was out of milk. I'm always out of milk. I should keep the powdered stuff on hand. Anyway, I've got sugar if you want."

"It's fine. It's good."

"What's so funny?"

"This feels weird. Normal. I don't know."

"Yeah."

We drank in silence for a while. There was something intimate about having spent the night on the couch together. I wanted to hang on to that closeness for as long as I could. And then there was that incredible kiss. A kiss he'd probably been too drugged up to remember.

But I would remember.

Unfortunately, last night's other events came rushing back at me. How Bree had rejected my help. Milo's goons' attack. I wasn't ready to process any of it yet.

"You tried," X said, guessing at my thoughts. "Gave it your best shot."

"It wasn't enough. She was too afraid to come with me."

"Was she?"

I frowned. "Of course she was. She seemed really agitated. Told me I was in danger just talking to her."

X's blue eyes lasered into me. "She told Milo we were there, Gabby. That's why his guys came after us. She could've given us time to get away, but she didn't."

I swallowed that information. Of course, it made sense. Milo's goons had appeared within seconds of Bree going back to the table. Still. "She must've been too afraid to keep it from him. If Milo found out that we were trying to get her to come with us, he could've taken it out on her."

X's grip tightened around his coffee cup. "We don't know if that's why she did it."

I remembered what Matador had said about Milo's girls worshipping him. "I guess she could be under his spell. She said she didn't need to be rescued. And she definitely seemed . . . different. Not herself."

"Exactly."

I narrowed my eyes. What was he getting at? "At least she knows there's help out there. She can let that sink in. Next time I see her, she might be ready to break away."

X held my gaze. "There isn't going to be a next time. You have to let this go, Gabby."

My mouth dropped open. I didn't want to believe what he was saying. "You're giving up on her?"

"My guys are still going after Milo. We're gonna do everything we can to bust up his operation. But I want you to let go of this fantasy that Bree wants to get away from him."

"Fantasy? You think she's happy with what's happened to her?"

"Look. We don't know how Bree got herself into this situation, but—"

"Got *herself*? Manny said that pimps are masters of manipulation. I thought we agreed she was the victim here."

"Maybe she's a victim. Maybe not. She ratted us out last night." I could feel the anger rising in his voice, like water starting to simmer. "That's all we know for sure. If one of his guys had been carrying a gun, we could all be dead right now. Pimps will do anything to hang on to their property. Murder's nothing for them. Do you understand that?"

If he'd wanted to shake me up, he'd succeeded.

"You saw Bree's Instagram page, Gabby. Chances are she's head over heels for Milo. It could take months or even years for her to see him for the scumbag he really is. That's when she'll be ready to get out."

My stomach sank. "So you're going to let Milo use her, then spit her out."

"I don't know when you appointed yourself her savior, but it's got to stop. Some girls are desperate to get out of the sex trade. Some girls would do anything for someone to reach out and help them. Those are the girls the Destinos need to focus on."

My mind was in overdrive. Give up on Bree? Focus on other girls? I couldn't accept that. "If she were *your* friend, you wouldn't give up on her."

His lips tightened, and I knew I'd hit a nerve. "I'd do anything for my friends. Including you. That's why I'm telling you to back off."

"I'm a little sick of you telling me what to do," I snapped.

"And I'm sick of you thinking you know what the hell you're talking about. I'm not gonna jeopardize my guys for you." X wrenched out of his chair and kicked it aside.

I froze, startled by his anger.

"I spotted Bree out on the street last week, Gabby. You wanna hear what she was doing?" He leaned in closer. "She was trying to recruit a sixteen-year-old runaway. She told her to come hang at her boyfriend's place. Luckily the kid was smart enough to say no, or else I would've had to step in."

"The Bree I know would never . . ." My voice broke. No matter how much I wanted to believe in Bree, I couldn't find an explanation for that. "Why didn't you tell me?"

"A lot of girls recruit for their pimps. It means they're totally under their control. But when I saw her last night, I thought it was still worth a shot. I figured that if you spoke to her, you might be able to convince her to go with you. You can be persuasive when you want to be." His hands balled into fists. "It was a bad call. I put you at risk. I should've known better."

He wasn't just angry at me, I realized. He was angry at himself.

I got up and took his hand. Whether he knew it or not, we were both upset, and we should be dealing with it together. But he slipped his hand out of my grip, turning away from me.

"Go home, Gabby. Your people are probably missing you by now."

My people. There it was again. I guess he wasn't one of them.

So I did. I left.

I took a bus back to the car only to find it was gone.

Shit.

In my hurry to get to Bree, I'd parked in front of a fire hydrant. And with the drama that had ensued, I'd forgotten all about it.

How was I going to explain this to my parents?

I got on another bus toward home, gazing out the dirt-streaked window. I was exhausted. Arguing with X this morning had zapped whatever energy I had left.

He thought I was stupid to hold out hope for Bree. And maybe he was right. But I hadn't been ready to hear it. Hadn't been ready to agree to give up the hope that we could bring her home.

Tears came to my eyes. I dabbed them away with a ratty tissue from my pocket. All I wanted was to crawl into bed and sleep the day away.

I realized I should apologize to my friends for running out on them last night. So I turned on my phone, which I'd put off when X had fallen asleep.

There were twenty messages waiting for me, mainly from my mom.

Holy shit.

I held my breath and listened to the first one. It had come at 8:09 this morning, about four hours ago. "Gabby, what's going on? We got a call saying our car's been impounded. Call me right away."

Ten minutes later. "Gabby, where the hell are you? Your friend Adriana says you never slept there last night."

And later. "Gabby, call me right away or we're calling the police!"

I closed my eyes. As if today could get any worse.

The next stop was mine. I called my mom as I walked up the street toward my house. She answered immediately. "Gabby?"

"Sorry for the confusion, Mom. I met up with a friend and—"

"Gabby, thank God!" Mom cried. "Where are you?"

"Down the block. I'm sorry to scare you. I had my phone off."

I had to yank my ear away from the phone as Mom shouted, "It's Gabby! She's okay!"

I could see them on the front lawn. Mom, Dad, and Sarita. And someone else, a female police officer. The squad car sat in the driveway.

Uh-oh. Mom hadn't been kidding when she'd threatened to call the police. They must've been worried sick. If only I hadn't parked illegally, they'd still think I was at Adriana's. But I'd been in such a rush, I hadn't had any choice.

I jogged the last couple of houses, and got caught in their hugs. It struck me that I couldn't remember the last time my parents had hugged me. The thought choked me up.

The cop turned to me. "So you're all right then, miss?"

I nodded. "It was just a misunderstanding."

"Where were you?" Mom demanded, her eyes red from crying. "Why would you do this?"

"I'm so sorry, Mom. I met up with a friend after Zombie-Mall and decided to crash at their place. I know I'd planned to spend the night at Adriana's. I should've told you about the change of plan."

Whatever relief my family was feeling turned to anger.

"You can't imagine how worried we were!" Mom shouted. For once, she seemed to have no concept of the fact that we were on the front lawn, and neighbors were watching. "Your friends had no idea where you went last night! Where did you go?"

"I told you, I was with a friend."

"What friend?" Mom challenged me. "The *undercover cop*?"

I turned to Sarita, who didn't look a bit apologetic. "Of course I had to tell them, Gabby. Nobody knew where you were."

This was so much more than I could handle right now. "He's not an undercover cop. I thought he was . . . I mean, he never actually said he was. I just sort of assumed it." I was rambling, and they were staring at me like I was high.

"We were going out of our minds, Gabby," Dad said quietly. "How could you pull a stunt like this, especially with what happened to Bree?"

"Bree. Yeah. About that." I took a deep breath. This was it—a perfect opportunity to say what I knew. Now that I'd confirmed with my own eyes that she was alive, it was time to talk, especially since the Destinos had taken themselves off the case. "I saw her last night at the Phoenix."

The cop, who'd been checking her phone, lifted her head. "You saw Brianna O'Connor? That's a very serious statement you're making."

"It's true. I spoke to her."

Dad paled. "Gabriella, if you think inventing some story about seeing Bree is going to deflect the conversation from your behavior, you're wrong."

"I'm not lying." I turned to the cop. "You can interview the staff at the Phoenix if you want. I tried to convince Bree to leave the club with me, and the guy she was with . . . he sicced his goons on us. There was a big fight."

"Who's the guy she was with?" the cop asked. "Do you know his name?"

"His name is Milo." I paused, bracing for their reaction. "He's a pimp."

I didn't stop to wonder if I was doing the right thing by telling the cops. I went with my gut, and my gut said *talk*.

The bright side was, instead of getting lectured by my parents at home, I got a field trip to the police station. They put me and Mom in a cold, bare interview room and left us there. After we'd waited for an hour, I got the hint that the cops weren't in a rush to hear what I had to say.

"You don't have to stay," I said to my mom. "I can call you to pick me up later."

"I'm not going anywhere. I want to hear everything."

"Fine. Up to you. Got any food?"

She dug into her large black purse, which must weigh twenty pounds. You could fit an entire bowling ball in there. There had to be something edible. She came up with a granola bar. I inhaled it.

Just as I was sweeping the crumbs off the table, a detective with a dated mustache and an iPad tucked under his arm came in. I assumed he was a detective—he didn't bother to introduce himself. And he wasn't wearing a uniform, just a rumpled shirt, cheesy tie, and cords.

The detective opened the iPad, then asked my name, my mother's name, my date of birth, my address, and my social security number. I might as well be at the DMV for all the paperwork he was doing. Then, finally, he asked for my statement about Bree, typing certain things into the iPad.

His half-closed eyes told me one thing: he considered this interview a waste of time. He might as well have called the file: *Troubled teen tells a tale to avoid the wrath of her parents.*

Screw that. When he'd finished asking questions and got up to leave, I said, "You don't believe me, do you?"

He turned around, like I'd startled him awake.

Mom put a hand on my arm. "*Gabby.*"

"Sorry, Mom, but I want to be taken seriously." I stood up, because I didn't like the feeling of him looking down on me. "I know you've probably had a bunch of people calling in bullshit tips. But I promise you, Bree *was* at the Phoenix last night. Why don't you call the club owner to confirm that the fight happened? Maybe they even have security cameras outside that spotted her."

The detective's eyes narrowed, but I had a feeling I'd gotten through. He walked out. To my surprise, Mom patted my arm as if to say, *good job.* It was a relief that she believed me. She might have had doubts about some of my choices, but she knew I wouldn't make up a lie and take it this far. I wished I'd never complained to X about my parents. When it counted, they backed me up.

Fifteen minutes later, the detective returned. "Sergeant Monchetta will see you in her office."

Sergeant? I really must've gotten through. Mom and I looked at each other, and we followed him down a maze of cubicles.

The sergeant was fiftyish with short, ink-black hair and plenty of makeup. Diplomas and medals were displayed behind her. The far wall had a huge map of Miami, color-coded by neighborhood.

I was hesitant to walk in. It felt like I'd been called to the principal's office, except this principal probably had a gun in her desk.

"Hello," she said. "Come in and sit down." She smiled at us, revealing perfect white teeth, and I realized she was a dead ringer for Kim Kardashian's mom, Kris Jenner. "I'm Sergeant Monchetta." She sat down behind her desk. I noticed the detective's iPad was in front of her. "Detective Clarke has relayed your story to me."

Story made it sound like I was making it up. Too bad—I'd thought we were making progress.

"How did you know Bree was going to be at the club last night?" Monchetta asked me.

"My friend spotted her and called me to come talk to her."

Her perfectly tweezed brows fused together. "Why didn't you call the police?"

The Destinos don't trust the police. "We thought they'd run off before the cops got near them. No offense, but when the cops enter a place, it's not subtle."

"So you spoke to her and she refused your help."

"Yes."

"Tell me what you know about the pimp, Milo."

"Not a lot. He's got a bunch of girls working for him. Apparently they all adore him."

"And you said in your statement that someone named X was helping you. What's this person's real name?"

The question caught me by surprise. Did she really care who X was? "I don't know his real name, and it doesn't matter. X was just trying to help find Bree."

A knowing smile. "I'm aware of what X does, Gabby. We've known about him and his group for quite a while now."

I bit my lip. So she knew about the Destinos, and had tried to trick me into spilling X's name. I guess that was the benefit of X never having opened up to me—I couldn't accidentally give him away.

"I worked in sex crimes for a decade," she went on, "and I'm fully aware of his group's mandate. If you're still in contact with him, do me a favor. Tell him I'd like to talk sometime, off the record. I believe that cooperation would be best for all of us."

That was interesting. I'd have to pass along the message.

The sergeant continued to ask questions, most of which I'd already been asked. Eventually I needed a bathroom break. Mom came with me, maybe because she didn't want to let me out of her sight. She waited by the sink while I peed. I figured it was my best chance to text X.

On the toilet, I looked at my phone and saw a bunch of texts from the zombie club and even Maria, whom Mom had called in a panic this morning. Those would have to wait.

> I told the cops I saw Bree. Her parents need to know she's alive. Maybe the cops can bring her home. P.S. Sergeant Monchetta knows about you guys and thinks you should chat sometime, off the record.

I knew what he must be thinking. I was some sheltered kid who couldn't have it her way, and ran off to tell the cops. But he'd be wrong. If the Destinos couldn't help Bree, the cops had to. Someone had to.

I left the stall and washed my hands. Mom gave me a random hug, I guess out of relief that I was okay.

Back in her office, Sergeant Monchetta had a few more

questions, then turned to my mom. "Can I speak to Gabby alone?"

"Of course. I'll be outside." She picked up her purse and left the room. Sergeant Monchetta got up and closed the door behind her.

"We've gotten hundreds of tips about Brianna O'Connor," she said, circling her desk and sitting back down. "Some of those sightings have been here in Miami, some as far as Texas." She steepled her fingers, leaning closer. "But since you knew her personally, your encounter with her is the most credible."

Monchetta looked over at her phone. "I'm going to call her parents and tell them what you told me. Right now, they don't know if she's alive or dead. But this news will change everything."

I knew what she was getting at. This was my last chance to recant before involving Bree's parents.

"If your account isn't accurate, please tell me, Gabby. I won't say a word to your parents. I know that you got in trouble for being out all night, and I can see why you might want to stretch the truth. Maybe you went out looking for Bree, but didn't actually see her?"

"I spoke to her last night, Detective. That's a fact."

"So you want me to tell her parents. You're sure about that."

"Yes, I'm sure."

She looked at me for a long moment, then nodded. "All right. Thank you, Gabby."

Mom drove me home.

When we pulled into the driveway, the impounded Honda was sitting there. Dad must've gone to get it while we were at the station. I vaguely wondered if the fact that I'd been trying to help Bree would get me out of footing the bill.

The smell of spaghetti greeted us when we walked in, Dad's go-to dinner when Mom wasn't around. Although I'd barely eaten, I didn't think I could stomach the heavy meal. I downed a cup of yogurt, then went upstairs to my room.

Sitting on my bed, I wrote a quick text to Adriana, knowing she'd pass the word on to the others. I'm fine, huge misunderstanding, sorry for running off like that, will explain tomorrow. xox I also texted Maria to say that everything was fine and I'd be in touch soon.

Then I saw a new text from X. I braced myself.

You made a good choice. For the record, I'm sorry things turned out this way.

Sadness came over me. I figured he was talking about Bree. But some part of me wondered if he was talking about us.

I remembered being glued to his chest last night, being in

a place of bliss with my head against his heart. It was beautiful. Too beautiful to last.

The truth was, X was never going to let me in. He'd warned me of that, and I'd chosen not to listen. But I had no regrets, not anymore. Everything about X was incredible, exhilarating. Despite the ache in my chest, I couldn't wish I'd never met him.

I gathered all my strength and texted him back.

I'm sorry too. Good luck.

The next afternoon, Sarita and I sat on her patio, shaded by a huge parasol. The day was cloudless and hot, which called for her favorite herbal tea—she'd always believed in the cooling powers of hot tea. I lifted the cup and took a sip, knowing I needed to do some serious damage control. Problem was, I didn't know where to start.

But Sarita did. "I'm glad you told the police you saw Bree."

"So am I. Once I knew for sure that she was alive, I had to."

She leaned back in her chair. "So the guy you've been hanging out with wasn't a cop after all."

She'd managed to say it matter-of-factly, without a hint of accusation. But I knew she must be wondering if I'd deliberately lied to her about it. "I hope you know I wasn't lying to you. I honestly thought he was a cop. But it turned out he's part of a group that helps girls caught in the sex trade."

She raised a brow. "What group is that?"

"They're called the Destinos."

"The Destinos?" Her back straightened up. "Aren't they a street gang?"

"Um, yeah." I'd been hoping she hadn't heard of them, but unfortunately the Destinos had done a great job of making a name for themselves. "They're not a typical gang. They help people. That's what they do."

She looked skeptical. "I have to be honest, Gabby. You don't often hear of gangs helping people. That sounds a little strange to me."

"It's a lot strange. I know that. But it's true. X is a good person. He does whatever he can to help girls caught in bad situations. He's . . ." My voice trailed off. "I love him."

Empathy took over, and she put a hand over mine. "I just want to make sure your feelings for him aren't clouding your judgment about what he's involved in. It scared me to hear about that fight at the club. I don't want you in the middle of anything like that ever again." She sighed. "It sounds like this X guy has good intentions. But please, let the police do their job."

"Don't worry, our investigation is over. It's up to the police to find Bree now." *I should have faith in them*, I told myself. I'd seen firsthand that Sergeant Monchetta was on the ball. She was even open to working with the Destinos. That had to be a good sign. "As for me and X, we're over too. Not that it was ever officially on. But I imagined it was. And boy, do I have a vivid imagination."

"Been there," she said softly.

"I thought he cared about me. But he won't let me in." Sadness took hold of me. "Why can't he let me in?"

"I guess his hands are full with that . . . that group."

"Fine, call it a gang. It's okay; that's what he calls it too. He's an artist, like you. He does these sketches for people, these incredible sketches. You'd think anyone who could do art like that would be more . . ."

"Open?"

"Yeah. But he isn't." I took another sip of tea, determined not to cry over him today. "What about Ben—things still going strong?"

She smiled. "We're having fun. Taking it day by day."

I'd thought, at one time, that I could do the same with X— that we could take it day by day. But he'd been right. I wanted more. Because with a guy like X, nothing less than all of him would've been enough.

ZOMBIE LOVE

DAMAGE CONTROL WITH THE PARANORMAL Twins was nowhere near as tricky as with Sarita. In fact, it was totally unnecessary. The moment I started into my rehearsed explanation about helping a friend in need Friday night, they diverted the topic to ZombieMall. They were dying to dish the deets.

"Be glad you got out of there when you did," Adriana said. "The zombies got faster as the night went on."

Caro nodded. "It was insanity. Can you believe Alistair and I survived until the end? Only eight of the two hundred people did."

"Congrats. How'd Rory do?"

Caro rolled her eyes. "When the guy in charge realized Rory wasn't one of the actors, he told him to get out of the game. All the actors are insured, and Rory was getting a little too hands-on with his victims. But Rory just ran off and hid, then came out a few minutes later in a different zombie costume. By the end, a few of the zombies were chasing *him*."

I laughed. "Can't believe I missed that." I turned to Adriana with a wry smile. "Was being bitten by a zombie everything you hoped it would be?"

She rubbed her chin. "On a scale of one to ten, it sucked hard. One arm bite, and I was out of the game."

Caro pulled a face. "Oh, come on, you could've kept going. It was so chaotic that most people got bitten two or three times before they stepped out. No one was keeping a tally sheet. You left the game because you were so freaked out."

Adriana bristled but didn't deny it. "*I* was all alone. *I* didn't have Sheriff Rick defending me."

"Sheriff Rick?" I asked.

They gave me a "duh" look. "From *The Walking Dead*!" Caro said. "Yeah, Alistair was a total Sheriff Rick. You should've seen him, Gabby. He was so pumped. He'd committed the mall map to memory, and had thought up these great hiding places. I wouldn't have survived if it hadn't been for him."

Behind the leopard-print glasses, her eyes were dreamy. Too bad Alistair was missing this. He was doing an extra-credit experiment for his bio class.

"When it was all over, Caro and Alistair started making out, right there in the mall," Adriana grumbled.

I turned to Caro. "Really?"

"Yes." Her face turned pink.

"It was quite disgusting," Adriana said.

Caro gaped at her. "Was not!"

"I meant because you were both covered in fake blood. You were a sloppy, bloody, kissy-kissy mess. Made me want to take a shower."

Adriana clearly wasn't thrilled about the hookup. She and Caro had always been a duo, and I doubted she wanted to make space for a guy. But I hoped she would go with it. I had a feeling that Caro and Alistair's kiss could be the start of something beautiful.

I nudged Caro. "So is it official? Or was it just a wild moment of passion since you'd survived the zombie attack together?"

"It's official." Caro beamed. "Miss Lisa was so right."

"She predicted this?" I remembered that Caro had asked about her love life, but that the answer hadn't given me much hope for her.

"Miss Lisa's exact words were, 'In the twilight of the apocalypse, you'll find love,'" Caro said.

At the time I'd had my doubts about the prediction. But apparently Miss Lisa had nailed it.

* * *

A benefit of my short disappearance last weekend was that my parents seemed happy to have me around. They were even giving me random hugs, which took some getting used to. The following Sunday, Mom did me the biggest favor of all: she let me sleep in instead of making me go to church. But at lunch, she dropped a bomb.

"JC's been asking for you."

I paused before my next bite of poached egg on toast. "What?"

"That was my response too," Mom admitted. "Obviously he's very fragile right now, and no one wants him to get upset. Camila says he's insistent that he see you. He's in the psychiatric ward at the children's hospital."

Dad's fork clattered to his plate. "You didn't mention this in the car."

"I'm passing the message along. That's all I'm doing."

"It's a bad idea," Dad said. "He's put her through too much already."

"This is Gabby's decision, not ours."

"It's fine. I'll go." I realized that I actually wanted to see him. I wanted to see for myself that he was okay.

"Fine," Dad said, "but don't stay for long. If you feel he's trying to manipulate you or guilt-trip you like he has in the past, leave. JC's not your responsibility."

"I know." Dad was clearly looking out for me, and it meant a lot. But my gut told me that visiting JC was the right thing to do. I turned to Mom. "When should I go?"

"Whenever you want. This afternoon, if you'd like to get it over with. Let me know and I'll call Camila."

"Go for it."

Visiting hours started at three, so that's when I went. Although Mom offered to come along, I insisted on going by myself. The only thing that could make this visit more uncomfortable would be if she was hovering. She insisted on paying for my parking, and I didn't argue.

I showed a security guard my driver's license, and he buzzed me in to the psych ward. A nurse led me down an eerie maze of hallways. There was a colorful mural along one side, with big, smiling, cartoony faces. I supposed it was there to cheer people up, but to me it was freakish and disturbing. X or Sarita would've done a much better job.

"Room two twelve," she said, leaving me at the door.

I stopped and steadied myself for a moment, then knocked. On the other side of the door, I heard JC's mom say, "Come in!"

The room was overrun with flowers and teddy bears, but that didn't make it any less a hospital room. JC and his mom were sitting on the bed, playing cards on an overbed table.

He looked pretty good. Pale, but healthy. He was dressed

in sweatpants and a Ninja Turtles T-shirt, his favorite lazy clothes. When he saw me, he smiled. There was no anger in his eyes. It was like I was looking at the old JC.

His mom slid off the bed. "Lovely to see you. Why don't I go take care of some business? I'll be back in a few."

She left us alone with silence. JC and I were the ones who needed to take care of business. I guess that's why I was here.

I sat on the edge of the bed. "So you got yourself a private room. Sweet digs."

He smirked. "If you're gonna go psych ward, you gotta do it right."

Silence again. I felt his eyes assessing me. I wasn't sure what to say.

"Gin?" he asked.

"Sure."

JC came from a family of old-school gamers—back when it was card games, board games, and charades. I'd spent far too many Friday nights playing them with his family. Games were never my thing, but I'd always thought it was cool that his family had an interest that brought them together. Mine didn't.

"I wasn't sure you'd agree to come," he said, dealing the cards. "You're probably wondering why I wanted to see you."

"Yeah." I took a card, then discarded one. His turn.

"It took literally two whole weeks for my mind to get straight again. I was fucked up, Gabby. Really fucked up."

He was right about that. "But you're okay now?"

He nodded. "It's not just the drugs that screwed me up—it was all the dumb stories I'd been telling myself since we broke up. About how it was all your fault."

My fault. That was no surprise. But it was still hard to hear him say it.

"So I'm seeing this counselor every day here, and she said I'm a self-centered prick."

My jaw dropped. "She didn't."

"Oh yeah, she did." His mouth quirked. "Not in those exact words, but she laid it all out for me. At first I thought she was a total bitch, but then it hit me. She was right. I kept blaming you for my shitty life, for my stupid choices. Like taking Blings, and selling them so I could afford to take more." Seeing the sadness in my eyes, he said, "Don't worry, I'm never gonna touch Blings again. Or weed. Nothing except a beer now and then. My counselor says it's not that simple. But for me, it is. That's the benefit of being a hardheaded bastard, I guess."

"You're too stubborn to fail." I smiled. "I know that for a fact."

He grunted. "I wish my parents had your faith in me. When they found out I was using this summer, they sent me to a shrink, for all the good it did. They're gonna keep me on lockdown for a while. And they won't let me go to U of F next year if they think I could mess up again."

Going to the University of Florida had been his dream ever since I'd known him. I hated to think he might lose his chance. "You won't mess up."

"I could've already blown it. My GPA's gone down this semester. I might not even get in." He caught my expression. "I don't deserve sympathy, especially not from you. I talked a lot of trash about you, Gabby. Don't blame the others. Blame me. They thought they were sticking up for me. I'm sorry."

A lump formed in my throat. "Thank you. I hope you know, I never meant to string you along."

"You didn't string me along. I just never listened to you. Hence the self-centered prick thing."

"We both screwed up, then. Let's say we're even?"

"Even." He sighed. "When I get out of here, I'm not going back to St. Anthony's. It's gonna be an alternative school for the rest of the year."

"Everybody will miss you."

He gave a snort. He picked up a card, looked at it, then put it in the discard pile. "I bet they will. But I'll tell you something. I'm done with Liam. The guy's fucked up, and he fucked me up. He's the one who convinced me to try Blings last spring when I was feeling really low." He shook his head in disgust. "He's a ballsy son of a bitch. Keeps a stash in the boiler room at school. Makes a ton of cash. He admitted to me that ever since Bree went missing, he's doing a lot more business. More people wanting to party, more people wanting to forget."

JC's face darkened, and I knew he was one of them. "I was at the party the night Bree went missing. We spent half the night talking. At some point I left the room to take a hit with Liam. I didn't come back." He took a deep breath. "I knew she'd been drinking. If I hadn't been high, I'd have made sure she got home."

His eyes were tortured. I realized that JC hadn't just been sad over Bree's disappearance; he'd held himself responsible for it. JC had often appointed himself DD, and even when he wasn't, he was still the guy who made sure everybody got home safely. That was one of the things I'd liked about him—he always looked out for people.

The guilt must've crushed him.

"Bree's alive, JC. Trust me. She'll be coming home."

His brown eyes searched mine, desperate to believe me. "You actually think there's a chance she'll come home?" His eyes misted up. For the first time in forever, I wanted to reach out and hug him. But I held back. He was still vulnerable, and I didn't want to do anything he could misinterpret.

"Yeah, she's alive. I feel it in my gut." I just had to trust that the police would, somehow, bring her home.

"It helps to hear that," he said.

I rearranged a couple of my cards, then took my turn. "You know, I think it's for the best that you're not coming back to St. Anthony's. That scene's old. You'll meet new people at another school." *Less-fake people*, I didn't add.

He sighed. "I know I've ruined your senior year so far. I'm gonna tell everyone that I was full of shit and that it wasn't your fault. I could probably get Ellie and Karina to hang out with you again."

"Don't bother. I have other friends now. I don't care what any of those people think of me."

JC nodded, admiration in his eyes. "That's the thing about you, Gabby. You never let anyone take you down. No matter what, you come out on top. I've always loved that about you." He put up a hand, a wry smile on his mouth. "Don't take that the wrong way. I'm getting over you, Gabby. I'm almost there."

It struck me just how much we had in common. We both loved someone who didn't love us back. Maybe it was my relationship karma; after breaking JC's heart, I was due for heartbreak of my own.

But there was one difference. As much as I missed X, losing him didn't make me want to self-destruct. He'd said I was amazing, and I believed he meant it. I'd take that with me.

I laid out my cards.

"You win," JC said. "Another game?"

"I should probably go. Got my show tonight to prepare for."

"All right, but I'll want a rematch someday."

"Count on it."

As I left the room, I knew there wouldn't be any rematch. My life and JC's would never be entwined again. But I had the feeling that he'd be just fine.

"Men!" Olive declared the minute I walked in the doors of WKTU. She was dressed in a frilly white dress and a jaunty orange cap, with a pair of just-for-show cat glasses perched on her nose. Between Olive and Sapphire, we must have the best-dressed staff in all of Miami radio.

"What about men?" I dared to ask.

She smiled sheepishly and lifted the tabloid she was reading. "They can't be trusted."

"Amen."

Enough said. I headed for the pink lounge and made myself some decaf green tea. I didn't feel like chatting with Caballero before the show. Seeing JC had gotten me thinking about X, about heartbreak, and my mood hadn't recovered. Knowing Caballero, he'd see it right away and call me on it. Best save it for the airwaves.

At one minute to nine, I stood in Caballero's doorway. He waved to me and said into the mike, "Get ready, everybody. Gabby Perez is here tonight, and you *know* that girl's got a lot to say. Some are calling her Miami's sassiest shock jockette. Stay tuned."

We slapped hands and I sat down, setting my notes beside me. Caballero left the room and appeared seconds later behind the glass with Olive. Damn. I was hoping he wouldn't be listening to this one.

"Hey, everybody, it's Gabby Perez with *Light Up the Night* coming to you from the soul patch of Miami. I want to thank you, my people. Since I've been doing this show, you've been open and honest with me—not only on the air, but through your emails and tweets. So tonight I'm gonna get personal in a way I never have before. Because I trust you. And because I know that whether it's a handbag or a radio host, you're shrewd enough to spot a fake.

"The truth is, I'm feeling sad. All because of a guy I met. A guy I can't stop thinking about.

"I want to tell you about him—about all the effing magnificent things that put me in awe of him. He's strong on every level. He's independent, knows who he is, doesn't let anyone tell him what to do. He's smart as hell. And he's talented and doesn't have an ego about it. And he's kind. You wouldn't know it to look at him, but he's one of the kindest people I've ever met.

"I don't know if we ever had a chance to be a couple. But I wanted more than he was willing to give, and he shut me down. I've asked myself what I could've done differently. Maybe I could've found a way to keep him in my life, just as friends. Well, screw that. I don't want to hide how I feel or what I want. Sure, I took a risk and it didn't work out for me. But it was worth a shot. Because this guy, I have to say, is freaking amazing.

"Let me tell you how it feels to miss this guy. It hurts. It's like a canker that burns a hole in your mouth and won't let you eat or drink. Like the headache that pounds away and makes you want to curl up into a little ball and shut out the world.

"I never understood what heartbreak is until now. I never even liked the expression—it's cheesy, isn't it? But I get it. Because something inside of me actually feels broken. And I can't think of anything that could heal me but him.

"Okay, so I've made this into a pity party. Thanks for coming. If any of you are going through this, I want you to know that I understand. That I'm with you in this.

"Anyone have a suggestion for a song we could play? Something that matches what I'm feeling, and maybe what some of you are feeling?"

The phones were lighting up. I pressed on line one. "Hey there. You got a song idea for me?"

"I do. How about some Macklemore and Ryan Lewis?" The guy had a smooth, black voice. "'Can't Hold Us.' You need some cheering up, honey."

I laughed. "I love that idea. Instead of bringing us down, let's bring us up."

"You've got a beautiful voice, baby." His own voice was playful. "It don't matter if you're skinny minny or big and beautiful. I'm here for you. I'll make sure you're never lonely."

"You're a sweetheart. Thanks for the cheer-up."

"My pleasure."

I put on the song, then took off the headphones for a minute. To my surprise, I felt lighter. It was a relief to talk about how I was feeling. Suddenly aware of myself, I glanced up and saw Caballero and Olive watching me with sympathetic smiles.

"It's cool," I mouthed.

The rest of the show was an emotional roller coaster of callers with breakup stories, getting-back-together stories, or new love stories. Afterward, I got hugs from Caballero and Olive, and went out to the parking lot. I half hoped to see X there, waiting by the car.

But there was no one.

OPEN

"WHO'S THE ASSCLOWN THAT BROKE your heart?" Alistair asked the next day.

That was the price of spilling your guts on the air. The people who cared about you brought it up. We were eating our lunches on the front lawn of the school, under a canopy of palm trees. It would've been idyllic if it weren't for the noise and stink from the traffic going by.

I put down the last of my ham-and-cheese croissant and dusted off my hands. "Why do you want to know, Alistair? You're gonna beat his ass?"

He pondered that. "Sure, I could inflict harm on his ass. We're learning about proctology in advanced biology—the study of the colon, rectum, and anus. All I'll need are some latex gloves and a headlight, and I'll be on my way."

We laughed. I didn't think much could amuse me today, but Alistair's deadpan humor had done the trick. Rory laughed so hard he snorted out a piece of food.

"Ew!" Adriana narrowly dodged the flying particle. "So who is he, Gabby? You never told us there was a guy."

I caught the note of accusation. She was right; I'd never told them. And I still couldn't tell them all the reasons why I'd kept X a secret.

"Yeah, about that. I didn't want to mention it until we were actually a couple. We'd started hanging out, and I kept thinking it would go to the next level, but it never did."

It wasn't the best of explanations, but Adriana seemed to accept it. Caro's response was to hold out a container full of teddy bear–shaped cookies. "They're homemade. I hope you're okay, Gabby. You sounded really depressed."

I knew that was true. WKTU's Twitter feed had blown up with well wishes. I'd probably overdone it. Oh, well.

I took a few bites of the chewy cookie. "Don't worry, I'm fine. Yesterday was pretty heavy. I visited JC in the hospital."

They went quiet.

"His mom said he wanted to see me, so I figured I'd go."

"Tell me one thing," Adriana said, lifting a finger. "Did he own up to being a complete jerk? Or did he use the *drugs turned me into a douchebag* defense?"

"He apologized. Didn't blame the drugs, just blamed

himself. He admitted that he had a hate-on for me after the breakup."

"Glad to hear he admitted it," Caro said. "When's he coming back to school?"

"He's not. His parents are going to send him somewhere else. It's a good call. There are too many bad influences here."

"In the form of Liam Murray," Alistair said with a sneer. "JC will have to pick better friends in the future."

I nodded. "It was Liam who got him into Blings in the first place. He even sells them at school."

"Too bad they didn't catch him in that raid a few weeks ago," Alistair said. "You'd think the dogs would've sniffed them out."

"Liam found the perfect hiding place. He keeps his stash in the boiler room. I'm sure the dogs didn't go to the basement."

"We should find the stash and destroy it," Rory said eagerly. "Liam would totally freak!"

Alistair made a face. "I wouldn't recommend destroying them. Blings are part of the lysergic acid family of psychedelic drugs. They're highly flammable."

Rory grinned. "Then I say we stick one of them up Liam's ass and watch him blow. Wouldn't you like that, after what he did to you?"

Alistair gave a grim nod. "Don't tempt me."

* * *

When I got home that afternoon, all I wanted to do was flop down on the couch and get lost in some mindless TV. But David was on the couch, his hand swallowed up by a huge bag of chips. "About your show last night."

I groaned. Was this another case of Melody listening on his behalf? I really wasn't in the mood to explain my deepest feelings to him. "What about it?" Instead of waiting for his reply, I went to the kitchen in search of a snack.

He followed me in, pulling a stool up to the island. "Melody and I were listening together. She gave me shit because I didn't know you were dating anyone."

I grabbed some yogurt from the fridge and tore off the top. "We weren't dating, not actually. I'd been hoping . . ." I broke off. Was I really talking about this with my brother? This had to stop right now. "Don't tell Mom and Dad."

He looked offended. "Of course not. You can trust me. Anyway, the guy's a dumbass if he doesn't want you."

Did my brother just say that? He'd done a convincing job of making me feel like a nuisance since birth. What had changed?

"Your show's popular in my dorm, you know." He crunched some more chips. "Some people don't even believe you're my sister."

Did I detect some brotherly pride? I wondered if Melody

was responsible for the change.

"So, how are things with Melody?"

He smiled. "Good. Really good."

Wow. My brother was in love. Cocky David had met his match. I was proud of him.

We talked some more, about Melody and his pre-med program. When our parents got home an hour later, Mom brought in the mail and put it on the kitchen table. "Something for you, Gabby. There's no postmark."

She handed me a scroll wrapped in newspaper, labeled with my name.

My eyes widened. Was it from X?

"Thanks." Without saying more, I headed upstairs and shut myself in my room.

My fingers shook as I tore open the newspaper wrapping, careful not to damage what was inside. As I unfurled the drawing, I held my breath.

It was an incredible Miami streetscape drawn in black chalk. I sat down on the bed with it, examining the details. There were street kids huddled together under a bridge. A pimp held court on a street corner as two innocent-looking girls walked by. Cops were parked in their cruiser smoking cigarettes. A street artist in a knit cap looked down at a canvas. It was X.

I knew why he'd put himself in it. This was his world—dark,

gritty Miami. It was nothing like the sunny, sheltered Miami where I'd grown up.

Then I spotted another detail. There was a girl on the ground floor of a glass building on Miracle Mile. She was sitting down, leaning into a microphone.

It was me.

Was this X's way of reaching out? Of saying we weren't done?

Then I saw it. The sketch wasn't signed with the usual *X*. It was signed with an actual name. *Jackson Marland*.

Oh my God. His name. He was telling me his name.

Jackson Marland. That was the name that carried the baggage.

I took out my phone. The temptation to search the name was overwhelming. He must have known I would do it. He was allowing me to do it.

I typed in his name and scanned the results. The only Jackson Marlands I saw were an aspiring actor in LA, and a quirky teen from St. Louis. Definitely not him.

I searched *Jackson Marland Miami*. The name Darlene Marland came up several times. I clicked on a *Miami Herald* article from four years ago. And then I knew.

Miami Teen on Trial for Stabbing Mother's Boyfriend

Alexander Horvat was in critical condition when he arrived

at the hospital with stab wounds. His girlfriend, Darlene Marland, confirmed that it was her estranged son who'd attacked him.

There it was. The ugly secret he'd been hiding.

The trial had taken place the following year. When I saw the next headline, my heart sank.

Mother Testifies for Prosecution in Son's Trial

The teen in the story, who wasn't named because of his age, claimed to have stabbed his mother's boyfriend in her defense. But his mother told the judge that her son had returned home after months on the streets, high and deranged, and had attacked her boyfriend without provocation. Alexander Horvat had a criminal record himself that included several counts of assault and drug possession. In the end, the teen was convicted of aggravated assault and sentenced to two years in juvenile detention.

I knew in my gut that even at sixteen, X would never have stabbed someone without provocation. That, I knew.

My eyes welled up. X was such a good person—a person who devoted himself to helping others. I'd seen the compassion in his eyes when we'd walked the streets in search of Bree. I'd seen the vulnerability in him when he told me he couldn't be my boyfriend.

Now I knew why. He hadn't wanted me to know about this. He probably thought that someone with my background wouldn't be able to see past it.

But last night he must've heard my show and decided it was worth the risk.

I called him.

"Hey," he said. I heard him exhale, maybe with relief.

The sound of his voice melted me. "It's me. Can I come over?"

"Yeah, please."

"Right now?"

"Right now."

On the sidewalk, half an hour later, we stood in front of each other, the Miami sky as blue as his eyes.

"Jackson?"

"That's me." He searched my face, needing reassurance. So I chose the quickest way: I put my arms around his neck and kissed him.

His mouth opened against mine, startled, but hungry. He squeezed me so tight I could hardly breathe. "Gabby . . ."

Our tongues danced, our mouths slanted. I was practically wrapped around him, right there on the sidewalk. He took my hand and we went inside.

With the door closed behind us, he gathered me in his arms again. But this time we didn't kiss; we just held each other.

"I looked you up. Read the news stories."

"And you're here." His eyes were questioning.

"Of course I'm here. I'm glad I know your name. *Jackson*. It suits you."

"Thanks. It's not a bad name, I guess. Growing up, my mom used to call me Jackie. God, I hated that. It was always, 'Jackie, pass me my booze. Jackie, find me my smokes.'" He scowled. "When they booked me at the police station, the cops took my fingerprints and had me sign my name. I signed an X. I thought, *I'm sick of being Jackson. I'll be X from now on.* Probably sounds crazy."

"No, it makes sense. Of course you'd want to be someone else after everything you'd been through."

He eyed me steadily. "My version of what happened that night is different from the one you read in the papers. My version's the truth."

"You don't have to go into it if it's too painful."

"No, it's okay. I want to. The thing is, I came home that day for my mom. Had this dumb idea that I could convince her to get clean and ditch the loser, who was always kicking the shit out of us. Alex is the one who did this to me before I

220

ran away." He pointed to his broken nose. "Mom blamed me for talking back to him."

He took a deep breath. "When I went home that day, Alex was there, high as usual. He told me to get the fuck outta there. Mom told him she wanted me to stay. That's when he turned on her." His jaw hardened. "I pulled him off her, but then he pinned me to the wall and was about to start pummeling me. I had a switchblade on me. I always carried it with me, for security." He grunted. "The judge didn't understand that I had to stab him a few times just to get him off me. That's how high he was. He wasn't feeling any pain."

My chest ached. "And there was no one on your side?"

"I did have someone, my soccer coach. He knew all about the shit Mom and Alex had put me through. He told the judge how, even after I'd run away from home, I'd been going to school."

"Wow. I'm surprised you found it in you to go, considering."

"School was a safe place. There were rules. Not like at home. You never knew what to expect, day to day. You never knew what druggie would show up looking for a place to crash, or looking to get paid." He shuddered. "I owe my coach for sticking up for me. My lawyer sucked. Told me plead no contest, to put it all down to being high that day. I wouldn't do it. I wasn't a user. I'd been surrounded by drugs my whole fucking life. When I was on the streets, I saw what drugs did to my friends. No, I wasn't a user, and wasn't gonna pretend to be. I told my lawyer I'd rather get locked up."

"I'm glad you didn't lie." That was Jackson for you. Even with his freedom on the line, he wasn't going to break, wasn't going to compromise the truth.

"If I had, I'd have gone to a rehab and gotten out in a few months. But I don't regret it. I met some guys there who became my band of brothers."

"The Destinos?"

"Some of them, yeah. We stuck by each other. I never knew a brotherhood like that before. My older brothers never gave a shit about me and my little brother. Guess it's what happens when you grow up fending for yourself. You don't give a shit about anyone but yourself."

"But that didn't happen to you." I knew from the way he talked about Kaden that he was looking out for him.

"You're right, it didn't. I don't know why." He shrugged. "In the end, juvie wasn't that bad. I got the rest of my high school credits there. Didn't need to worry about where I'd sleep every night. When you're used to being on the street, that's a big plus. The shitty part was not being able to look out for Kaden. Since Mom and Alex were as fucked up as ever, social services finally stepped in and put him in foster care."

"Is your mom still with Alex now?"

"No. He's dead. Got shot by another drug dealer a couple years later." He said it casually, like he felt neither satisfaction nor regret.

"Have you seen your mom since then?"

"Why would I? She was never a mom to me. A kid's supposed to feel safe, right? A mom's supposed to spend money on food for her kids, not on getting high. That woman is . . . diseased." There was regret in his voice, as if there was still some part of him that didn't want to accept it.

"The one thing I never understood was why, when social services wanted to take my brother and me away, she'd do whatever she could to keep us. I deluded myself into thinking it was because she loved us. Took me years to figure out she just wanted the welfare check." He broke off suddenly. "So you'll forgive me if I've got trust issues." He attempted a smile. "I'm working on them."

I smiled back. "You've made a lot of progress."

"You think so?"

"I know so."

"Good." He hesitated. "I've been listening to your show, Gabby. Ever since I found out about it, I've been listening. Sometimes I just need to hear your voice." He looked at me. "I heard you last night."

My heart turned over. "I figured that's what the drawing was about."

"I'm sorry I hurt you."

"Thank you."

His mouth curved up. "I loved the part about the canker that won't let you eat or drink."

I smiled. "Got the point across, didn't I?"

"And that caller who requested Macklemore—he was awesome." We laughed, and then he was kissing me senseless.

I felt the tightness of his muscles, the incredible strength of him, and the need making his body tremble.

"God, Gabby," he said, trying his best not to be rough as his hands went all over me.

A bell rang in my mind. The words of Miss Lisa came to me. *Someone needs your help.* Had it been Jackson all along? Had he needed me to open him up and teach him to trust?

My gut said yes.

The rightness of him was all through me. Our kisses escalated, and we went to the bedroom, flopping down on his unmade bed.

"I could drown in you," he said against my ear.

His shirt had come off at some point, and I marveled at his broad, muscular chest. His body was perfect, despite all of the scars. I was half afraid to touch him for fear he'd fall away from me. My hands flattened on his chest. And suddenly it was real. Jackson trusted me. He was letting me into his life and into his heart. I could see it in the way he couldn't tear his eyes away from me, like he, too, was afraid I'd vanish.

"You're beautiful," I said, rising up and kissing his neck, biting it gently.

"You tell me when to stop," he said, out of breath now.

"What if I don't?"

He gazed down at me, a question in his eyes.

"Yes," I said simply, and pulled him over me.

We stayed in each other's arms for a long time, till the sky outside his bedroom window had fallen dark. His walls had come down, and there he was, bared to me. Laying my head against his chest, I felt as if I were in an ethereal place between earth and heaven.

"It's scary, feeling like this," he said softly.

I knew what he meant. When you love someone, you're vulnerable. And he had done everything in his power *not* to be vulnerable. "I'm not going anywhere."

He stroked my hair. "You don't have to promise me anything. I'm gonna take this moment and any other one you give me. I've learned that when you're happy, you've gotta stay in it. Because we don't know what'll happen next. I don't mean to sound morbid."

"You're not being morbid. It's true."

"I'm not sure if I'll know how to do this, Gabby. I've never been a boyfriend before. You'll have to help me get it right."

"So what *have* you been, then?"

He shrugged. "The guy on the side. The guy who comes and goes. It never mattered until now. You'll have to tell me how to make you happy, because I have no clue."

I thought about it. "Just be honest with me."

"That's it? Not flowers and chocolate?"

I looked up at him, saw the lazy smile on his face. "My last boyfriend did all that. He was constantly taking pictures of us and posting them. Making us look like the happy couple. I felt suffocated. I should've been honest with him a lot earlier."

"I'm sure you were just trying to give him a chance."

He was right. I hadn't wanted to hurt JC or disappoint everyone who'd believed we were a done deal. But somehow my own needs had gotten lost. I'd put JC's happiness, my parents' happiness, above my own. An arrangement like that could never last.

"The problem was, I listened to everybody's opinion and not to my own. And when you don't listen to your gut, nothing good can come of it. That's what I learned."

"I get what you mean now, about being honest. It's not just about being faithful. It's being honest about who you are and what you want."

I smiled up at him. "You're a quick study."

"I hope so."

CRAZY IN LOVE

AT THE ZOMBIE CLUB MEETING the next day, I wasn't exactly with-it. All I could think of was Jackson and the breakthrough we'd had last night.

Just thinking of him made joy zing through me. I now knew where the expression *crazy in love* came from. But at the same time, being with Jackson felt anything but crazy. Being with someone I loved and admired, someone who respected me and my opinions, was the sanest thing I'd ever done.

As I was thinking all of this, Alistair was giving us the latest zombie-sighting rundown. "There were two significant incidents in Tucson, Arizona. A puppy that was stillborn miraculously came back to life several hours later. And a man who was pronounced dead after a heart attack woke up on a slab in the morgue." He passed around two newspaper articles.

"That's a happy guy," Caro said, looking at the smiling man in the picture.

"You'd be smiling too if you woke up minutes before your scheduled cremation," Alistair said.

"It's got to be the zombie virus. Let's keep this one." Adriana took the article and put it in our file of zombie cases.

It was a good thing Rory wasn't here today, because he'd probably want to talk about his latest zombie-killing techniques. Since his premature death at ZombieMall, he was keen on improving his zombie-fighting skills.

"I have an update," I said. "Not zombie related. You know that guy I was upset about?"

"Oh my God," Caro said. She and Alistair were sitting knee-to-knee in a pew, holding hands. "He heard your show and called you?"

I nodded. "We're together."

They burst into applause. Then the questions came.

"*Now* are you going to tell us his name?" Adriana demanded.

I laughed, because it was so ironic. "Jackson."

I felt all warm and fuzzy saying his name. It was becoming more and more natural to think of him as Jackson. The fact was, X was never a name. Jackson felt like *him*.

"What does he do? Is he a student, or does he work?" Caro wanted to know.

"He's an artist." It was true, and it sounded a lot better than saying his main work was heading up a street gang.

"Realism or abstract?" Alistair asked.

"Urban realism," I said, using a term Jackson had mentioned.

"Very cool," Adriana said. "I'm happy for you, Gabby. Now that you're settled with the new man, maybe you could help me find one. How about putting the word out on your show? You could say: 'I've got this friend. She's got thick healthy hair and a cute little nose ring. She's a curvy girl. Looking for a guy for fondue parties, walks on the beach, and psychic channeling.'"

We all laughed.

"I could do it, but it's risky," I said. "Some of our callers are a little loopy. I mean, creepy loopy, not cute loopy."

Adriana sighed. "I feel like I'm the only single person left in this world. In the event of an apocalypse, my bloodline will die out. My eggs will shrivel. I'll have only my cats for company until they decide to turn on me."

"Rory's still single," Caro said, and Adriana shot her a look of death. Caro put up her hands. "I wasn't saying that you two should get together, I just meant that you're not the only single—"

Adriana scowled. "If Rory and I were the last human male and female on earth, we still wouldn't procreate. I'd put on one of those medieval chastity belts and pray for the plague to finish me off. Let's face facts here. I'd rather live out an eternity in the second circle of hell than have to deal with Rory!"

Alistair considered that. "Dante's second circle of hell is for those led astray by their own uncontrollable lust. I think the seventh circle would be worse—that's where the violent offenders go."

"The seventh circle then. You get my point."

"I'm on the lookout for a guy for you," Alistair said. "There may be someone in my Young Inventors organization. I'll keep you posted on my efforts."

Adriana gave a nod. "Thank you. And remember, don't you two do a séance behind my back, okay? I'd feel so betrayed."

Music blared from the car's stereo system, rattling the windows. I sat in Jackson's car outside his brother's group home, waiting for them to come out. I knew that for Jackson, inviting me to meet his little brother was a very big deal. Although we'd only been going out for two weeks, I saw this as a sign of his complete trust in me.

The group home was an L-shaped house with puke-colored stucco and a red-tiled roof—the type of place that might've once been stylish but now looked jarring and odd. The lawn was one big flowerbed, and I couldn't help but wonder if gardening was among the boys' chores.

The front door of the house opened. When Jackson walked out with a six-foot-two light-skinned black guy with a fluffy Afro, I did a double take. I guess there was no need to ask if they had the same father. Despite the difference in skin color, the resemblance between them was clear. The eyes, the mouth, the way they carried themselves. It fit.

I got out of the car. Kaden looked me over and grinned. "You're the girlfriend, huh?"

I liked him instantly. "Do I get a hug, or will I have to earn it?"

He laughed. "What's with girls and hugging?" But then he gave me one.

I gave up shotgun and slid into the back. Jackson pulled away from the curb, and we drove toward Five Guys, Kaden's favorite burger place.

When we arrived, Jackson ordered enough food for four people.

"Wait till you see my little brother eat," Jackson warned me. "It's epic."

"Group home food is shitty," Kaden said, grabbing some fries off the tray before we'd even paid for them. "Everybody's got their cooking night, so we mostly have pasta. It's the only thing those idiots can cook. If I fill up tonight, it'll help me get through the week."

"Sounds like the Paleo diet," I said. "Cavemen would binge

on meat and fat whenever they made a kill. Most of the time they only ate nuts and veggies."

"Yeah, well, I'm supplementin' a shitload of spaghetti."

We sat down in a green leather booth. Kaden dove in, very much like a caveman. Jackson slid me an embarrassed look.

"Big brother here used to cook for me growing up," Kaden said, his mouth full of food. "He tell you that?"

"No, he didn't mention it." But I had the sense that Jackson had taken care of his brother in all the ways his mother hadn't. And still did.

"Chili and toast was my favorite. Remember, Jackson?"

"The chili was from a can. And I usually burned the toast. We had a piece-of-crap toaster."

"I still love burnt toast," Kaden said, smiling at the memory. "I'm always setting off the smoke alarm when I make it. Usually at two a.m."

Kaden bit into his burger, juice dripping from the corner of his mouth. After a few bites, he said, "Thanks for taking me to the radio station. Hope you're not gonna get in trouble."

"Not at all. Caballero's going to give you a tour while I'm doing my show."

"DJ Caballero? Seriously?" Kaden was starstruck. "I love that guy."

"I do too. He's the best. He'll show you the equipment, anything you want to see."

"Cool. Will any hot chicks be there?"

"Um, well, technically we have a hot chick at the front desk. But she was born a man." Since I knew Sapphire was scheduled to work tonight, I figured it was best to mention it in case the Adam's apple fazed him.

"You got a tranny working there? What's her name?"

"Sapphire. And she calls herself transgendered, or trans."

"Don't worry, Gabby." He waved a hand. "I got no problem with trannies, or whatever you want me to call them. When I used to run away, they were the nicest people on the streets. They'd always offer to buy me hot dogs." He burst out laughing. "Oh shit, don't take that the wrong way! I really mean hot dogs. It was the only cheap, hot food you could get."

I couldn't help laughing. Kaden was hilarious.

"Now don't be surprised if Caballero asks a lot of questions," I said to Jackson. "He'll want to make sure you're a quality guy. He's got the fatherly thing going on."

"Maybe it'll prep me for meeting your parents," Jackson said, and I caught the undercurrent. I'd mentioned to him a couple of times that he should meet them, but I hadn't set a date. I was sure he knew why. He'd once said that my parents probably wouldn't let him through the door, and some part of me worried it was true. Although I was getting along better with them these days, my parents still weren't the most open people in the world. And things were going so well between Jackson and me that I didn't want my parents to mess anything up.

"I forgot to mention that my aunt Sarita invited us to her art show at the Orange gallery next Saturday night. What do you say?"

"Sounds great. I'll try to be there."

By now, I was used to the "I'll try." If he had Destinos business, it took priority. Dating the head of the Destinos definitely wasn't easy. He was always on call, often having to run off somewhere, giving apologies but no details. That was the deal with Jackson, and I was handling it the best I could. Because being with him was worth it.

"Aren't you gonna invite me too?" Kaden asked, dipping multiple fries in a mountain of ketchup.

Jackson glared at him. "Since when are you interested in art?"

"Since never. But events like that usually have fancy hors d'oeuvres, like those little pastries with meat and cheese inside. They melt in your mouth. I crash those things all the time."

"Well, you're not gonna crash this one."

The dynamic between them was so clear—serious older brother looking out for impulsive younger one. It didn't surprise me, since Jackson had told me about his brother always getting into trouble. But he hadn't mentioned how talkative and charismatic Kaden was. In the short time we'd spent together, Kaden's charm had already won me over.

Later on, we parked in the lot outside WKTU.

"Hola!" Sapphire greeted us as we went in the door.

"Hey, Sapphire. This is Jackson and his brother Kaden."

"So nice to meet you two!" Her eyes drifted over Jackson, and she gave me an *Mmm-hmm* of approval. "I hear Caballero's giving Kaden a little tour of the place while your show is on." She looked at Kaden. "You must've done something special to deserve it. He doesn't show just anyone around. Off you go, now. Gabby, you're on in twenty."

"Got it. Thanks, Sapphire."

We headed for the lounge. Jackson was holding my hand, and Kaden trailed behind us, checking out the celebrity photos on the wall. "Holy snap, that's Jason Derulo!"

"All the big hip-hop and pop artists stop in here," I told him.

Kaden was awed. Even Jackson looked impressed.

I had to admit, when I'd thought of bringing Kaden to the station, I'd also liked the idea of Jackson being here. Of seeing what I do up close. Of seeing why I love it so much.

Just before nine, I hovered in the doorway as Caballero finished his spiel.

"Hey," I said when he took off the headphones. "The boys are in the lounge."

Caballero frowned. "What boys?" Then he cracked a smile. "Just kidding. Can't wait to show them around. And I'm gonna get to know this boyfriend of yours too. Gotta make sure he's good enough for our Gabby."

We switched places and he shut the door behind me. Through the glass, I saw Sapphire in the control room, examining her fake nails.

I cleared my throat, then started, "Miami, it's me. Gabby Perez. Your favorite hundred-percent-real no-faker mover and shaker. I'm the brains and the brawn, the queen and the pawn. And I'm coming to you live from Miracle Mile, where the most incredible things are known to happen.

"Let's talk about miracles, shall we? When I came to you two Sundays ago, I was hurting. Because there was a guy I wanted to be with who'd kept the door to his heart shut. But that's all changed now. It changed because I let him know how I felt. And he decided that opening up was worth the risk.

"Tonight I'd love to hear from callers who've taken a chance on love, and had it pay off. Anyone?

"I know I'm only eighteen. Or eighteen next month, if you want to get technical about it. But there's something even I know at this age. It's that loving someone is always a risk. But here's the truth of it. If you don't take that leap of faith, if you don't tell them how you feel, you'll always be alone. And you won't ever know what it's like to be in their arms. If you're lucky, the gamble will pay off. That's my wish for all of you tonight."

The phones lit up, and I pressed on line one. "Hey, it's Gabby here. Do you have a story about taking a chance on love?"

"Yes, as a matter of fact, I do." To my surprise, the woman sounded old, like a grandmother. "My husband, Rex, and I were high school sweethearts, and married with a child before he ever told me he loved me."

"Really? You married him even when you weren't sure if he loved you?"

"Oh, I knew. I always knew, dear. But it wasn't easy for him to say how he was feeling. Men of his generation were used to keeping their emotions inside."

"But you were able to open him up eventually?"

She chuckled. "I didn't have to, dear. The birth of our first daughter broke him wide open. That was the first time I ever saw him cry. He was overcome with love for her. After that, he wasn't so afraid to let his emotions show."

"That's a beautiful story. How many years have you been married?"

"We were married forty-five years. He passed away last August."

Sadness came over me. "I'm so sorry."

"Thank you. Rex gave me three beautiful children, and he

loved us until the end. So I say to all the young kids like you out there who are listening, love is worth it."

"Wow. You've got me choked up. Thank you for sharing your story."

"My pleasure, dear."

At that moment, I noticed that Jackson and Kaden had come into the control room. Kaden was looking down at the switchboard, fascinated, as Caballero showed him this and that, but Jackson's eyes were focused on me. I could tell he was as moved as I was by the caller.

"That lady's story about love and patience speaks for itself, doesn't it? She trusted her instincts that Rex was worth waiting for, and she never regretted it. I want to share some advice that my new man gave me. He said that when you're happy, stay in the moment. Live it. Don't waste it worrying what'll come next."

I dared a look at Jackson. He reached up and pressed his hand against the glass. A sign of solidarity. An unspoken *I love you*. And it hit me that the elderly caller was right. You didn't need to hear the words to know you were loved. You could feel it.

After taking more calls and playing some music, I wrapped up the show and handed off to Caballero. "Thanks for showing them around."

"My pleasure, Gabby. That Jackson's a solid dude. You

have my blessing. And Kaden's got spunk. Reminds me of myself at that age." He winked and put the headphones on, spinning once in his chair before going live.

In the car on the way home, Kaden went on and on about his mind-blowing WKTU experience. His worship of Caballero had reached a new level.

"Caballero said they sometimes take interns, especially over the summer," Kaden said. "I could totally do that."

"Absolutely," I said, loving his enthusiasm. "It would be unpaid, but it's great experience if you want to work in radio or TV one day."

"If? Are you fucking kidding me?" Kaden practically jumped from the backseat into my lap. "I'm all over that. Could you tell Caballero I wanna sign up right away?"

"Easy, Kaden," Jackson said. "Why don't you focus on getting all your credits this year first?"

I nodded, turning back to Kaden. "He's got a point. If you pass your classes, Caballero will be more likely to take you on."

Kaden groaned. "I don't see why that should matter. School's not my thing."

"It doesn't have to be—you just have to get through it," I said. "Caballero was impressed by you. But he'll want to know that you're responsible and that you live up to your commitments. Passing in school is your best way to prove that."

"All right, I'll do it. Whatever it takes. Just watch me."

When we dropped Kaden off, he slapped us both five and went back inside, a new bounce in his step.

"He's excited," I said. "It's so good to see."

Jackson pulled back onto the road. "Yeah, it is." His voice held zero enthusiasm.

"Why am I sensing a *but*?"

He sighed. "It's nice that you want to help him out. But you don't know him like I do. I love the kid, but he's always messing up. You give him the right choice and the wrong choice, and nine times out of ten he'll choose the wrong one. If he interned at WKTU, I'd be worried he'd steal those autographed pictures off the walls and sell them on eBay."

"But what if he didn't?"

He stopped at a light, glancing over at me. "I don't want him to screw things up for you."

"Don't worry. I'd tell Caballero all about his past to cover myself. It might not happen anyway, right? He's got to get all his credits at school next semester before I'll even talk to Caballero about him. If he does that, it's worth giving him a shot."

"I don't know what to think of this. But it's good to see him so pumped. Even if it doesn't last."

"It might last. People can change, right?"

"You make me think anything's possible."

He reached over and took my hand as he drove. I knew he

was taking me home, but I wasn't ready to be dropped off. I didn't think I'd ever be okay with leaving him.

A few minutes later, he pulled into my parents' driveway. "It was great to see you do your thing tonight. You're a pro, Gabby. I was like, *I can't believe that's my girl.*"

I smiled. It felt so good to hear him say that. "I wanted you to see me there. To see why I love it so much. It's the same when I see the art you create. I can't imagine how you do it. It's such a gift."

"I've been drawing my whole life. I guess it was inevitable that I'd get good at it."

I shook my head. "You have it or you don't. And you have it. That's how I see it."

"I like how you see it. How you see the world. How you were with my brother. You see the best in people."

"And you don't?"

"I expect the worst."

"Kaden's got charisma. If he uses it for good, he'll be unstoppable."

"Be careful, you're giving me hope for him."

"But hope feels good, doesn't it?"

His eyes glittered. "Hope is dangerous."

UNTOLD

THE FOLLOWING WEEKEND, THE TIME had come for Jackson to meet my parents.

It was seven o'clock Saturday night. I sat in the living room, tapping my foot.

David raised a brow, amused. "Antsy?"

"Maybe a little."

I was glad Mom had invited David to join us, because that would take some of the heat off Jackson. Unlike my parents, David knew the real story. He knew that Jackson was the "Mystery Guy" who'd helped Maria and me at the club that night, and the guy I'd gushed about on my radio show.

But I couldn't risk my parents guessing that Jackson was the X I'd talked about at the police station, so I'd made up a story about how we met. I told them we met at a coffee shop while I was waiting for Maria. There were no free tables, so he'd asked to share mine. I'd noticed him sketching, and he'd told me he was an artist. The conversation had flowed from there.

Despite the guilt I felt for lying to my parents, I'd actually enjoyed inventing a mythology of our relationship. It was a much lovelier story than a tale of a club, a pimp, and a tainted drink.

"Why didn't you bring Melody?" I asked David. My parents loved her. And if they were gushing over Melody, that would mean even less pressure on Jackson.

"She had to take a shift at work. She's off at nine, then we're going to a candlelight keg party on campus."

"A *candlelight keg party*?" I repeated. "Now that's a fire hazard if I ever heard one."

"It's being put on by the Environmental Action Club. We'll keep the lights off to save power. And a keg is more environmentally sustainable than lots of beer bottles."

"Sounds lovely. A bunch of drunk coeds in a room full of candles. Good luck. I'd stay by an open window, just in case."

He laughed. "Will do."

I continued to tap my foot.

"It'll go fine," David said. "An hour and a half, then we'll be outta here."

"An hour and a half? I say one hour. It's only dessert."

"Depends on whether Mom serves it right away or makes him work for it," he said.

I'd managed to talk Mom out of having Jackson for a whole dinner, which would be course after course, hour after hour, question after question. JC had usually handled it well, nodding and smiling as Dad rambled about politics and Mom told us about all the "problem kids" at Rivera. But I didn't want to put Jackson—or myself—through that.

At five minutes past seven, the doorbell rang. I jumped off the couch and swung open the door. Jackson looked incredible in a crisp striped shirt and jeans.

"Hey, you." I hugged him, catching the scent of his yummy cologne. "One hour, tops, then we're off to the art show," I whispered in his ear.

"No worries. Your parents are teachers. I know how to deal with teachers."

He didn't seem nervous at all. But I guess when you're a Destino, when your job is life and death, meeting your girlfriend's parents is no big deal.

I wished I shared his confidence. Last night I'd tried to give him some coaching over the phone, but he'd refused to listen. *I'm not gonna pretend*, he'd said. *That isn't me.*

Generally, I admired that about him. *Generally.*

My family came up, and I made the introductions.

Jackson shook everyone's hand.

"So nice to meet you," Mom said. She was froufroued up in a floral dress, and her hair was freshly cut and colored. "Come on in."

We all went into the dining room. I noticed Jackson taking stock of the place, and I looked around self-consciously. Hopefully my mom's love of religious icons and designer wallpaper wouldn't throw him off.

"I'll get the pies; they're keeping warm in the oven," Mom said. "I made pecan and apple-blueberry. Gabby assured me you like pie."

"I do."

Mom went to the kitchen, and the rest of us sat down at the dining room table, under the glitziest chandelier Home Depot had to offer.

"I hear you're an artist," Dad said.

Wow, the pie wasn't even served yet, and the grilling had begun.

Jackson shrugged. "I don't call myself that, but yeah. I draw, I paint. I take the cash."

My teeth snagged my lip. I knew he was trying to be unpretentious—he *was* unpretentious—but I wished he'd stop. I'd told my parents that art was his career.

"Jackson's work is unbelievable. I showed one of his pieces

to Sarita last week, and she thought it was stunning."

Mom swept into the room and served the pies. Jackson agreed to have a slice of each.

"Can't be easy to make a living as an artist," my mom said, pouring several glasses of iced tea. "My sister struggled for many years to make a name for herself. It's nice to see how well she's doing now."

"She's a big deal in the art community, from what I hear," Jackson said.

Mom sat down and placed her napkin in her lap. "Gabby told us she brought you and your brother to the radio station. Did you enjoy yourselves?"

Wiping his mouth after a bite of pie, Jackson replied, "It was great. Gabby's gonna try to score an internship for my brother next summer at WKTU if he stays out of trouble. Kaden's taken a few wrong turns, but hopefully we can get him on the right track. The chance for a summer internship should motivate him."

My parents nodded, to my relief. That must be the teacher-speak he'd been referring to.

Jackson looked at David. "You're in pre-med, huh? I hear they're close to passing the stem-cell bill. Think it'll get through this time?"

Clearly Jackson had prepared for tonight. I squeezed his

hand—my way of saying *Thank you for trying to make a good impression.*

"Yeah, hopefully it'll pass." But I could tell David had no clue what he was talking about.

"Are you from Miami, Jackson?" Mom asked.

"Yeah, born and raised in Opa-Locka."

To her credit, Mom didn't flinch. Opa-Locka was ghetto Miami, with sky-high crime rates. Mom had probably never set foot in that part of the city.

"And do your parents still live there?"

"My mother does. My father passed away a long time ago."

Although Jackson had told me he didn't know who his father was, I figured it was a good explanation to give to my parents. No need to open that can of worms.

"I'm sorry to hear that," Mom said, and had the decency not to ask anything more about his family.

Thankfully, David managed to steer the conversation toward his pre-med program for a while. I owed him one.

"So then last week," David said between bites of pie, "I had to write a paper about when someone should be declared clinically dead—after two minutes, five minutes, or even twenty minutes, like in Italy. It's a big deal, because every second counts when you want to harvest someone's organs."

"David." Mom was horrified.

I slid Jackson a look, and we both tried not to laugh. Do-no-wrong David had chosen an inappropriate topic for dining room conversation.

"I'm sure Sarita will be pleased that you'll be at her show tonight," Mom said, swiftly changing the topic. "Where do you showcase your paintings, Jackson?"

"I mostly sell them on the street to tourists. And there's this coffee shop in South Beach that'll sell some for me. But they take twenty percent, so it's not really worth it."

With that, I figured it was time to get going. I placed my hands on the table. "Well, we'd better head off. I told Sarita we wouldn't be late."

"This was excellent pie, Mrs. Perez," Jackson said, folding his napkin and putting it beside his plate. For someone who'd grown up the way he had, Jackson had excellent table manners. "Thanks a lot."

"You're very welcome," Mom said, pleased.

It took another ten minutes to get out the door and into his car.

We both gave a huge sigh as we sat down.

"How'd I do?" he asked, turning the ignition.

After checking that my parents weren't at the window, I answered him with a kiss. "Fabulous."

"I did the best I could." His hands stilled on the wheel.

"But I wasn't gonna bullshit them or it would just come back to bite me."

"You were perfection. Gorgeous, hot perfection." And we kissed again, slow and deep this time.

"Damn," he said against my mouth. "If we don't stop this, I won't be driving us to the art show."

"Gotcha." I peeled my hands off him reluctantly. "We'll pick up where we left off later."

The gallery was called Orange. A small, boutique-like space downtown, it was crowded with rich Miami art people and hipsters. The moment we walked in, I caught the scent of Sarita's favorite jasmine candles. She firmly believed in the importance of stimulating all five senses when encouraging people to buy art.

Sarita looked glorious in a sleeveless mauve blouse and a black flared skirt, her garnet hair spilling down her back. Since she was surrounded by people, I figured we'd chat with her later, when she had a minute.

"Nice turnout, huh?" I said as we approached the first painting.

"I can see why." Jackson stopped in front of it. The painting showed a white woman in a translucent blue dress lounging on a yellow hammock, a fiery red sunset behind her. A black man's hand appeared from the corner, caressing her naked calf.

"The show's called *Untold*." I glanced down at the brochure I'd picked up at the door. "'An exploration of the hidden passions that stir within us.'"

"Hidden passion is awesome." His blue eyes burned into me. "Out-in-the-open passion is even better."

I pressed myself into him, feeling his hard body against me. "I agree."

Someone cleared his throat, and a silver-haired couple moved past us with disapproving looks.

We checked out more paintings, then had some hors d'oeuvres from the white-linened buffet table at the side of the room. Although there were flutes of champagne for the taking, we didn't touch them—the last thing we needed was to be caught drinking underage and embarrass Sarita.

We came to a painting of a young girl with curly black hair, muddy clothes, and a gleam in her eye. I put a hand over my mouth, knowing that it was me. The painting was called *Little Sweetheart*.

"Cute kid, wonder who it is," Jackson said, squeezing me to his side. "When did she paint this?"

"I don't know. There's a photo of me in her dining room just like it. She must've used it for inspiration."

Jackson gave a low whistle. "It's selling for thirty-eight hundred. Hope she gives you a royalty."

"Gabby!" Sarita descended on us, sweeping me into her arms. "I've already had several offers on this painting. We're going to have to auction it. Turns out your immense cuteness inspires people to open their checkbooks. Too bad you lost those delicious chubby cheeks."

I laughed, putting a hand to my cheek. "I hope so." I turned to Jackson. "Here's the guy I've been talking about, Jackson."

Sarita kissed his cheeks. "Gabby showed me one of your paintings. One word: stunning. I would love to see more."

Jackson looked startled. "That means a lot, coming from you. Thanks."

I said, "I've been telling him that he can get way more for his artwork than he's charging."

"Of course he can," Sarita said. "We'll talk." Then she turned to a short man in a bow tie who'd been waiting to speak to her, and let him lead her away.

It was ten by the time we got back to the car.

"Was that the coolest thing ever, or am I biased?" I said, buckling my seat belt.

"Both." He turned the ignition and pulled onto the road. "Where we heading? My place?"

"Sounds good to me." I hadn't had my fill of him yet. I

never would. "That could be you one day."

He released a slow breath. "I don't know about that, Gabby."

"I'm sure Sarita would mentor you. We were talking yesterday, and she said she could look into funding options for art college. You obviously know the techniques already, but they can teach you how to market your work."

He grunted.

"Did I say something wrong?"

"I don't need my future planned out for me. And I don't have to make five thousand dollars on a single painting. That's not why I do it."

I blinked. "Of course it's not *why* you do it. But you could be a well-known artist one day, if you want."

"I'm paying my rent and I've got food on the table. That's all that matters to me now."

"Yeah, but . . ."

He braked at a stop light, glancing at me. "But what?"

"Nothing." My excitement was quickly dissolving. "I thought you might want to make your art into a career. It's what you love, isn't it? There's no harm in making a plan."

His eyes narrowed. "Is that you talking, or your parents?"

"Me," I said, trying to keep my cool. "My parents don't approve of me going into radio, but I'm still going to do it. I think it's important to . . ."

"Have goals?"

"Exactly. So you see what I'm saying."

"Yeah, I do. I hate to disappoint you, Gabby, but I'm focused on the Destinos. My art is a distant second. And now that we're seeing each other, I hardly even have time for it."

That got my back up. "I hope you're not blaming me for that."

"Of course not."

"Good. I'm not trying to plan your life for you. I just thought the possibilities were exciting." Jeez. Couldn't I give him some feedback without being accused of trying to make him into someone he wasn't?

"They *are* exciting. I'm just not sure if . . ." He broke off. "You're ambitious, Gabby. Driven. I'm like that too. But my ambition isn't to be some fancy artist who gets worshipped by all those snooty art people. I'm helping people the best way I know how. And if that's not enough for you . . ."

I stared at him. "Who said it wasn't enough?"

"You did. We've been together less than a month, and you're already trying to plan my future and my brother's."

I was speechless. *Is that what he thought I was trying to do? To control him?* My mouth opened to speak, but my throat closed up.

"I think you'd better drop me off at home," I said finally.

"Are you sure? I didn't mean to—"

"I'm sure. I'm tired." The truth was, I was holding my emotions in, and I'd prefer not to burst into tears in front of him.

We were silent the rest of the way to my house. When he parked in the driveway, he turned to me. "You said I have to be honest, Gabby. So I'm being honest. I wasn't trying to hurt you."

"I know. You don't need to explain. Good night." I quickly kissed him on the cheek, then got out of the car. I ran inside and slipped upstairs to my bedroom. That's when I started to cry.

I lay on my bed, going over what had happened, trying to understand how it had gone wrong.

We've been together less than a month, and you're already trying to plan my future and my brother's. That really got me. I wasn't sure if I was more hurt or angry. I'd wanted to make him feel good about his art and what he could accomplish. He'd interpreted that to mean he wasn't good enough just as he was. It was ridiculous.

Or maybe . . . maybe he was right.

I was hopelessly in love with Jackson, and it was a hell of a lot easier to think of him as a struggling artist than as a gang leader. But the Destinos were his calling. He had no interest in a real career. If that's what I was hoping for, I was going to be disappointed.

I remembered him telling me about Lobo, the former head of the Destinos. Jackson had turned against him for leaving the Destinos and starting a new life with a girl. In spite of that,

I'd still secretly hoped that Jackson would do the same thing. That I'd be enough to make him change his life.

Was I supposed to envision him as a Destino five, ten years down the line? How long could he play this cat-and-mouse game with the local pimps before it caught up with him?

The truth was, he was already a target.

I sank back against my pillow. Tears streamed down the side of my face. I'd made a huge mess of what started out as a great night.

Sitting up, I was about to text him when his message appeared.

I screwed up. I'm sorry.

Tears filled my eyes again, this time with relief. I texted back:

No, it's my fault. I came on too strong.

I shouldn't have shut you down. I just got freaked out. Think I was afraid you were gonna try to convince me leave the Destinos. I can't do that.

I'm not asking you to. But it scares me to think you're in . . . forever.

I don't know where I'll be in a few years. I take it day by day.

Then I will too.

He was leaving the future open, thankfully. He wouldn't necessarily be committed to the gang for life. I couldn't ask for more than that.

So we're okay? I texted.

Of course we're okay. Now come and give me a real goodnight kiss. I'm parked across the street.

I bolted to the window. His car was there. My heart soared.

On my way down right now.

BLUR

THE NEXT NIGHT, AS I breezed into the hot pink offices of WKTU, I realized that something was different. *I* was different. For the first time, my stomach wasn't knotted with nerves.

Caballero once told me that confidence is what happens when you forget to second-guess yourself. He was right. I was looking forward to tonight's show without any of the usual anxiety.

Just before nine, I stood in the doorway of the control room. Caballero did his sign-off and put on Chromeo's latest track. He must've seen my reflection in the glass, because he immediately spun around in his chair. "Yo Gabby-Gabby." He rocked a vintage red velour leisure suit with white stripes up the sides. Another piece of Caballero wisdom—when your butt is in that chair, comfort is key. "You gonna wow us tonight?"

"You bet your ass."

He grinned. "That's what I'm talking about." He got up to leave the room, then paused in the doorway. "When you gonna bring that Kaden back? He was something else, that kid."

I smiled. "I'll let him know you said that. He says he's going to pass all his classes this year. Then he'll be back."

Olive made a hand signal, and I knew it was ten seconds to launch. Nine, eight . . .

"Miami, it's me. You know, Gabby Perez. The Sunday night second-in-command of the WKTU spaceship. The verbal virtuoso of the airwaves. The Latina lover of the—okay, you get the picture. Tonight we're talking about fate. Do you believe in it? Is everything happening the way it's supposed to in your life?

"There's something I never told you. I've been too embarrassed to tell you until now. Confession time: I'm no radio star at my school. I'm a social pariah. You see, I broke up with the best-loved guy at school last spring. And everybody wanted to punish me for it. My former friends completely turned their backs on me. And so, coming into senior year, I was alone.

"But there were these people at school—people I might not have gotten to know otherwise. They let me sit with them, hang with them, join their club at lunchtime. They never judged me because they were used to being judged themselves. I'm lucky to call them my friends.

"That's fate, people. If I'd never gone through the difficult breakup, if I'd never been treated badly by my former friends, I wouldn't have found the true stick-by-you kind. The keepers.

"So tonight, let's talk about fate. About how sometimes that crappy thing that happened to us ended up being for the best."

I glanced through the glass, and saw the surprise in Caballero's eyes. My confession had been as much for him as for my listeners. Somehow, it was easier to say it on air than to his face.

Olive sent through a caller.

"Hey, caller one," I said. "What's your name?"

"Um, Britney," said a girl about my age. She sounded a little shaky.

"Do you have a story about fate for me?"

"It's more of a question. What happens if you miss your fate? Like if you made the wrong decision and you regret it and you keep suffering for it?"

The word "suffering" brought my antenna up. "Can you tell me about that wrong decision?"

"It's, um, it's . . ." Then a dial tone.

"That's too bad," I said. "I wish you well, Britney. I'm sure that whatever decision you made, you can turn it around. Next caller—Hi, this is Gabby Perez. What do you think about fate?"

"Hey, Gabby. I loooove your show, by the way. A couple of years ago I had to find a new apartment really fast, and I found this place on Craigslist. When I went to see it, the guy I'd be living with seemed kinda shady, but I didn't have much of a choice, and I could afford the rent. Well, the day I was supposed to deliver the deposit check, I waited at the bus stop for like, an hour, and it never came. Then I got a call from a friend whose roommate had left her high and dry."

"So you moved in with your friend and not the shady guy?"

"Exactly. If the bus had shown up on time, I'd have already given him the deposit check. How weird is that?"

"Very weird. I love that story."

I took more callers, and heard story after story about how a twist of fate made things turn out for the better. By the end of the show, anyone who wasn't a believer in fate might have changed their mind.

When ten o'clock came, I handed off the reins to Caballero. He put up a finger to stop me from leaving, making me wait until he did his intro and put on a song. Then he turned the chair to face me. "There's this Ani DiFranco song you should listen to. It's called '32 Flavors' and I used to play a pop version of it in the late nineties. It goes, 'God help you if you are a phoenix and you dare to rise up from the ash. A thousand eyes will smolder with jealousy while you are just flying past.' That's you, Gabby."

I could've hugged him. "Thank you."

"Now, this might shock you, but I was no prom king myself. It's all right, though. People like us, we win." Then, with only a second to spare, he turned back to the microphone and continued his show.

With a smile on my face, I went out to the car. I loved driving on a clear night with the windows down and good music blasting. The only thing that would make it sweeter would be if I were heading to Jackson's instead of going home. But he had Destinos business tonight. I'd see him tomorrow night for sure.

As I drove, it struck me that my eighteenth birthday was two weeks away, and I was in a better place than I could've ever hoped for. My radio show was going strong. I had a new group of friends. JC and I had made peace.

And I had Jackson. And Jackson had me.

I'd only been driving two minutes when my phone rang. I figured it might be one of my friends calling to say they'd heard my tribute to them on the show. But it was a private number.

I put the Bluetooth on, turning down the music. "Hello?"

"G-Gabby, is that you?" It was a panicky female voice.

"Yes, who's this?"

"It's me, Bree." She was panting, as if she'd been running. "I got away from him! You said you'd help me. I called your show and . . . I don't know what to do."

My stomach clenched. *Oh my God. It was Bree.* "Where are you?"

"I'm at Los Pablos on Miracle Mile. It's at the corner of . . ."

"I know it. I'm three blocks away. Wait for me. Don't go anywhere."

"Y-you promise?"

"Yes. Two minutes. Stay on the phone with me. I'm about to park the car."

Adrenaline was pumping through my veins. I parked the car crookedly, then ran the last block to Los Pablos. There was a blinking sign outside, saying "Two for One Tacos."

I walked into the crowded restaurant, blaring salsa music filling my ears. I scanned the place twice before I spotted her.

Bree was sitting in a booth at the back of the restaurant. Her blond hair was unbrushed, and she wore rumpled gray sweats.

"Oh, Bree, I'm so glad you called." I gave her a hug, catching a whiff of perspiration. She felt thin, too thin.

"I'm sorry, Gabby. I wanted to go with you that night, but I was too scared. Milo gets crazy angry . . ." She took a slow breath. "I can't go to the police. No way. Milo says if I talk, he'll kill me."

I took her hand, which was clammy inside mine. "Don't worry, we'll figure this out. Let me call a friend who can help." I slipped out my phone to call Jackson. He'd know what to do.

She shook her head, frazzled. "Please, not yet. I need to think. My mind is so jumbled right now. Do you think they'd give me a beer? It'll calm me."

"I wouldn't risk it. They'll probably ask for ID."

"Fine. Can you get me a 7Up?" She patted her hips, as if feeling for some money, but her sweatpants didn't even have pockets. "I don't have any money."

"Sure." I flagged down the waitress and ordered a 7Up and a Coke.

"Does Milo know you've left?" I asked.

She shivered. "He'd know by now. I convinced him to let me go buy a snack at the deli across the street. That was over an hour ago."

Fear snaked down my back. I remembered that terrifying moment when Milo's guys had attacked us at the club. "Could he have tracked you here?"

"No. I got on the first bus I saw. Then I took another bus here. I knew you'd be doing your show and I thought you'd . . ."

"You made the right choice, Bree. We're good. We're safe." I said it as much to reassure myself as to reassure her.

The waitress came back with our drinks. Bree guzzled a quarter of her soda in one swig. I sipped mine, trying to think of what to say next. I sensed that she was volatile—that the wrong words could freak her out and send her running back to Milo. I had to be careful.

"I won't pressure you into doing anything you don't want to do," I said. "Do you trust me?"

She nodded. "I trust you." She looked past me, toward the door, and gasped.

"What is it?"

She put a hand to her chest, shaking her head. "Sorry, I thought I saw him come in. Wasn't him. I must be seeing things."

My anxiety was spiking. "I think it would be better to go somewhere else. To my place, maybe. Or to your house. Or I could get you a hotel room where you can have some space to think. Whatever you're comfortable with."

She chewed her lower lip. "Maybe the hotel idea. My mom and stepdad—I don't want to see them. No way." She wrung her hands. "All they ever did was ruin my life with their stupid rules."

Is that how she saw them? If so, she'd been damned good at hiding it. Her mom and stepdad had always seemed reasonable to me—more than my parents ever were.

"I understand. We'll leave them out of this. Let's get you a hotel room, then. Are you ready to go?"

"But I'm hungry."

I sighed. "Okay, then. Let's order some food."

If only I could slip into the bathroom and text Jackson to let him know where we were. But I wouldn't dare let her out of my sight. I didn't trust her not to bolt out of here.

Patience, I told myself. Milo shouldn't have any idea where we were. If I could get Bree to relax a bit, then she would eventually come with me.

"How about an order of wings?" I asked her. "Honey garlic?"

"Sure. That would be great."

I ordered a dozen wings. Then we sat there, sipping our drinks. I tried to find topics that would calm her. I mentioned school, the zombie club, the latest love triangles. But her eyes, like mine, kept darting to the door.

When the wings arrived, Bree picked one up and took a couple of bites. But instead of digging in, she stared into her glass, steadily drinking until the soda was gone.

The next time the waitress came by, I paid the bill—I didn't want anything to delay us getting out of here. I made myself eat a couple of wings, then I balled up my napkin, finished off my Coke, and said, "Ready to go?"

She nodded very slowly. "Almost."

A feeling of tiredness swept over me. "Okay then. Let me know."

Bree wobbled. Her face wobbled. I rubbed my eyes, but it didn't clear my vision. Everything seemed to slow down around me. I lifted my hand in front of my face, and it felt like it wasn't attached to my body. When I moved it, it streaked in front of my vision.

Something was happening to me. And I knew exactly what it was.

Bree's face contorted into a wide, joker-like smile. She looked past me, over my shoulder.

I managed to turn my head, bright lights streaking on either side of me. Sitting at the bar, right in front of the bartender, was someone I recognized too well.

Milo.

I placed my hands on the table, and opened my mouth to scream. But instead I saw the table rushing at my head. Then it was dark.

ALIVE

"WAKE THE FUCK UP."

Someone was shaking my shoulders. I was pulled from a dark, swampy place. My eyes opened a crack. It was Bree shaking me. My hope that this was just a vivid nightmare vanished.

"S-top, stop. I'm w-waking up."

"Finally." She released me, and I flopped back against the couch.

My head felt like a ten-ton weight on my shoulders, but I forced my eyelids to stay open. An apartment. Fast-food wrappers, empty liquor bottles, pizza boxes. The aftermath of a party, or many parties. I didn't know how long I'd slept, but it was still dark outside.

Why had she brought me here? My brain immediately

267

shut down the question, because I didn't want to know the answer. Instead I wondered how she'd gotten me out of the bar. For all I knew, I might've walked out on Milo's arm, a drugged-up zombie.

Milo. An icy shiver went down my spine. He wasn't in the room now, but he was close by, I knew it.

Bree's face zoomed in close to mine. "Sorry I couldn't let you pass out for long. But it's eleven already and we have to get started. If your parents are anything like mine, they're already wondering where you are."

My brain was slowly powering up. Get started on what? What did that mean? And my parents . . . they wouldn't realize anything was wrong. I usually met up with Jackson after the show. As long as I was home by midnight, they wouldn't suspect anything. Even then, they'd probably be in bed and not even notice.

"My mom might've called the police already," I said. "I told her I was meeting you."

"How'd you manage that? You stayed on the line with me until you got there."

Shit. I hung my head, only because I didn't want to look into her eyes. She was cool and calm—her agitated state in the restaurant had been an act.

Everything about Bree had been an act.

I raised my eyes. "I was only trying to help you."

"Yeah, I know." She patted my shoulder. "I wish you'd listened when I said I didn't need your help. Do I look like I need it?"

Even with the fog still in my brain, the answer was clear. Bree looked nothing like the frightened girl in the restaurant; she looked sleek, stylish, and in control. She wore a translucent white shirt with a lacy black bra underneath and black leggings. Bling glittered on her hands, neck, earlobes.

She gave a snort. "You should've backed off instead of siccing your boyfriend and his Destinos on us. Those motherfuckers have been putting us through hell."

I played dumb. "I don't know about the Destinos, but I never meant to cause you any problems. I didn't realize that you and Milo . . ."

"That Milo's my man? Yeah, I kinda figured. I'm a little disappointed that you thought I was one of his girls. C'mon, do you think I'd put up with that?"

"I thought he'd manipulated you."

"Don't worry, I'll give you the benefit of the doubt," she said. "It's true that Milo and I aren't your average couple. Just like you and the X man, huh?" She gave me a knowing look. "But isn't that part of the thrill? I can't tell you how sweet it is to have a real man who knows how to treat me."

I worked up a smile. "I totally know what you mean. How did you meet him?" I was hoping to draw her out. Hoping she could see me just as Gabby, her old friend.

She blushed. "A dating app, if you'd believe it. Sometimes he recruits girls that way. But he knew right away that I was different." She smiled at the memory. "Love is such a rush, huh? Unfortunately, you picked the wrong guy."

I shuddered, terrified to ask what she meant.

"She's awake!" Bree called out, blasting my ears.

Milo came in from the next room, wearing a Dolphins jersey and board shorts. Behind him were his two goons—the ones who'd attacked us at the Phoenix.

Milo stopped in front of me. I kept my head down, fixated on his pristine sneakers. He didn't speak until I lifted my eyes.

"This is how it's gonna go. You're gonna text your boyfriend and tell him to come over. Once you get him here, we let you go. How easy does that sound?"

My gut tightened. It was Jackson they wanted. But I wouldn't lure him here. I couldn't.

Not knowing how to respond, I stalled. "I—I don't understand. My mind's still messed up. I—I can't think."

He slapped me, sending me back into the couch cushions. I cradled my throbbing jaw.

"You awake now?" He grabbed the front of my shirt, getting in my face. "If you don't cooperate, Malik's first in line." He indicated the big black guy, who watched me menacingly. "Then it's Eddie for sloppy seconds." The greasy white guy's mouth contorted in a smile. "Then we slit your throat and throw you in a Dumpster. And here's the kicker: we still get X anyway."

I burst into sobs. How could I send Jackson into an ambush? And yet, if I refused to contact him, those guys would . . . My whole body shook.

"Do you know how much those Destinos have fucked with us?" Bree snarled into my ear. "Did they think we were gonna put up with it? They even got the cops on us. So now we've got the Destinos *and* the cops trying to shut us down."

I was the one who'd gone to the cops, not Jackson. Thank God they didn't know that. They'd probably kill me right now.

"Okay, okay!" I shouted hysterically, taking my phone from my pocket. "I'll call him."

Bree snatched it from me. "Yeah, right. In the state you're in? No, Gabby, you're gonna text him. And if you try to pull anything or put in some secret message, you'll regret it." She bent close to my ear, whispering, "Eddie's the worst. That's why Milo's saving him for last. He's the one who punishes our bitches for us."

A tremor went through me. "Y-you do it then." With her bad spelling, Jackson might catch on that something was wrong.

"How stupid do you think I am?" Bree asked. "You have to text him the way *you* text. And don't worry, I've been looking at old texts you sent me—I know how you write. I'll read it over before you send it."

I took a deep breath, trying to get a hold of myself. It was up to me. I'd have to find a way to get a message past Bree and through to Jackson. I had to find a way to alert him.

Finally I reached out for my phone, but Bree held it back. She was going through my contacts, looking for the number.

"It's under Jackson," I said, "his real name."

Bree looked suspicious, but then she scrolled through my last few texts, and saw it was true.

"Awww, how sweet," she said. "'*Good luck with the show tonight. See you tomorrow.*' Kiss hug kiss." She handed me the phone. "Go to it. If you send the text before I approve it, you know what'll happen."

Looking into her eyes, it suddenly struck me: Rory had been right. Bree had slammed our lunch table that day. She was an instigator, not a follower. The difference between her and the others was that she was two-faced about it. She was nice to me in class, then went around bashing me like everyone else.

I only wished I'd figured that out sooner.

"Tell him you're at Caro's dad's place finishing up a history project," Bree said, "and that the shit car you drive won't start."

So she'd done her research. She knew that Caro and I were

in sixth-period history class together, and that Caro's parents were divorced. Jackson would know that most of my friends lived in Coral Gables, but he wouldn't know about Caro's dad; I didn't know where he lived either.

I started to text.

Hey hon. At Caro's dad's. Just finished our history project. Car won't start. Come get me? Bree told me the address. I ended with, Pretty please Jackie? G xox

I held my breath as Bree read it over, then handed it to Milo. They both nodded, and Bree sent it.

Jackie. That was the clue. He'd told me his mother had called him that, and he'd hated the nickname. It would be strange of me to ask him for a favor while using a nickname he didn't like. *If* he even remembered he'd told me.

Another part of me hoped that he wouldn't see the text at all—that maybe his phone was off. But that would be rare for him.

We didn't move as we waited for the reply. After five minutes, Bree said, "You better hope he answers."

Then the phone buzzed in her hand. She read it. "'*Sure, twenty minutes. Hope you'll make it worth my while. Haha.*'" She looked at me with a grin. "Horny motherfucker, is he? Not as horny as Malik and Eddie, I'll bet. They can go at a moment's notice. Right, boys?"

I didn't look to see their reactions, but I felt their stares burning into me. I clenched my jaw, fighting back a wave of nausea.

Milo loomed over me, waving his gun in my face. "You're going to answer the door and invite him in. Once he's in, he's ours. If you're smart, you'll get out before the fireworks start. Do you hear me?"

"Yes." I put my head in my hands. I wanted to shatter into a million pieces. If Jackson wasn't suspicious of my message, I'd be luring him to his death.

I couldn't let that happen.

There was no way I was going to let him walk through that door. I would have to warn him. If I got shot instead, fine. Better die that way than face what Milo's goons were promising to.

I suddenly remembered the quote from Bree's Instagram page, written in blood. *Would you die for him? If you hesitated, you're not in love.*

Yes, I would, I realized. I would die for him. And the weird part was, there was some peace in that.

"It's been twenty-eight minutes." Milo stared down at me. "Where the fuck is he?"

"He's always late," I said quietly. But Jackson was never late.

It gave me hope. Maybe he was talking to the police right now.

The minutes had passed with excruciating slowness. Bree had insisted on brushing my hair and cleaning up my face. If I looked like I'd been crying, Jackson would know right away that something was wrong.

Thirty-five minutes. The goons were restless. I felt Milo's anger rising, directed squarely at me.

Forty minutes.

Then the buzzer rang. I moved to get up, but Bree pushed me back down. Milo went over and pressed the release button to unlock the building's main door. Then he came over to me, pressing the barrel of the gun to my temple as everybody took their positions. Eddie headed for the kitchen, while Malik slipped into the bathroom. Bree took refuge in the bedroom, closing the door.

Then Milo went into the front closet, keeping the door open just a little so he could watch me.

There was a knock at the door. Taking a breath, I got up from the couch and walked toward it. As I reached for the handle, a stillness came to me. *This is going to be over very soon. And whatever happens, it's going to be okay.*

I opened the door. Jackson was there, a warm smile on his face. My chest tightened. *If this is the last sight I see, I'm good with that.*

"I told you that car was gonna break down one of these

days," Jackson said. "It's a write-off."

But I wasn't listening to him. Milo was creeping up behind the door, gun raised.

"Run!" I flung myself forward, trying to push him away from the door. But it was like pressing against a brick wall; he didn't move. Jackson grabbed me and pushed me to the ground.

Bullets sprayed the air.

I covered my head. Heavy feet trampled over me, squeezing the breath out of my lungs. More shooting and shouting. Someone was crushing me into the carpet, and I knew it wasn't Jackson. I didn't know who it was, but he was protecting me.

Then I felt myself being yanked to my feet. We ran down the hall into the stairwell. "Stay down!" the guy in black barked, as a stray bullet shattered the glass in the door and ricocheted off the wall.

More gunfire. I covered my head and my ears.

"How many in there?" the guy demanded. I dared to look up, and saw that he was familiar. He had a scar running down his face. I knew he was the Destino named Matador.

"Three guys," I said. "Bree's hiding in the bedroom."

"Okay. Stay here." Gun in hand, he reached for the door.

"Wait. Bree's probably got a gun too. Be careful."

"Thanks." Then he was gone.

Gunfire kept blasting. I hunkered down, staying clear of

the broken window. Had Jackson actually gone into the apartment? Had he been shot?

The shooting stopped.

What was happening? Screw Matador's command to stay put. I needed to know that Jackson was okay. Cautiously, I got up and opened the door. The hallway was littered with glass. I approached the apartment and looked inside.

My eyes swept over the scene. Jackson was standing in the middle of the room, gripping Bree's arm. She was sobbing and struggling like a crazed kid. There were several Destinos standing around, black bandannas over their faces. Milo, Eddie, and Malik were dead, sprawled on the floor.

Jackson's eyes met mine across the room. I saw relief in them. He said to the Destinos, "Time to head out. Gabby and I'll greet the cops."

Without another word, the Destinos rushed past me.

"I can hear the sirens," Jackson said, a sense of inevitability in his voice. "I'm thinking two minutes."

No. You can't do this. "Get out of here, Jackson," I said. "Don't risk it. They might think you . . ." I gestured toward the bodies. He probably *had* killed them, I realized. He'd been the first one in the apartment. But he wasn't carrying a gun that I could see; he must've slipped it to one of the Destinos.

Jackson wasn't fazed. "I can defend everything I've done here. I'd do it all again. For you."

That was Jackson, always doing the right thing. His refusal to lie in the past had resulted in two years of juvie instead of a short stint in rehab. But this was different—his entire life was at stake. Did he really think the cops would hear his explanation? The truth was, the moment he admitted to these shootings, it would be over for him.

I moved in front of him. "If you want to do something for me, then you'll get out of here. Now." I grabbed Bree's arm from his grip. She wasn't struggling anymore. Her sobs had turned to whimpers, as if she'd lost the energy to cry. "We'll tell the cops that a rival gang stormed in here and we didn't know who they were. Right, Bree?"

Her head swung my way, her hair falling in a messy curtain over her face. "Fuck you."

"Back atcha." My hand tightened around her arm. "I'll tell them everything, Bree. How you kidnapped me. Drugged me. How you played us all. You like the sound of that? Or I could make it all go away."

She lifted her tear-stained face, pushing her hair out of the way. "Like I can trust you."

"I'm serious. I'll tell the cops you called me over here to help you and that we got caught in a gun fight. All you have to do is not mention Jackson or the Destinos. How easy is that?"

She fell silent. Through the tearful glitter in her eyes, I saw that clever mind of hers working. She might be torn up with grief over Milo, but she also wanted to save herself.

Jackson picked up her bling-covered phone from the couch. "I bet there are some texts that show you weren't the innocent victim after all. That you were a pimp's partner in crime. Best you can hope for is that they'll try you as a minor. But if you're eighteen by the time it goes to trial . . ."

"Fine," she bit out.

"Good choice." He went around grabbing cell phones off the bodies. "I need your phone too, Gabby."

Right. If the cops found my phone, they'd see that I'd texted Jackson to come over. They'd know he'd been here.

The sirens were drawing closer. Panicked, my eyes scanned the room. I had no clue where my phone was. After I'd been forced to text Jackson, Bree had held on to it.

"It's in the bedroom," Bree said reluctantly. "I probably dropped it in the closet."

Jackson ran into the bedroom, and came out seconds later. "Got it." He looked at me, and his expression was a caress. Then he ran out the door.

It was me and Bree now.

Although I still held on to her arm, it was more to hold her up than stop her from running. She stared at Milo's body.

"Love, huh? " I said. "Was it worth it?"

She turned to me, a strange look in her eyes. "It was . . . an adventure."

"Freeze!"

We didn't move.

Two cops, guns drawn, entered the apartment. Several more crowded the hallway behind them.

"They're all dead," I said to the cops. "This is the missing girl you've been looking for, Brianna O'Connor."

"Are you Brianna O'Connor?" one of the cops shouted back, not lowering his gun.

I saw the pathetic expression on her face, the *help me* look in her eyes. Bree had effortlessly slipped back into the role of innocent victim. She'd play the cops, of course. She'd play her family. She'd play the press.

"Y-yes," she said weakly. "It's me."

When the two-day blur of questioning was over, Jackson was waiting for me. I knew he would be.

I drove to his place at dusk, spotting him on the steps outside his building. By the time I parked the car, he was waiting at the curb, and when I got out, he immediately enfolded me in his arms. I breathed in his comforting scent, reveling in his strong arms around me. He was here and he was real, but I had to kiss him a million times just to make sure.

As he caught my hand and led me up to his apartment, relief flooded through me. After walking on eggshells for two days, I was finally free. Both the cops and my parents had bought my story. They'd had no reason to doubt my version of events, since it was the same as Bree's.

I'd done my best to be strong and stoic during the questioning, to not give any hints of my true feelings about Bree. My goal was to protect Jackson and the Destinos, and I'd done that. My parents had hugged me and kissed me and chastised me for trying to run to Bree's aid without calling the police first. They didn't know that I'd been kidnapped, that a gun had been put to my head. And I couldn't ever tell them.

In the apartment, Jackson searched my eyes. "So Bree stuck to the story?"

I nodded. "She knows that if she rats on the Destinos, the truth about her will come out. Bree's too smart to let that happen."

"So it's all tied up neat and tidy with a bow, huh?" His eyes were full of admiration. "You saved my ass, Gabby. But I want you to know, I could defend what I did that night. They were shooting at us. I had no choice but to fire back."

"I know that. But you would've gone to jail." I looked at him, taking in a shaky breath. "I'm the one who put you in that situation. I could've gotten you killed. I'm so sorry." Then it happened—the dam burst. I threw my arms around him and started to cry. For two days, I'd kept my emotions on lockdown. But the realization of what had happened, of the choice I'd made, was now hitting me.

He pulled back slightly, tipping up my chin so he could look into my eyes. "I know what Milo would've threatened to do if you didn't cooperate. That's how he controls his girls." A cold rage took him over. "You had no choice but to text me. *I'm* the one who's sorry, Gabby. If I weren't in charge of the Destinos, they wouldn't have kidnapped you to get to me."

I shook my head. "Milo blamed you for going to the cops. But I'm the one who did that."

"Yeah, but I fucked with him, trust me. We were on the verge of shutting him down. He had to do something about me sooner or later."

"I was terrified that you wouldn't catch on to my message."

"I knew what 'Jackie' meant. You're too careful to call me that by accident. But that wasn't the only reason I knew it was a setup. It was weird for you to go to a friend's place to work on a project after your show on a Sunday night. And Caro's dad doesn't live in Overtown. He lives in Coconut Grove."

"How do you know?"

"It's a pretty seedy neighborhood for someone who can afford to send their kid to Catholic school. There's no one with his last name in that area. Plus, that apartment was only rented a month ago. I looked up the address, and saw a For

Rent ad that hadn't been taken down."

I was impressed. "You did your research."

"Point is, you didn't need to go throwing yourself at me like that."

"I couldn't risk that you were going in blind."

"You're brave, Gabby." He cupped my cheek, his blue eyes tender. "You've always been brave."

"Me, brave? You could've run but—" I broke off. "You killed Milo and his guys. It was you, right? I didn't think you ever carried a gun."

"Yeah, it was me. Normally I don't carry a gun. None of us do. If we had guns, we'd end up shooting people—and we couldn't keep doing what we do with a trail of dead bodies around. But I knew what we were walking into that night." His jaw tightened. "My guy, Matador, found Bree hiding in the bedroom. She shot at him. Luckily her aim was way off."

"God." But I could believe it. Bree would've done anything to protect what she and Milo had going. "I knew her for years, but I never really knew her. I shouldn't have trusted her after you told me she'd been recruiting for Milo."

"There are a lot of people who get screwed up but are worth saving." A wistful look came into his eyes. I wasn't sure if he was talking about Bree, or about himself. "Sometimes it just takes a person who can see through the darkness."

And now I had no doubt who he was talking about. I remembered the words of the psychic. *"They're in a place of darkness.... You can help them break free."* But I also wondered if, by loving Jackson, I was the one who was truly free.

JUSTICE

ON THURSDAY, I WENT BACK to school. The upside was I got to see my friends and catch up in my classes. The downside? I had to hear everyone cheering about Bree's *rescue* from some horrible pimp.

If they only knew.

Adriana had rescheduled the zombie club meeting for today at lunch. The atmosphere in the basement chapel was suitably spooky, with the overcast day blotting out the sunlight from the windows. The chapel smelled funkier than usual, like a mix of mustard and mothballs. Or maybe it was whatever Rory was eating for lunch.

"Are you feeling better?" Adriana asked me.

"Oh yeah, it was just a cold. All gone now. I probably

could've come back yesterday."

They didn't question anything, and as usual, I felt bad for lying. Telling my friends that I'd missed school due to a cold was a little lie. Telling them nothing about what *really* happened to me was the bigger lie.

On the outside, I probably looked normal. But inside, I was reeling. Sometimes, a sudden feeling of elation swept through me—*I survived*. Other times, I felt a shiver of terror at how close I'd come to being dead.

I'd spent yesterday with Jackson. Being in his presence was healing. There was nothing I couldn't say in front of him. He'd let me rehash every detail of what had happened that night—details I would never be able to share with anyone else. Jackson had assured me that I would move forward from this, that the mark of that night, the fear I still carried, would fade with time.

"That was nice what you said about us on your show," Caro said sweetly.

Rory put a hand to his chest. "I was touched. Thoroughly touched." And Adriana made a face like she was glad she wasn't the one who'd touched him.

"Well, it's true," I said. "You guys rock." I'd forgotten all about having sung their praises on the show. But I was glad they hadn't.

Sudden noises brought our heads up. Shouting filled the

corridor outside the chapel. Heavy footsteps thundered down the hall.

We all jumped to our feet.

"What the hell?" Caro said, grabbing Alistair's arm. "What's happening?"

"The zombies are here!" Rory declared. He lifted the only weapon he had—a fork from his lunch bag. "Stay behind me, everyone. I'll check it out." He slowly headed toward the door.

"Open the damn door, hero," Adriana said.

Rory turned to us. "Stay back, everyone. I'll tell you if the threat is alive, or undead." Lifting his fork, he opened the door and peered out. "Holy zombieballs!"

"What?" we asked.

"Liam Murray has officially screwed himself."

We looked at one another, then pushed Rory aside to look out the door. There were four cops in navy jackets and bullet-proof vests standing outside the boiler room. One of them was frisking Liam Murray.

"It's not mine, I swear!" Liam shouted. "I don't touch that shit!" Liam saw us, his eyes going huge. "There! I was meeting with my friends down here. Right, guys? You can back me up?"

We didn't say a thing. As if we were going to help him out of this mess after what he'd done to Alistair!

The cops didn't bother to look at us—they were focused

on removing several backpacks from the boiler room. Back-packs full of Blings and cash, I'd bet.

"Calm down," one of the cops warned him. "I'm going to cuff you now."

Liam went ballistic. "Fuck you! Don't touch me! I'm gonna sue!"

Unimpressed, the cop pinned Liam to the wall and snapped the handcuffs over his wrists.

"Stop! Ow, you're hurting me! This is harassment!"

I glanced at Alistair, seeing the slight smile on his face. Did he have something to do with this?

Liam dragged his feet as one of the cops led him down the hallway. When they passed us, Alistair gave him a cheery wave. "Bye-bye, Liam."

A week later, I walked into math class to find a surprise waiting for me.

Bree was back.

I did a double take.

Holy. Shit.

I knew that she'd been planning to return to St. Anthony's. Since her *rescue*, she'd been in touch with Ellie and Karina, and they'd spread the word around school that she'd be back. But I hadn't expected her so soon.

I had to make a quick decision. Did I sit down beside her

in my usual seat, or grab a free desk at the back of the class? If I didn't sit beside her, people would think I was avoiding her because I felt awkward about her ordeal. It would only add to my heartless-bitch reputation. But really, what harm could a little more hate do?

Spotting a free seat, I made a beeline for the back of the class. Then I saw it—the challenge in Bree's eyes. She was daring me to sit beside her.

No way would I let her think I was afraid of her. No way.

Circling around the last desk, I sat down in my usual seat.

"So you're back," I said. Since the whole class had their eyes on Bree, I tried to act upbeat.

My words seemed to cut some unseen tension in the room, because others started piping in.

"Glad you're back, Bree."

"You look great, really."

"We all missed you."

"Excellent to have you back, Bree," Ms. Saikaley said, standing in front of the class. "Come on, everyone. Let's welcome her back properly." She started to clap, and the whole class joined in.

Bree smiled and her green eyes shimmered with tears, as if she was genuinely touched. Hell, maybe she was. Who knew?

When the clapping died down, Ms. Saikaley launched into the lesson.

On the surface, everything was strangely . . . back to normal. I copied the question on the board. Bree did too, along with the usual doodling in her notebook.

"So, are you passing the class?" Bree whispered to me.

I looked at her, astonished. Seriously? She was going to act like nothing had happened? Part of me wanted to laugh, and part of me wanted to smack that innocent look off her face. But in the end, it was best if I played along.

I finally said, "Heading into exams with a seventy-two."

"See, I knew you'd be fine." I shouldn't have been surprised that Bree had come back to school so soon. She wouldn't want to miss all the attention. I glanced down at the words *Bordom is evil* that she'd scratched into her desk back in September. That said it all, I realized. She'd wanted an exciting life—that was why she'd run off with Milo.

Now that the dream of Milo was over, her excitement would come from being the center of attention. I could see it now—*Dateline NBC*, maybe a guest appearance on *The View* with all the ladies nodding sympathetically. Not to mention a book deal. I could picture her face on a book cover, all sweet and serious. The title would be *Survivor* or some bullshit like that.

When class ended, everybody filed out except Bree, who stayed behind to talk to Ms. Saikaley.

Ellie and Karina were waiting for her in the hallway. As I

walked by, Ellie said, "Hey, Gabby."

I narrowed my eyes, waiting for the dig. But there wasn't one.

"Your birthday's coming up next week," Ellie said, giving her face a quick scan with her compact. Spotting some freckles, she swiped at them. "We should do something, the four of us, like we used to. I bet Bree will be up for it."

Karina nodded, her shiny black ponytail bobbing. "She'll want to have as much fun as possible before she moves to Nowheresville."

I frowned. "To where?"

"Her mom's sending her to live with her dad in Iowa. She's leaving December thirtieth, right before New Year's Eve. Can you believe that?"

"It's the most boring place ever," Ellie said. "I can't believe they'd do that to her after everything she's been through. It's like they're punishing her."

Interesting. Was the move an effort to keep Bree safe, or to keep her out of trouble? Had her family figured out that she wasn't the innocent victim—that she'd run off with Milo willingly?

Either way, the exciting life Bree had dreamed of was about to take a turn for the boring. How tragic.

"So are we doing a birthday thing or what?" Ellie asked me. "I say we do. Remember last year when we all went to that place for dinner? What was it called?"

"The Urban Bistro," I answered. This was JC's doing. He must have convinced them I wasn't a snobby bitch after all. I wished he hadn't bothered.

"Guess who called me this weekend?" Ellie asked, as if I hadn't already guessed. "JC. Nobody's heard from him in forever. Not even a thank-you for the gift basket and card we sent him. And then, out of the blue, he calls and asks how Bree's doing."

It seemed like a reasonable thing to do, since they were Bree's closest friends, but Ellie and Karina weren't impressed.

"JC still won't return Liam's calls, his *best friend*," Karina said, disgusted. "Liam's devastated. He's in so much trouble right now with the charges."

Even more good news. Liam was finally getting his. "I wouldn't be too hard on JC," I said. "He's focused on staying clean. He can't manage his own problems and Liam's right now."

Ellie scoffed at that. "I'm surprised you're so sympathetic considering what he put you through. He told me that all the smack he talked about you was a pack of lies."

Karina nodded. "JC had everybody believing him. You didn't deserve it, Gabby."

"Yeah, you totally didn't," Ellie said.

Was that supposed to be an apology? *Sorry we believed JC*

and treated you like dirt; let's be friends again?

I started to walk away, but Ellie called after me. "We'll see you at lunch, Gabby?"

I said over my shoulder, "Thanks, but I'm good."

SURPRISE

"PACK FOR A SLEEPOVER. WE'RE picking you up at six thirty. And *don't* eat dinner."

That was all Adriana would tell me.

My birthday plan was to spend Friday night celebrating with my friends, Saturday night with Jackson, and Sunday (my actual birthday) with my family.

From the passenger seat of Alistair's parents' SUV, I asked for the second time, "Where are we going?"

"You'll see. We have to pick up one more person," Alistair said, making a left turn.

The SUV already contained Rory, Adriana, and Caro. I didn't know who else Alistair could be picking up. That is, until we reached Maria's street.

She was waiting on her doorstep in a bright pink dress, her

hair freshly bleached blond. "Birthday girl!" She came running, stumbling in her high heels, then threw open the door of the SUV. Perfume flooded in.

"Hey!" I blew her a kiss from the front seat.

Maria slid in next to the Paranormal Twins, who'd dressed as if we were going to a funeral. She looked momentarily puzzled, then shrugged.

I'd never gotten them together as a group before, since I knew Maria was freaked out by anything paranormal. But for my birthday, why not? There was no need to ask how my friends had tracked her down; they'd probably seen her comments on my Instagram.

"Do *you* know where we're going?" I asked Maria over my shoulder, hoping she'd give me a hint.

"Sorry, hon. I've been sworn to secrecy."

After twenty minutes of stop-start traffic on the expressway, we arrived in North Miami. Alistair pulled into the underground parking lot of the Redmond Hotel. Soon after, we were entering the lobby.

We settled onto some yellow couches. "We have a room here?" I mouthed to Maria, looking over the glitzy lobby.

She made a sign indicating her lips were zipped.

"Stay here. I'll be right back." Alistair walked away.

Five minutes later, he came back, holding an electronic room key. "Ready?"

Buzzing with excitement, we got into an elevator, where Alistair pressed the button for the fourteenth floor. A businessman came in after us. As he reached for the button, he saw that we were also on the fourteenth floor. He glanced upward, as if praying that we didn't have the room next to his.

Lucky for him, when we got out of the elevator, we went in opposite directions.

"Here we are," Alistair said, opening up a room for us.

It was a posh suite with a comfy living room and a bedroom with two queen beds. We dumped all of our stuff in a corner of the bedroom.

Rory looked at Maria, his brows winking up. "This could be ours." He bounced his butt on one of the beds.

Maria's mouth opened in horror.

Alistair cut in quickly. "Rory, you're on the pull-out in the living room. I've got a foam mattress with me. We're good."

Rory heaved a sigh and brought his duffel bag to the living room.

"Guys, this is so sweet," I said. "I don't know how much you paid, but I'm chipping in."

Everybody shook their heads.

"It wasn't that much," Alistair said. "We got a discount through my dad's corporate membership. Now, who's hungry? We have a reservation across the street."

We headed across the street to Yolanda's, a loud, boister-ous restaurant with cute waiters. According to Alistair, the place had the most authentic Mexican food in Miami. Trust Alistair to have done his research.

Wow. A fabulous restaurant and hotel room—my friends had gone all out for my birthday. For the Paranormal Twins, it was all very . . . normal. I'd half expected we'd be spending my birthday at a cemetery or a UFO convention.

We ordered, we ate, we laughed. I was forced to stand up on a chair wearing a sombrero and holding sparklers as my friends and the waitstaff sang "Happy Birthday." Maria ogled the waiters, which was a good sign. She was back in her *moving on* phase. I hoped it would last.

When we finally returned to the hotel, we were happily stuffed. I figured we'd find a movie on TV and watch it until we conked out. But when we got back to the room, Adriana dimmed the lights.

"It's time, everyone," she said.

I looked around. What was this about?

Everyone sat down in the living room.

"There's something we haven't told you, Gabby," Caro said with barely contained excitement. "This isn't some ordinary hotel."

Alistair was sitting next to her, holding her hand. "It's

known as the most haunted hotel in Miami. The Redmond has been on this land for more than a hundred years. Before that, it was a sanatorium."

"A *what*?" Maria gripped my arm.

"Sanatorium," Alistair explained. "It's where they locked away patients with tuberculosis. Those poor people never saw the outside world again."

"There have been dozens of reports of ghostly patients walking the thirteenth floor late at night," Caro said.

Maria's hold on my arm relaxed a bit. "Let's hope they don't make it up to the fourteenth floor."

Caro and Alistair glanced at each other. "Actually, we're on the thirteenth floor," Alistair said. "Some hotels call the thirteenth floor the fourteenth because so many of their guests are superstitious. In this case, they have reason to be. Didn't you notice that there was no thirteen button in the elevator?"

"No." Maria turned to me. "Being attacked by a ghost is not on my bucket list."

"I can tell us if a ghost is present." Alistair picked up his backpack, and took out a handheld device that looked like the meter the gas guy used. "This is an EVP reader. It detects changes in the electromagnetic field." There was a small click as he switched it on.

"That is so cool," Rory said. "Where'd you get it?"

"eBay." Alistair moved the EVP meter around the room.

"The reading is completely normal. Should we attempt to make contact?"

"Yes!" said everyone but Maria.

Adriana and Caro closed their eyes and started to hum.

"Loving God and all-powerful angels, please protect us with the white light of your love as we seek to communicate with the spirits," Adriana prayed. "Everybody, visualize white light around us."

Maria whispered to me, "I'm having trouble visualizing it."

"It's okay, I'll visualize it around both of us," I said.

Caro cleared her throat. "Are there any spirits who would like to communicate with us? Only spirits who mean us no harm are welcome."

Alistair lifted his eyes. "The meter spiked. There must be something in the room with us."

Maria shivered.

"Now, somebody ask the spirit a question," Alistair said. "Let's see if we can get the meter to spike again."

Rory asked, "Did you suffer a slow and heinous death?"

"No change," Alistair said.

"Is your soul trapped between here and the light?" Adriana asked.

Alistair's eyes went big. "It moved. Keep talking."

"Don't be afraid of the light, whoever you are," Adriana said. "You'll find happiness and peace there."

Rory huffed. "Hey, don't tell it to go the light yet! We gotta ask it more questions first."

"It obviously wants to move on, Rory," Adriana said. "We should be thinking about the spirit's well-being, not our own entertainment."

"But—"

"Quiet," Adriana snapped. "Spirit, is there something holding you back from the light? Something you've done that you can't forget?"

Alistair nodded, looking down at the reader. "Major response to that one."

"This is freaking me out," Maria whispered, holding my arm too tight.

It freaked me out a little too, but I didn't want to admit it. "Adriana and Caro do this stuff all the time. It's not a big deal."

"Ahhh!" Maria jumped to her feet, waving her hands.

I stood up. "What's wrong?"

"A c-cold hand touched my back! It slid up and down. . . ." She hugged herself, hyperventilating.

Alistair got up and put the lights on.

"Holy shattering eardrums," Rory said, hands over his ears. "That was *my* hand, okay? No need to freak out about a friendly pat on the back."

"That was more than a friendly pat on the back!" Maria said.

I had to laugh. Trust Rory to use a séance as a chance to make his move.

"How about we see if there's a movie on?" I suggested. "Maybe a comedy?" I figured we'd let the spirits rest tonight.

Everybody agreed. We grabbed the duvets and pillows off the beds to snuggle with, then settled down and turned on the TV. Looking around at my friends, I couldn't help smiling.

Happy birthday to me.

Saturday night. My too-high heels were squeezing my toes. I didn't know where Jackson was taking me, or why he'd parked several blocks from our destination.

"Are we almost there? My shoes are pinching."

"Two more blocks." He slowed his pace, his mouth curving up at one corner. "Want a piggyback?"

"Nah, I'll manage."

I wondered where we could possibly be going. Since this was a quiet, residential part of Kendall, I didn't expect to see any restaurants or cafés. The narrow streets were lined with small, tidy houses, their yards decorated with garden gnomes, American flags, and bird feeders.

"Can I find out where we're going?"

"Sorry, it's a surprise."

Another birthday surprise. Not that I was complaining, although I was still tired from last night. We'd stayed up late watching movies, and Maria had slept restlessly beside me. I didn't know if it was our contact with a ghost or Rory's creepy-crawly hands that had bothered her—both were equally terrifying.

"So I went out for coffee today with an older woman," Jackson said, sliding me a look. "She's a dead ringer for that Kardashian lady, can't remember her name."

My jaw could've hit the sidewalk. "You took Sergeant Monchetta up on her offer?"

"I figured I should get a sense of what I was up against."

"Up against?" I'd hoped Monchetta could be an ally for the Destinos. With her background in sex crimes, she seemed to have a unique respect for what they did.

He looked at me. "Monchetta knows what really happened that night. She knows it was Destinos who busted in there, that it was Destino bullets that killed Milo and his guys."

My eyes widened. "Did she say that?"

"She didn't have to. I just wanted to get a sense of whether she planned to do anything about it."

"And?" I bit my lip. Was Monchetta holding a trump card against the Destinos, to play whenever she wished?

"She made it clear that she's not interested in locking me up. Reading between the lines, I'd say that another unsolved gang murder isn't her top priority. Bree's back home, and the heat is off. Going forward, Monchetta's goal is to help as many girls out there as possible."

"Sounds like the same goal as the Destinos."

He nodded. "I get the feeling Sergeant Monchetta's a realist. She knows that playing by the book doesn't work when the system itself is screwed up. She's more about the endgame than policies and paperwork." He slanted me a look. "That's the kind of cop I could see working with."

I smiled. This was good news for the Destinos, and mostly for the girls who needed them.

A few minutes later, we arrived at the surprise destination: a tiny blue stucco house. It sat farther back from the street than the other houses, fronted by an overgrown lawn and a chipped white picket fence.

We went through the gate and approached the door. Jackson did a rhythmic knock. Manny answered, beer in hand. "Hey hey! C'mon in!"

As we walked inside, Jackson said, "Since I met your people, I thought it was time you met mine."

There had to be ten or twelve guys there. *The Destinos unmasked*, I thought. They all appeared strong and tough, like an elite sports team. Some had tattoos from gangs they used to be in; others looked clean-cut. I recognized Matador, the scarred guy who'd steered me to safety during the shootout.

These were Jackson's people. And now they were my people too.

He introduced me, one by one. Several of them must've come to my rescue that night, but they'd worn black bandannas over their faces. I shook their hands, resisting the urge to hug them all.

"Good to see you again," I said to Matador. "Thanks for . . . that night."

He waved a hand, like it wasn't a big deal that he'd shielded me from bullets, or that Bree had shot at him. Like it was an everyday sort of thing.

The Destinos were watching a basketball game. As I'd suspected, guy-only gatherings centered more around sports-watching than conversation. Two of them moved to the floor so we could sit on the love seat. While the guys concentrated on the game, I looked at them, wondering what drew each of them to the Destinos.

"Who owns this place?" I asked Jackson.

"It's rented. We keep a place for a few months, then we move on to another one. We use it as a safehouse for girls when we need to. No one's here now, though. We also use it for meetings."

"Thanks for bringing me here."

Our hands locked together.

"We won't stay long. I made a dinner reservation for us. A nice little bistro. You'll see."

There was a knock at the door, the same beat of knocks that Jackson had used. He stood up immediately, looking around.

"Is something wrong?" I asked.

"Hope not. Thing is, everybody's already here." He headed for the door. Manny butted in front of him, peering through the peephole.

"No worries, X. I invited some old friends." Before Jackson could ask who, Manny swung open the door.

It was a good-looking, dark-haired couple about our age. Manny grabbed the girl into a bear hug. "Diaz! I missed you!" Without releasing her, he turned to the guy. "You better be taking good care of her."

"He is," the girl assured him. "You're looking great, Manny. Been working out, huh?" She curled a hand around his bicep.

"Eat your heart out, Diaz. I'm beating them off with a stick these days."

The Destinos got off the couches and came over to greet the couple with fist bumps and hugs. Jackson hung back.

"Who are they?" I whispered.

"Lobo and his girlfriend. He's our former leader." Jackson shuffled his feet, as if debating what to do. I knew he was pissed off at Lobo for leaving the group. But it didn't seem to me like Lobo had done anything wrong. It was his life, his choice.

When the last of the Destinos had greeted them, Jackson walked over. "Hey, Lobo, Maddie."

Lobo's handsome face broke into a smile. "Wasn't sure you'd let us in the door. It's really good to see you, bro."

"Same here," Jackson said. "This is my girlfriend, Gabby."

"I heard about her." Lobo's eyes settled on me. "So you're the one."

"Guess I am." I felt Jackson's arm slide around my waist.

"This is Maddie," Lobo said.

I shook Maddie's hand. "Nice to meet you," we both said at once.

"How about I entertain the lovely ladies while you two hug it out?" Manny put his arms around us, then steered us into the kitchen, where several cases of beer sat on the counter.

"Thanks for setting that up," Maddie said, looking relieved. "That went better than we expected."

"Well, it had to be done sooner or later. X is the most stubborn sonofabitch I've ever met." Manny looked at me. "But I think fiery Gabby here's meltin' our boy down."

I wasn't sure if Jackson's change of heart had anything to do with me, but I was glad for it.

"I've missed you," Maddie said to him.

"Of course you have." Manny gave that crooked grin, but I could tell there was an undercurrent behind it. They obviously had a soft spot for each other. "Now that I'm a Destino, I've got the whole sexy-dangerous thing going on. Your boyfriends are going to have to keep a close eye on you with this much sexy around."

We laughed.

"Help yourselves to some beer or . . ." He looked around. "Or water. I'm going out to get pizza. What kind do you like?"

Maddie shrugged. "Anything."

"We're going out for dinner later," I said, feeling a little awkward.

"Cool. I'm gonna go ask the others." He left the kitchen.

Maddie turned to me. "You'll have to tell me how you and X got together. He's a tough nut to crack, that guy."

"You're telling me. I want to hear how you met Lobo, too." I paused, thinking. "Hang on just one sec, will you?"

Returning to the living room, I found Jackson sitting on the floor, talking to Lobo and the guys. I tapped him on the shoulder. "Why don't we stay and have pizza? You could cancel the reservation."

He frowned. "But it's your birthday. Are you sure that's what you want?"

I nodded. "Let's spend it with your people."

"All right." He took out his phone.

I kissed his cheek, then went back to Maddie. I had a feeling we were going to get along really well, me and her. "You first."

"I'm glad you made peace with Lobo," I said later that night as we walked back to the car. "I wasn't sure what you'd do when he showed up."

"Me neither. I've spent the past few months mad as hell."

"So what changed?"

"Maybe I changed." His hand tightened on mine. "I could never accept that Lobo had walked away. The way I saw it, he'd built us up, then abandoned us. But I think I was just scared."

"Scared?" That was a surprise. Jackson seemed so fearless to me. "Of what?"

"Scared that I couldn't lead the Destinos. That I wouldn't be good at it." He glanced at me. "Lobo was an awesome leader. He controlled every situation as much as humanly possible, anticipated every outcome. The guy was a machine, on day and night. I sometimes wondered if he even slept."

I could see what he was getting at. "A tough act to follow?"

"Yeah. I needed to show the guys I could do it. Show *myself* I could do it."

"You seem like a natural leader to me." It was true. He had the smarts, the confidence, and the dedication. He must've known it himself, or he wouldn't have stepped up to the plate.

"I don't know how much of it comes naturally, but I learned on the job. I proved that I can handle being in charge. That I *like* being in charge."

"I bet you do. As long as you don't expect to be in charge of *me*, we'll get along nicely."

He laughed. "I'd be crazy to try to boss you around, Gabby Perez. You'd roast me on your radio show."

I gave him a sly look. "Yeah, I would. And don't you forget it."

He stopped walking and turned to me. "Well, you make me happy, Gabby. Don't *you* forget it." He wrapped his arms around me. "I'm glad that I'm the first person to tell you happy birthday on your birthday. It's twelve-oh-three."

I grinned. "And I'm glad that my parents finally changed my curfew to twelve thirty."

He smiled, but his eyes were intense. "I love you, Gabby."

I closed my eyes, feeling his words wash over me. It was the first time he'd said it, but I'd already known that he loved me. I thought about the old woman who'd called my radio show, about how she knew her husband loved her long before he said it.

"I love you too."

He cupped my face, kissed my cheeks, then my forehead. "Because I love you, I'll always be honest with you, Gabby. Being a Destino is what I do. That's why I brought you to meet the guys tonight. It's what I'm destined to do. I hope you can live with that, because I can't be without you." He searched my face. "Can you live with that?"

"I can," I said softly, then raised my lips for his next kiss.

ACKNOWLEDGMENTS

Many thanks to Kari Sutherland, Jen Klonsky, Alice Jerman, Emilia Rhodes, and John Rudolph. To the entire wonderful team at Harper. To the Firkin writers for friendship and encouragement over the years—Cynthia Boyko, Opal Carew, Christine Enta, Lucy Farago, Rowan Keats, Vanessa Kelly, Debbie Mason, Teresa Morgan, Sharon Page, Joyce Sullivan, and Randy Sykes. To the Swan Valley writers for their warmth and willingness to share ghost stories—Jay Asher, Linda Gerber, Kristin Harmel, Alyson Noël, Aprilynne Pike, Wendy Toliver, and Emily Wing-Smith.

Thanks to Alison Halsall, Jennifer Cruz, Carol Ann Dillon, Charles de Lint, Melanie Donald, Chantelle Lajoie, Anne-Marie McEvoy, and Simone Elkeles. Shout-outs to my colleagues here in Ottawa and back in Brooklyn who keep on getting it done for kids. To Kelly Blake for doing what she does best. To my super supportive family—Mom and Pop, Sarah and Jeff, my in-loves Lorraine and Evert, Justin and Julie, Jon and Candace, Char and Frank, Phil and Mary, Jeremy and my two sweeties.

Most of all, to you, my readers. Many of you have told me that my books have made a difference in your lives. I wish I could wrap my arms around all of you. It's always been for you.

Read on for a sneak peek of

RUN THE RISK

DÉJÀ VU

I SAW MATEO THE MOMENT he entered the movie theater's concession area, sensed him like a dog senses a tsunami.

Should I run for cover?

I turned away and focused on wiping powdered sugar off the counter. I'd never expected to see him again.

Feenix waved a hand in front of my face. "You okay, Grace? You see a ghost or something?"

He might as well be a ghost, because as far as I was concerned, the boy who'd been my first love was gone. I hadn't seen him in four years.

"Do you know the new security guy?" she asked, jabbing my waist.

"I used to." I grabbed a J-cloth and sprayed the counters.

It was almost time to close up the pretzel booth for the night.

Feenix looked him over. "He's damn juicy, if you ask me." She made a point of objectifying guys—it was part of her feminist role-reversal plan.

Back when I'd dated Mateo, she wouldn't have said that. He'd been tall and lanky then, with more than his fair share of acne. I'd seen past the acne, though—and what I saw was the cutest, smartest guy around.

He looked different now; the boy had turned into a man. His broad shoulders had filled out and his tanned arms were ripped, like he could do pull-ups without breaking a sweat. The dark ink of a tattoo peeked out from beneath his left sleeve. *Probably a gang tattoo*, I thought bitterly.

"Juicy or not, he's with Los Reyes," I said. "Or used to be."

Feenix's eyes widened, and I wished I could swallow back my words. The fact was, I had no idea what he'd been up to the last few years, and it wasn't fair to mess with his reputation on his first day.

"Luke wouldn't let any gang members work here—you know that," she said. "He can smell 'em a mile away."

It was true. Our boss was a former member of the Brothers-in-Arms biker gang, and he didn't put up with any gang drama among staff or customers. Luke was up front about the fact that he'd done time in his early twenties, but he'd cleaned up his act. Now he owned Cinema 1, one of the few successful independent movie theaters in Miami.

Feenix gave me a meaningful look. "Security Guy screwed you over, didn't he." It wasn't a question.

"It was a messy breakup, but I was like, fifteen. I can't even remember the details."

"We *all* remember when we were fifteen. But since Kenny's waiting, I'll give you a pass for now." She grabbed her velvet clutch and hugged me. "We'll talk tomorrow. Bye, sweets."

"Bye."

I couldn't take my eyes off Mateo as he walked the hallway past the theaters. Until now, I'd stayed partially hidden by the glass pretzel display. He might notice me anytime, so I'd better quit staring. But I couldn't. I'd always wondered what happened to him. My ears had perked whenever someone mentioned him, but it had been rare.

Here he was, in the flesh. I wasn't surprised that Luke thought he'd be good security. He definitely looked tough enough to scare the shit out of any troublemakers.

Maybe he wouldn't recognize me right away. I'd been dyeing my mousy brown hair blond recently. And he wasn't the only one who'd filled out.

His eyes scanned past me, then stopped dead. Question answered.

Uh-oh.

Should I smile or give him a *who cares* look? Unable to

decide, I looked away. My heart pounded in my chest. Out of the corner of my eye, I could see him starting to walk in my direction. Before he got too close, a customer stopped him to ask a question.

I grabbed a broom and swept the floor. Our concession was the smallest one at the theater, just a few square feet between the popcorn stand and the burrito bar. As I cleaned, I stayed low. I didn't want to talk to him. Not now. Not ever.

Mateo was a bruise that was still achingly sensitive when touched. Maybe it was because we'd never had real closure. Or maybe it was because we'd broken up just four months after Mom died. In my memory it was all wrapped together in a big, twisted knot of pain.

The knot of pain was in my closet now, in a box full of love notes and pictures. That's where I kept the promise ring. Just the thought of it made me want to gag. How stupid was I to believe that the promise ring meant we'd be together forever? That *I will always love you* meant just that. What a joke. I hadn't been mature enough to see that it was simply a horny sixteen-year-old guy talking.

Maybe Mateo caught my vibe, because he didn't approach me after all. Minutes later, I closed up the booth, dropped the register with Eddie, the assistant manager, and headed out into the night.

The sudden temperature change—from air-conditioning

to April heat—slapped me in the face. I took off my cardigan and slung it over my handbag, looking down at my phone. The bus was coming in four minutes. If I hurried across the parking lot, I should make it.

"Long time, huh?" said a voice behind me.

"Jesus!" I put a hand to my chest. Mateo had materialized at my elbow like a ghost.

"Sorry." His dark brown eyes were watchful. "You took off fast."

"Got a bus to catch." I did a double take. A scar slashed down his left cheek, from the corner of his eyebrow to his mouth. God, it was as if someone had tried to rip his face off. How the hell had that happened?

His eyes shuttered, and I felt bad for making my reaction so obvious.

I told myself not to feel sorry for him. He'd made the choice to join Los Reyes. I'd done everything I could to convince him not to. Getting hurt was part of the game.

I sped up, squelching the urge to run across the parking lot. He kept pace easily. "You should probably get back," I said. "I don't want Luke to think you're skipping out. He's a hard-ass, you know."

"Is he?"

"Yeah. Good guy, but a hard-ass. You full-time or part-time?"

"Twenty hours a week. Thursday night to Sunday night."

"That's all?"

"I'm in the paramedic program at Miami-Dade. I've got training shifts earlier in the week—seven at night till seven in the morning."

I blinked. I couldn't believe that *he* was in college and I wasn't. In what universe?

I bet he thought he was hot shit, too. "Paramedic, huh? Good for you." I didn't mean it to sound snarky, but that's how it came out. "Look, I've gotta run. My bus—" Just as I said it, the bus shot by.

"Shit!" I had the worst bus luck ever. Way too early or seconds too late. That was my life.

"Sorry if I slowed you down," he said with genuine regret. "I can drive you home. I'm due for a break."

"No thanks, it's fine." I kept walking toward the bus stop, then sat down on the bench inside the shelter and took out my phone. The best way to shut a guy down, in my experience, was to start texting.

He came into the bus shelter, his head almost touching the ceiling. It was just him and me and the dirt-streaked, graffiti-tagged walls around us. His nearness made my pulse pound and my armpits go slick. *All this time, and he still affects me, damn it.*

"Guess I'll see you tomorrow," he said.

I could feel his eyes on me, but I refused to look up. My throat felt dry. "Yep, see ya."

I held my breath, waiting for him to leave. Out of the corner of my eye, I saw him finally head back toward the theater. Only then did I exhale.

When I opened the door to my house an hour later, my stomach sank.

There were five guys in my living room, reeking of sweat and cologne. Pizza boxes, crumpled napkins, and beer cans littered the room. Did they have to be here tonight? Hadn't seeing Mateo shaken me up enough?

I shouldn't be surprised, though. Dad had left this afternoon to drive a load to the Northeast, and he'd be gone for two weeks—probably more if he visited his girlfriend in Atlanta.

"Hi," I said, but nobody looked up. They were all enthralled by a video game.

"Alex?" I said to my brother.

"Shhh!" He had a controller in his hand and waved me away. Alex looked like Mom's side of the family, the Hernandezes, but with Dad's blue eyes. His black hair was buzzed short with lightning bolts on the sides. He was five nine, but he had a seven-foot-tall chip on his shoulder.

Living with Alex was like living with a live wire. You tip-toed around it. Tried not to touch it because it just might spark and burn you.

Animale got off the couch and walked up to me. "Hey there, *hermana*. How's it going?"

"Fine," I said.

Animale was slightly shorter than me, and good-looking in a slick, disturbing way. Piercing green eyes raked over me, as if assessing my ripeness. He was the only one who ever bothered to talk to me—and I wished he hadn't.

"We'll take off when their game's finished," he said. "It could be a while, though. My boys here think they can make it to Level 13."

As if Level 13 meant anything to me. "He's got school tomorrow."

"Of course he does, Grace." He gestured as if there was a feast laid out. "We've got pizza and beer. Help yourself, honey."

I wanted to refuse the pizza as a matter of pride, but damn it, I was starving, and I knew the fridge was empty. I grabbed a middle slice—one their grubby hands hadn't touched, hope-fully—and sat down on the couch.

I chewed slowly, too upset to actually taste the pizza. I'd told Alex so many times not to bring them here. But the moment Dad went out of town, they were back. As usual.

Alex had started hanging around with these guys almost a

year ago. I didn't like them on sight. Why would they want to hang out with my brother, who was several years younger than them? My instincts had been right. Alex had gone from a regular kid to a thug overnight. Although they never talked about it in front of me, I knew they were members of the Locos—the most violent gang around.

I hated them.

Last May, they'd all gotten arrested for armed robbery—no doubt Animale had masterminded it. The last two months of my senior year of high school had been turned upside down. With the stress of Alex's arrest, I'd had a bit of a breakdown. I didn't finish two term papers and failed three exams. It was a wonder I'd graduated at all. But my GPA had plummeted, and my acceptance to the Early Childhood Education program at Miami-Dade had been revoked.

After a few months of hell, the charges against them were dropped due to some legal loophole. I'd been left to pick up the pieces of my life—just like I had to pick up the mess they left whenever they came over.

As I finished the slice of pizza, I could feel Animale's eyes on me. I finally raised my head. His eyes sharpened. He saw the hatred on my face.

He had a tiny teardrop tattoo below his right eye. I always wondered if the teardrop was meant to represent his tears or other people's.

I held his gaze, telling him without words that I wasn't weak, that he wasn't welcome here, and that in the tug-of-war for my brother, I intended to win.

A smile pulled at his lips, revealing sharp incisors. For him, this was a game. Maybe even a turn-on. It made me sick.

I got up and went to the kitchen, cleaning up the dishes from this morning. When I finished, I took out my phone and killed time, waiting for them to leave. I never went to bed while they were here, no matter how late they stayed. I'd even thought about getting a lock for my bedroom door.

If Alex wanted to leave with them, I'd have to stop him. If he left with them now, there was no way he'd get up for school tomorrow. He was fifteen, for God's sake. School wasn't optional.

An hour later, I heard them getting ready to go.

I stood in the kitchen doorway as they filed out, eyes on Alex. He was sitting on the couch in the midst of the mess they'd made. A good sign. He wasn't leaving.

Animale was the last to step out the door. He gave me a slick smile. *"Hasta luego."*

I stared at him coldly. I hoped there wouldn't be a next time.

Once the door closed, I turned to Alex.

"I told you not to bring them here!"

He shrugged. "So? We needed someplace to hang tonight."

"Maybe they should get jobs instead of *hanging* all the time. That's what most people do."

His chin jutted. "I'm sick of you judging my friends."

"*Judging* them? They're the reason you almost got locked up! They're the reason I lost my college acceptance!"

He rolled his eyes. "Don't start with that again. Ain't their fault you couldn't keep your shit together."

I wanted to slap him. I didn't even know who he was anymore. He used to be a good kid.

"Animale's crazy," I said. "If you follow him, he's gonna ruin your life. I don't want to see you get arrested again or . . . or worse."

"Don't you dare talk shit about Animale," he said through gritted teeth. "He's awesome. The guy gets total respect wherever he goes. He ain't afraid of anyone or anything."

And that's a good thing? I wanted to say, but I bit my tongue. Alex looked up to Animale. He was his hero.

And there was nothing I could do about it.

GREAT BOOKS BY
ALLISON VAN DIEPEN

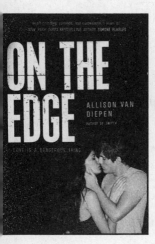

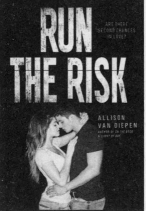